"I love you very much." Field Marshal von Blomberg spoke the words with undisguised tenderness. He reached for Eva's hand. "Knowing you has been a joy to me."

"Please don't say things like that." She tried to pull her hand away, then surrendered it. "I'm fond of you, too. You mean a lot to me. Knowing you has made me just as happy, but..."

"There can't be any buts if you really mean that."

Her face clouded. "You know what I'm getting at. Some people would say I'm not good enough for you."

"But you are!"

"You're all I've ever wanted. Being with you is like a dream come true, but I wouldn't want you to risk everything for my sake. You deserve better than that."

She nestled against the field marshal. Gently but ardently he put his arms around her. "You aren't trying to break it off, are you?"

"I'd never do that. I'm your girl, and happy to be— happy deep down inside, now that I've found you at last."

"It's heaven to hear you say that. I've known nothing but happiness since the first day we met, and I don't intend to lose it. Stay with me."

But this was not to be. Hitler and Göring had other plans....

THE
AFFAIRS
OF THE
GENERALS

Hans Hellmut Kirst

Translated from the German
by J. Maxwell Brownjohn

FAWCETT CREST ● NEW YORK

THE AFFAIRS OF THE GENERALS

THIS BOOK CONTAINS THE COMPLETE TEXT OF THE
ORIGINAL HARDCOVER EDITION.

Published by Fawcett Crest Books, a unit of CBS Publications, the
Consumer Publishing Division of CBS Inc., by arrangement with
Coward, McCann & Geoghegan, Inc.

First published in Germany under the title *Generals-affären* © C.
Bertelsmann Verlag, GmbH. München 1977/54321.

ISBN: 0–449–24258–7

Printed in the United States of America

First Fawcett Crest Printing: February 1980

10 9 8 7 6 5 4 3 2 1

To those who die by the word

It is no exaggeration to say that a domestic incident constituted the prelude to tragedy.

> Sir Nevile Henderson,
> British Ambassador in
> Berlin, 1937–39.

When a German field marshal marries a prostitute, anything can happen.

> Adolf Hitler, Führer
> and Reich Chancellor.

Adolf Hitler's peculiar genius for recognizing and pouncing on a purely fortuitous occasion to further personal designs was seldom more in evidence...

> Professor Harold C. Deutsch,
> US historian.

That girl Eva Gruhn has made history!

> Alfred Jodl,
> German general.

Hitler will lie to you and cheat you and in the end drop you just as he did me...

> General Ludendorff to
> General von Fritsch,
> early summer 1936.

The letter that triggered this book

Dear Sir,

A word of warning about the author of this missive, in other words, your humble servant. If I don't put you wise to myself, other people very soon will. I have been variously described as a controversial figure, a shady character, a member of a military conspiracy, and a man of (reputed) integrity with a rather debatable record.

It would be truer to say that I was just an observer of the contemporary scene, though one who found it hard to look on idly. I couldn't have been better placed because my coordinator's job at the Prussian Ministry of the Interior afforded me a bird's-eye view of Berlin in the nineteen-thirties. I also possessed a wide—by present-day standards, extremely wide—range of personal contacts in every part of the political spectrum. Last but not least, it was my exceptional and momentous privilege to have been a boyhood friend of someone at the very top of the Nazi tree.

Thanks to my ringside seat, I had first-hand knowledge of the events which historians have christened "the Blomberg-Fritsch affair"—a mean, dastardly, and deliberate plot to ruin Germany's two most senior soldiers.

Although the echoes of their personal tragedy were almost drowned by the thunderous approach of World War II, both cases involved a crucial struggle for power inside the Third Reich. In stooping to fraud, slander, and forgery, Hitler's minions were aiming at nothing less than absolute control of the Wehrmacht, or armed forces, and an irrevocable break with German military tradition. It was an ominous development—perhaps the single most important step on the road to national disaster.

My notes, records, and collected depositions relating to this squalid backstage drama are yours if you want them. I surrender them with some trepidation. Use them as you think fit.

Yours sincerely
(Counsellor) Erich Meller.

THIS BOOK has turned into a novel. My hope that it will excite compassion and human understanding need not conflict with the fact that it also tallies in very many respects with records and documents of the period.

That it should strive to do so is essential. Historians of every complexion, some partisan, some objective, and others autobiographical, have since been busy on their own detailed "documentary" accounts of the Third Reich. This has involved them in an analysis of every ascertainable current of opinion and power grouping, every sphere of influence and official measure, every opportunity seized or neglected, every blunder and sin of omission.

The disadvantage of this method is that human beings and the human element tend to be overlooked, if not swamped, by a deluge of carefully accumulated facts and figures. Every phase of the political and military power game is described without conveying a hint of what it meant to its agonized, bleeding, and expiring victims. All they represent to the reader is a necessary application of fertilizer to the soil of history.

This is not to dispute the value of actual reportage or the virtues of diligent research. The following points have been established beyond doubt:

1. A senior German general and decent human being was publicly pilloried for being a homosexual. At the time, this trumped-up charge meant more than a social death sentence. It was a secret weapon which could be used for the permanent destruction of any selected target.

2. A German field marshal holding the highest rank and appointment in the armed forces was stripped of all his posts on the strength of forged and doctored evidence purporting to show that he had married a prostitute.

Faced with these facts, none but the most unthinking

observer can fail to wonder what actually happened. What went on inside these victims of a criminal regime, and how, having been so deeply injured and foully slandered, did they contrive to go on living?

The only logical explanation is twofold. The first soldier had the sort of naive integrity which, however commendable in abstract, proves totally self-destructive in a world ruled by criminals. As for the second, the most crucial phase in his existence revealed him to be a mere man. Worse still, he was a man in love, and the object of his love fell prey to a ruthless smear campaign.

Both "scandals," which are closely linked by other than chronological factors, developed into a human tragedy remarkable for its touches of pathos.

We can attach a precise time and place to the start of this tangled and often preposterous web of events. It all began in Potsdamer Platz, Berlin, on the evening of 22 November 1933.

1

Obscure Beginnings

The dark and rainy day was drawing to a close. The sky above Berlin, ten-month-old capital of Adolf Hitler's Thousand-Year Reich, seemed to sag like sodden canvas. There were no policemen in sight and few people walking the streets. Below street level, in the Wannsee suburban line station, a female ticket clerk yawned behind her window. If she noticed the pale shadow of a man leaning against one of the scuffed and dirty pillars, she didn't show it. He looked like a loiterer. On the other hand, he might be Gestapo. It was wiser not to notice him. No point in asking for trouble, not these days.

Somebody flushed a toilet in the men's washroom for the third time in half an hour, but nobody came out. The woman at the counter took care not to notice that either.

The man propped against the pillar grinned broadly, nodded sagely, and went on waiting. He knew what for.

The man's name was Otto Schmidt—"Otto-Otto" to his friends. To someone of Otto's breed, the current sequence of events was a routine but often lucrative occurrence in the world of flushing toilets, whispered confidences, and stifled mo:.:s of pleasure.

The inevitable had yet to happen, but it soon did. Four or five male figures clattered downstairs from the street, chatting and joking loudly among themselves. All but one wore dark-blue uniforms.

Army officers painting the town, thought Otto, very alert now. The single civilian was an elderly man with a high-pitched voice and strutting gait. His once-smart black overcoat had a brown fur collar.

"Splendid evening," he fluted, swaying from the waist as he minced along, "—simply splendid! We must do it again sometime."

Everyone enthusiastically agreed. The officers had dined well after a hard day's training. Now they were on their way back to barracks or bound for some nightspot in the city center—Friedrichstrasse or the Kurfürstendamm. Their friend in the fur-trimmed overcoat had given them some promising addresses.

They pumped his hand and gave him a boisterous good night before boarding the next train, waving from an open window. The train vanished into the darkness. The man with the fur collar stared after it for several seconds, his face pale and forlorn. He might have been all alone in this white-tiled limbo.

Then, like a signal, came the sound of the nearby toilet flushing yet again.

Otto Schmidt was familiar with various forms of nocturnal entertainment. Though not unique to Berlin, they aroused particular disapproval in the capital city of a country whose new rulers laid such strong emphasis on the virtues of propriety, morality, and clean living. Undesirable elements had to be weeded out and Otto Schmidt was—in his own way—helping the campaign along.

He even made an income out of it—quite a decent income sometimes, but only as long as he fed the police a fairly regular diet of names and addresses. It never occurred to him that he was about to hook a really big fish. If it had, he would probably have done his utmost to avoid landing it. Otto liked to collect, but he also liked a quiet life.

All he knew at that moment was that the men's room at Wannsee Station functioned as a meeting place where one of his confederates pursued his trade between urinal and lavatory bowl. The flushing toilet was his call sign.

The gentleman with the brown fur collar headed for the source of the sound like a homing pigeon. To quote a later interrogation transcript, he looked "itchy."

Excerpt from Counsellor Meller's notes—

Detective Superintendent Georg Huber gave me the following information:

"The character in the men's room was one Josef Weingartner, known to clients and associates as 'Bavarian Joe.' He'd caught my attention early on, probably because 'Bavarian George' was what they used to call me at police headquarters and later in the Gestapo.

"Anyway, this Josef Weingartner was a male prostitute, and a sorry specimen at that. He looked shop-worn, but that made him all the more eager to please. He wasn't choosy and kept his charges low.

"He must have serviced several hundred clients between 1933 and 1937. Business was usually transacted on the station premises but not in the men's room itself. That was just a rendezvous. Actual customer contact took place as far off the beaten track as possible—preferably in the open, in order to give adequate warning of the approach of a third party. The police, for instance.

"Weingartner was a modest performer—middling at best. His rates ranged from ten to forty marks, depending on the form and extent of the treatment required. He certainly never made more than fifty marks a session.

"I'm not telling you all this to give you a thrill of moral repugnance, Counsellor—you're a man of the world. I'm simply drawing your attention to a couple of salient points.

"To begin with, Weingartner had no pretensions to class. He serviced hundreds of clients but didn't know their names—in fact, he hardly knew what they looked like, because he preferred to operate in the dark. There was a sound commerical reason for this. As I already indicated, he was no pinup.

"My own considered opinion is that no one of any refinement would have chosen the boy as a source of sexual gratification. But that, Counsellor, is precisely what the Gestapo claimed.

"Human nature's capable of anything, you may say. Quite right, in principle, but it surely doesn't apply in cases where someone's income and social status give him a certain freedom to pick and choose. In other words, I simply can't imagine a general—and a senior general at that—consorting with a pathetic creature like Weingartner. Can you?"

Otto Schmidt continued to hug the shadowy lee of his pillar in Wannsee Station. All he had to do now was wait, and patience was part of Otto's stock-in-trade.

To a connoisseur of such scenes, the next phase was a daily or, rather, nightly spectacle. As Otto put it later under interrogation: "The pair of them got down to business, the filthy bastards."

Hot on the heels of Bavarian Joe, the man with the fur collar followed him outside, down a dark alley, and across several disused tracks to where a rusty chain-link fence separated the station from its adjacent freight depot. Then, amid stacks of building materials—bricks, timber, and sacks of cement—there occurred what is commonly termed a homosexual act. Duration: seven or eight minutes. Probable charge: thirty marks.

Otto Schmidt knew it all by heart. Without budging from the spot or watching what went on, he would later be able to swear to anything he was asked.

> **More extracts from the records of Counsellor Erich Meller, then employed at the Prussian Ministry of the Interior, Berlin—**
>
> Quite absurd, these recent and reiterated attempts to white-wash the events of the time as "politically understandable." They were mean, malicious, and criminal manoeuvres undertaken by men who paid lip service to the military code of honour. Their object was to discredit that code and, if possible, destroy it.

After our defeat in World War I, the remains of the officer corps—a conservative and class-conscious bunch—sought refuge in the "Hundred-Thousand-Man Army" permitted to Germany by the Versailles Treaty. The Commander-in-Chief of this so-called Reichswehr was General von Seeckt, a gifted and masterful leader whose aim was to build up a neutral force with no party political ties. Then came Hitler, who succeeded in squashing even the most self-assured of his generals, though not Seeckt, who died before the Führer's power over the armed forces became absolute.

Among the victims of Hitler's systematic campaign were the twin stars of World War I, Hindenburg and Ludendorff.

Ludendorff, who had been extolled as a military genius while Chief of the Grand General Staff of the Imperial Army, was the first to go. His association with Hitler's abortive Beer Hall Putsch in 1923 turned him into a failed revolutionary. It also transformed him into a frustrated and embittered man who devoted the rest of his life to racist and anti-Semitic daydreams.

Field Marshal Paul von Hindenburg, that personification of German martial glory whose proud boast it was to have remained "undefeated in the field," became President of the German Republic in 1925. Hitler disposed of him later, when he was already in his dotage. This he did, as he had once done with Ludendorff, after brazen attempts to ingratiate himself and loud protestations of loyalty. He, Adolf Hitler, who had fought in the trenches and won the Iron Cross First Class, proclaimed that he would leap to defend the Army's reputation at all times.

He probably meant what he said, but only from his own perverted standpoint. What is certain is that the military took him at face value. They told themselves that a man imbued with the spirit of the trenches could be relied on to organize the masses and quell subversive elements such as communists, socialists, and pacifists.

In the firm belief that he would "toe the line," Field Marshal President Hindenburg appointed the corporal-turned-politico Reich Chancellor on 30 January 1933, or what became known as "Assumption of Power Day."

Hitler actually showed some willingness to venerate Germany's military traditions, if only verbally. In the garrison church at Potsdam, where Hitler had just delivered an address on "true national values," Hindenburg shook his hand with solemn appreciation. The generals saw high times ahead, rich with plum appointments and fat military appropriations.

The Party's brown-shirted "storm detachments," or SA for short, a militantly ambitious organization millions strong, were swiftly and brutally put in their place by the murder of Ernst Röhm, their chief of staff, and numerous senior SA officers. Hitler now proclaimed that the Wehrmacht was the sole force in Germany entitled to bear arms. This was an announcement worthy of Hindenburg himself. The generals' hopes rose still higher, but they had yet to know their Führer—their "leader"—for what he was. They continued to nurse the grand illusion that he was a mere corporal, an Austrian upstart, and, when all was said and done, their social and military inferior.

In his galloping senility, Hindenburg was quick to praise Hitler in lofty, well-nigh reverential terms. One evening after a dinner I attended at the presidential palace, he listened thoughtfully to the sound of a passing aircraft. Then: "That's *him*," he declared, meaning Hitler. "He's worrying about this Germany of ours—he's always on the move..."

After a feebleminded reaction like that, anything was

possible. On 1 June 1935, Hitler announced two key appointments. General Werner von Blomberg was promoted field marshal. He also became Commander-in-Chief Wehrmacht and War Minister. Simultaneously, as though to mitigate the predictable resentment aroused in conservative military circles, General Baron Werner von Fritsch was appointed Commander-in-Chief Army.

This second appointment was a very subtle move. Blomberg, who was reputed to be in sympathy with National Socialism, had been harnessed alongside Fritsch, a soldier in the old Prussian tradition. They made a promising team—from Hitler's point of view.

It would seem at this distance in time that Hitler foresaw the whole course of events. Thanks to my boyhood friend in high places, I watched the ensuing *pas de deux* or *danse macabre*—however you choose to regard it—from a front-row seat.

Otto Schmidt felt sure of his ground when he saw the man with the fur collar returning from the far side of the Wannsee Station tracks. He was looking relieved but apprehensive. Like a forest creature terrified of being cornered, he glanced nervously in all directions.

Reassured because he seemed to have the platform to himself, the man drew a deep breath and relaxed. He produced a white handkerchief from the right-hand sleeve of his overcoat and wiped his perspiring face. Then he caught sight of Otto emerging from the gloom at the end of the platform.

Otto advanced at a leisurely pace, trench coat flapping and hat pulled down low over his eyes. Two paces away, he stopped and said calmly, "Your activities have been observed and noted. In detail."

The man with the fur collar winced. One hand drew the white silk scarf even tighter round his neck. The other shielded his face, which had gone the colour of milk. He did not reply.

Otto was an old hand at this kind of situation. Knowing that its inherent menace would only be heightened by a pause, he stood there and smiled. There was nothing friendly about his smile. It was wary, contemptuous—ominous.

At that moment, a train pulled into the station. The man with the fur collar fled inside. Still leisurely, Otto followed. His quarry was almost in the bag. All that remained was to set a price.

Closer inspection suggested that it would not, unfortunately, amount to much. Otto sat down opposite his victim and took stock. A retired officer, from the look of him. The effete and ravaged face possessed a sort of vacuous dignity, but the darting eyes pleaded for mercy.

"Who are you? What do you want?"

Otto did his best to look easygoing, broad-minded, and sympathetic—the sort of man you could talk to. "Kröger's the name," he lied. "Detective superintendent, Vice Squad. You can figure out the rest for yourself."

The train continued to rumble across Berlin.

"I'm not a hard man," Otto announced. "Never have been. That ought to be worth something."

"Two hundred marks," the man with the fur collar replied quickly. "I could pay you right away."

"What the hell do you take me for?" Otto looked genuinely affronted. "You wouldn't want me to march you into the nearest police station with that cocksucker in tow, would you? Okay, but it's only kindness of heart that's stopping me. That should be worth at least five hundred. Is it a deal?"

"I don't have that much, not on me."

"Where, then?"

"Back at my apartment. If you'd like to come with me..."

"You bet I would—with the proper precautions." Otto was a practical man. He knew every trick in the book. "So don't think you can give me the slip. Like in at the wrong door, out at the back. That game won't work with me, friend."

"I give you my word of honour..."

"Five hundred marks, that's what you're going to give me—two hundred here and now and the rest at your apartment. Okay, let's have your name and address."

The man with the fur collar turned out to live in Lichterfelde-Ost, a fairly prosperous residential district favoured by senior civil servants and members of the armed forces. General Beck, the Army Chief of Staff, lived there too.

The man's identity card bore the address 20 Ferdinand-strasse. Occupation: captain of cavalry, retired. Place of birth: Austria. Name: von Frisch, Achim.

Achim von Frisch handed over the two hundred marks. Later that night, he gave his blackmailer three hundred more, sadly remarking as he did that it would leave him very short because he wasn't a wealthy man. He found it hard to make ends meet on his modest Army pension.

Otto Schmidt pocketed the money without a flicker of remorse.

More notes by Counsellor Erich Meller—

The relationship between Hitler and his generals was strained and uneasy from the outset. Simplifying, one might say that they despised him and he detested them.

To them, the Chancellor was an ambitious little ex-corporal with an inordinate appetite for public acclaim. To him, they were a bunch of arrogant, pig-headed careerists. Neither impression was completely wrong.

"They don't understand me!" mourned Hitler during a monologue which I and a few others were privileged to hear one night at the Chancellery. It was a performance worthy of the State Theatre. With exalted fervour—more Schiller than Shakespeare—he went on to lament that they were incapable of comprehending his grand design.

"That gentleman doesn't speak our language!" snapped General Ludwig Beck, the Army Chief of Staff. He made this observation at a small and, so he believed, sympathetic gathering to which I had been graciously invited. A reserved and dignified man, Beck wasn't one of those who referred to Hitler as "the corporal." To him, the Chancellor was "that gentleman" or "Herr Hitler." "Herr Hitler," he said, "obviously can't see where our efforts should be directed."

The general enlarged on this theme with defiant and unflinching candour. "The purposeful expansion and development of our armed forces will make a vital contribution to European stability. Indeed, the millions invested in them should prove a peace-keeping factor of the first magnitude."

Adolf Hitler let his generals wallow in this cosy misconception. If only during his early years as head of state, he took every opportunity to express his absolute reliance on the sense of solidarity bred by common experience of war. "We *are* Germany," he declared. "There can be no greater obligation!"

He felt well able to afford such pleasing pronouncements, because his immediate circle now included not only the worthy Werner von Fritsch but the noble Werner von Blomberg, who seemed capable of neutralizing even the most die-hard reactionaries in the German military establishment. Nobody could have foreseen that Blomberg himself would become a top-level "security risk" or, rather, be criminally manoeuvred into that role because of a woman.

But that was what happened, thanks mainly to the efforts of Hermann Göring. Even the stirrings of the human loins were grist to his political mill!

Preliminary attempt at a dramatized reconstruction of the events surrounding Eva Gruhn ... Subject: maternal warnings—

"Honestly, my girl, what's come over you!" Frau Gruhn threw up her hands in despair. "Seems to me you're getting too greedy. I don't see what you're after."

"I want to live a little, that's all," Eva said. "I want to get out of this stinking, overcrowded hole. Surely you wouldn't begrudge me that?"

They were in the basement laundry room of a shabby Berlin tenement. Flaking walls, soiled concrete floor, battered washtubs, and mangle. There was a rank smell of cheap soap and dirty washing on the boil.

"I'm just an honest, respectable woman," Frau Gruhn persisted. "I've always tried to be a good mother to you—you can't pretend otherwise—but lately you don't listen to a word I say. You're heading for trouble, my girl."

"Oh, stop it, Mother! All I want is security. I want the kind of love worth having—and I think I've found it at last. Please don't try to stop me."

"I'm only trying to warn you, Eva. You're a good-looking girl. Everyone falls for you, but that's the whole trouble. Men are unpredictable, believe me. I ought to know."

"Only one man matters in the long run, and that's the one I think I've found. He was worth waiting for."

"But you always seem to get friendly with men so much older than yourself, Eva. It worries me. Isn't that what they call a father fixation?"

"Maybe." Eva shrugged. She could hardly remember her father, who had died in the Great War. "Personally, I'd call it realism. From all I've seen, experience makes older men a lot more gentlemanly and understanding, not to mention generous."

Frau Gruhn disapprovingly shook her head of slightly greying hair. She could still lay claim to a certain rustic beauty, but her face bore the imprint of a hard life.

Eva, at this time just over thirty, was a curvaceous young woman with unmistakable sex appeal.

"That reminds me," said Frau Gruhn. "What's going on with the landlord? They say there's something between you."

"Do they?" Eva smiled at her. "Some people will say anything, especially when it's what other people want to hear. I'm a favourite topic of conversation, I know. You expect me to like it?"

"Of course not. Still, if he's really serious about you, he wouldn't be a bad catch. I've heard he owns at least two apartment houses besides this one."

"I'm not that easily impressed, Mother. I don't care what a man owns. What matters to *me* is whether he loves me the way I love him, not for any selfish reason."

Frau Gruhn sighed. "And what about the tenant on the third floor? You're friendly with him too, so I hear, but he's got one foot in the grave—must be fifty if he's a day. Fancy fluttering your eyelashes at a man like that!"

"Herr Vogelsang, you mean? Why shouldn't I be nice to him? He's got important connections in the Party—and the police. Besides, he's not so bad. He runs a high-class delicatessen in the Kurfürstendamm."

"When I was young," Frau Gruhn proclaimed firmly, "I always did my best to lead a decent, respectable, hardworking life. I saved myself for one man, and that was your father. I never loved anyone but him."

"You're bringing tears to my eyes, you and your respectability!" Eva gave her mother a pitying smile. "Still, at least Father died a hero's death, as you always put it so beautifully. I'm going to borrow that phrase from now on. The way I'm heading, I can use a war hero in my family tree."

"But what about your background? We're ordinary people. You can't just wipe that out."

"I don't want to, Mother, but I'd like to forget a couple of things. That's where my friend can help me. He's a wonderful man, a kind man —a real gentleman. The sort of man I've dreamt of ever since I was a child."

Frau Gruhn looked thoroughly perturbed. She brooded in silence for a moment. Then she said darkly, "It'll end in tears. You, a girl from a humble home, and him, an important and powerful man—it's bound to go wrong."

"There's no bound to about it. I'm not saying that just because he keeps telling me not to worry—I can feel it deep down."

"So who is he? Come on, it's time you told your mother."

Eva laughed aloud, radiant with self-assurance. "Maybe you'll read about him in the paper one day."

"In the paper?" Eva's carefree smile only intensified her mother's forebodings. "Where in the paper—in the crime section? Eva, I'm worried sick. The whole thing could turn out to be a disaster, for me as well as you."

More notes made by Counsellor Erich Meller—

"Bavarian George"—a departmental nickname for which my friend Georg Huber cherished an understandable aversion because of its resemblance to "Bavarian Joe," one of the seediest figures on his Vice Squad books—was a first-class detective.

He was justly regarded as an acknowledged master of his craft. More than that, he had a firm belief in his absolute dedication to truth and justice. In this lay the seeds of his own dark and depressing fate. Like many others, he came to grief because of a desire to preserve his personal integrity. I ask you—in *those* days!

I myself headed Section C at the Prussian Ministry of the Interior. The "C" might have stood for all manner of things from coordination to criminology—and so in a sense it did.

My section had been made responsible for ensuring the smoothest possible cooperation between the various official bodies currently jockeying for political power— Party, civil service, SA, SS, police, Military Intelligence, and the rest. At the same time, I managed to grind an axe or two of my own. I couldn't have done so without some protection—naturally not, or I wouldn't be here now.

"Bavarian George" Huber dropped in regularly, always pleading that the sight of my name on the office door had reminded him that I kept several dozen boxes of choice Havanas stored in a cool office cupboard. His yearning for these Henry Clays, which dominated the cigar scene at a time when Castro was still in knee pants, had then—so Huber used to claim—become too much for him.

I always made him welcome, however inscrutable his manner. Ceremoniously selecting a Havana from my ample assortment, he would test the outer leaf with his fingers and run his nose along it like someone savouring the fragrant skin of a beautiful woman. Before lighting up, however, he never failed—offhandedly—to deposit some papers on my desk.

He never actually pushed these police files or sheaves of loose papers straight at me—that I can swear, though I was free to pick them up, examine them, and ask any questions I chose. Huber's "consultations" lasted for as along as it took him to smoke his cigar. Depending on size, this could mean forty to fifty minutes.

As time went by, I plied him with the longer and fatter varieties because his material consisted of ammunition ideally suited to the jungle warfare waged by our Nazi rulers. Some of his consignments were well worth a Corona Corona. This, for instance:

Memo to Vice Squad, Police Department, Berlin. Confidential. Re Gruhn, Eva, for personal particulars see card index. Classified "of doubtful character" but not to be kept under direct surveillance. Any further information to be noted for precautionary purposes.

"An extremely questionable mode of procedure, my dear Huber," I said, confident of my familiarity with the tricks of his trade. "Add one chance memo to another equally random report and—surprise!—the police have the makings of a case. It happens a hundred times a year."

"A thousand times in Berlin alone," said Huber, outwardly engrossed in his cigar. "But don't be side-tracked. Read on—take a look at item two."

This referred to Eva Gruhn's mother, who had often clashed with the authorities. To judge by what I read, she was a woman whose outspokenness was deeply resented by some of the civil servants she had badgered in the past. Their accumulated comments on her included such boldly underscored remarks as *Hard to handle, Deliberately uncooperative*, and—more ominously—*Antisocial tendencies*.

"One of the world's unfortunates," I theorized. "The sort of woman who knows her rights and antagonizes everyone by insisting on them. She's obviously the bane of the local authorities. Is her daughter like her?"

"Yes and no." Huber took a pleasurable pull at his cigar. "I'm a policeman and you're an administrator, but I suspect we both tend to generalize when something fails to fit our preconceived pattern. So the mother sounds like an argumentative old washerwoman. Who says the daughter isn't a natural-born lady—or couldn't become one?"

That interested me. "What are you getting at, Huber?"

"You'll see. Run your eye over the third item."

This read:

Departmental memo re Gruhn, Luise. Subject was originally employed as a charwoman at the Royal Palace, Berlin-Charlottenburg, where her husband, Paul Gruhn, worked as a gardener. They were married in 1903. Their only child, Eva, was born the same year. Paul Gruhn appears to have broken with his wife at an early stage, because he left her and took

a variety of jobs, usually at a safe distance from
Berlin.

It also happened that Paul Gruhn had obeyed his
country's call in 1914—with fatal results. He served as an
infantryman at Verdun and died the conventional hero's
death there in 1916, when the lower part of his anatomy
was rearranged by several pieces of shrapnel.

With tigerish tenacity, his widow struggled to support
herself and her daughter throughout the hectic postwar
period, the dark days of inflation, recession, and political
ferment. No form of employment deterred her, however
menial. She helped out in hospital laundries and kitchens.
Later, she tried specializing in "therapeutic massage,"
most of her clients being war-wounded veterans.

Between 1923 and 1927, she officially described herself
as a masseuse—a respectable profession in those days,
though she was repeatedly questioned by the police and
business registration authorities on the strength of several
complaints. Unfounded complaints, it seemed, because
no charges were ever brought

"You'll notice," said Huber, still reverently preoccupied
with the butt of his Havana, "that even the objective
professional who compiled that report betrays a certain
sympathy for the mother and daughter."

"Why not?" I said. "I'm beginning to feel the same way
myself. It sounds as if they're just another two casualties of
our age—a couple of poor, harassed women with an
understandable craving for the security they've never had.
I not only respect that sentiment, I sympathize with it. Am
I wrong?"

"Probably not, but I can't say for sure—not yet. Not
even after reading item four, which sounds equally

suspicious. Better read it yourself—it could be another piece in the puzzle."

May 1933, Eva Gruhn arrested on suspicion of theft. She was accused of stealing a ring set with diamonds or diamond chips. The missing article was later discovered at the owner's home. Furthermore, the diamonds turned out to be high-class imitations, probably manufactured at Idar-Oberstein. In view of her proven innocence, Eva Gruhn was released.

I was suddenly stung by the sight of all these carefully husbanded specks of police-dug dirt. "My God, Huber," I said irritably, "I don't admire your department's methods. This is nothing but a tissue of unfounded charges and bureaucratic gossip. If it ever fell into the wrong hands, it could lead to an appalling miscarriage of justice."

"You should know, Counsellor, you're an expert." Huber studied the remains of his cigar. "But who's to distinguish between the wrong hands and the right? We're living in the age of the card index and filing cabinet. Random bits of information like these are preserved for one of two purposes—exposure or concealment. They're like an ammunition dump. Blow it up and you can destroy an enemy, refrain from blowing it up and you may acquire a useful friend."

"Good God, are we still talking about the Gruhns—two obscure women struggling to survive in a tough world? Don't the police have anything better to do than fill their files with trivia? I call that pretty despicable—disturbing too."

"You'll be even more disturbed when I tell you they're being watched, especially the daughter. I've still to

discover who placed them under surveillance, but it may
be a purely routine move—for the moment. Better look at
item five."

The fifth item concerned someone named Volker
Vogelsang. Records had him listed as a habitual offender
in the "several previous convictions" category, but his
offences were only minor cases of misrepresentation or
fraud and one extremely clumsy attempt at embezzlement. In the expert opinion of a detective who knew him
well, Vogelsang was "a congenital bungler." That was just
what made him so useful.

As a matter of routine, the police requested Vogelsang's
"official cooperation." He obediently performed some
odd jobs of a not entirely insignificant nature. Before long
he was registered as "Informant No. 134" and had become
one of several hundred similar pigeons.

Vogelsang passed on whatever he could—whatever
came his way. Then, quite unwittingly, he hit the jackpot.
Again as a matter of routine, somebody fed him a code
word which galvanized him: Eva Gruhn.

His very first "informant's report" on the subject began
as follows:

I happen to know the said person. We live in the same
building. Her mother, Frau Luise Gruhn, used to
work as a "masseuse" specializing in war wounded
amputees. As far as I can gather, she sometimes
persuaded her daughter, i.e. Eva, to assist her for a
share in the proceeds.

Their work entailed massaging the stumps of the
patient's severed limbs, also his back muscles and
cardiac region. It must have been a rather depressing
job because Eva tried to get out of it.

I helped her—without any ulterior motive, I

should add—by getting her a job in a department store. She soon switched to a high-class restaurant, where she waited table to the entire satisfaction of the proprietor and his customers. And that was when it happened . . .

"When what happened?"

But Huber had already risen and was mashing out his cigar stub in my big glass ashtray. He retrieved his papers from the desk.

"What happened next may be wholly innocuous." He paused. "As long as it doesn't go any further."

"Further than what, for God's sake?"

"The standard Hollywood fairy tale. Handsome prince falls for village maiden but remembers his duty to the throne just in time. For both their sakes, let's hope they don't insist on a happy ending."

"Eva Gruhn and who else?"

Huber, who had reached the door, was looking very pensive. "I'm afraid you're not going to laugh at this, Counsellor, though it does have its funny side. The lucky man is one of the restaurant's regular customers, Field Marshal von Blomberg."

The news left me slightly dazed and more than a little worried. It was an extremely delicate situation. "How many people have access to these records?"

"At least half a dozen detectives plus their immediate superiors, but they only know the story as far as it goes. If it isn't already too late, I'm going to keep it under wraps from now on."

"What are you afraid of?"

"The same as you, of course. That's why I think the matter should be looked into a bit more closely, but not by somebody from the police department. Don't you agree?"

With a farewell flourish, he tossed me a plain envelope. Inside were a photograph and two addresses, one belonging to Eva Gruhn and the other to the restaurant where she worked. Huber was actually trying to enlist me in his hazardous scheme on the confident and, I fear, well-founded assumption that I'd rise to the bait.

Otto Schmidt was busy exploiting his latest victim. The professional in him felt dissatisfied with the measly five hundred marks extracted from Captain von Frisch. He wanted more—as much more as possible.

And so, only a few weeks after the events at Wannsee Station, he paid the captain another visit. He knew the address, after all, and there was no real need to vary his approach. Without a blush, he continued to pose as a member of the CID. He didn't care whether Frisch believed him or not. It was an old but effective story, and he blandly repeated it as he elbowed his way into the captain's apartment.

"I never welsh on a deal, sir, so don't get me wrong. You paid up like a gentleman. As far as I'm concerned, we're quits."

"But... In that case, what are you doing here?"

"Because we're not alone in the world, you and me. I've got superiors, sir. Very awkward superiors. The long and the short of it is, they want their cut."

Frisch turned pale. "How much?"

"Policemen have to live too," Otto told him. "Being practical men, we've run a check on your financial assets. Don't worry, we won't ask more than you can afford."

"So how much?"

"Two thousand marks."

"My God, that'll just about bankrupt me!"

"Exactly, sir. Have the cash ready by the day after tomorrow. We'll meet in the subway restaurant at Lichterfelde-Ost at one P.M. sharp. My boss'll be there too."

"What if I refuse?"

"That's easy. You'll be charged."

"And what if I charge you with blackmail?"

"Think about that for a moment, sir. You really want me to give evidence against you—me, a police officer? I wouldn't be the only witness either. There's our old friend Bavarian Joe, who did you that little favour. You really want it to come to that? Of course not, so what choice do you have?"

Frisch bowed his head. "None."

From Counsellor Meller's notes—

Months before the pace of events began to pick up, the Berlin vice squad possessed two files. They were kept in the same office but on different shelves. Nobody, not even my friend "Bavarian George" Huber, that expert on human frailty, had any immediate inkling that they would some day be closely related.

One of these files contained a random and sketchy assortment of information about someone called Eva Gruhn. The other, which was appreciably fatter and much more conclusive, referred to Otto Schmidt, a useful and cooperative "observer of the Berlin homosexual scene."

The custodian of these records was a detective inspector named Singer, whose antlike industry was exceeded only by his ambition, and Singer enjoyed the favour of an influential superior. This was Detective Chief Superintendent Meisinger, a confirmed Nazi sympathizer with an urgent desire to jump on the new regime's bandwagon. Reinhard Heydrich, who headed the RSHA, or Central State Security Bureau, had instinctively grasped this and earmarked him for a senior post in the Gestapo. Meisinger was now grooming himself for promotion. As he saw it, this meant accumulating as much information as he could find, no matter how incomplete or indiscriminate.

Commenting later, Huber said, "I didn't have a clue what was going on, even though these records and card indexes were part of my province. But that's the way it was. When the kings of the jungle join battle, even the warthog tries to roar like a lion. In our case the outcome was a tragedy none of us foresaw—and tragedies often come in pairs."

But this was just another aspect of the forthcoming poker game. The players had gathered round the table, and the chips, as they say, were down.

Although he could never have been called unimaginative, Adolf Hitler tended to judge others by himself. He firmly believed that all who became involved with him were bound to react in the same way, even generals. This shocking but far from baseless assumption prompted him to think them capable—like himself—of everything from political duplicity to an insidious power struggle. He simply couldn't grasp that even his generals included many honest men—or, at least, many who aspired to be and remain so.

If he had realized this, he need never have subjected them to criminal pressure. One word of command from the Führer, one order from the Chancellor and head of state, and the two men most directly affected by these events, General von Fritsch and Field Marshal von Blomberg, would have obeyed. After all, they were soldiers.

But Hitler seems never even to have considered such a

course. I suppose his real aim was to stage a deterrent political drama in collaboration with Göring and Heydrich—and Heydrich, of all people, was the "boyhood friend" I mentioned earlier. The inevitable result was a series of wantonly provoked and lethal confrontations between adversaries armed with unmatched weapons—duelling foils versus meat cleavers.

My God, what a massacre!

2

More
Manoeuvres

Colonel Friedrich Hossbach, Wehrmacht adjutant to the Führer and Chancellor, Adolf Hitler, enjoyed a high reputation for reliability, sincerity, and honesty—and rightly so. Hossbach was a soldier who did his best to remain one, even in present surroundings.

Just lately, however, he had been oppressed by a feeling that the Chancellery's gleaming parquet had turned to ice beneath his feet. He felt this now, as he hovered in front of Hitler's desk.

"My Führer, Commander-in-Chief Luftwaffe wishes to know if all three armed services will be represented at this afternoon's conference with the War Minister and Commander-in-Chief Army."

Expertly, Hitler contorted his face into a mask of resentment and anger. His suspicions could erupt like lightning. "What!" he yelped. "Since when has Göring had the run of my appointments book? Is there a leak somewhere, Colonel—in your office, for instance?"

Friedrich Hossbach did not show how hurt he was by this imputation. He confined himself to saying, with studious courtesy, "According to my information, sir, Field Marshal von Blomberg and General Göring dined together last night, so it's quite possible the subject came up during..."

"All right, my dear Hossbach, all right." Hitler's mood seemed to mellow from one moment to the next. He made no attempt to apologize, of course. That he never did nor was ever expected to do.

"Kindly tell Göring to mind his own business," was all he said. "He'd do better to concentrate on that Air Force of his—it could use his undivided attention. My first concern is the Army. With me, the Army always takes priority."

This little speech embodied three important statements specially intended for the ears of Hossbach, who occupied a key position midway between the Chancellery and the Wehrmacht. In the first place, Hitler had conveyed that, although regarded as his heir apparent, Göring struck him as undesirably pushy—something he knew would be welcome news in many quarters. Next, he had gratified those who harboured similar doubts by questioning the general's professional competence. Last but not least, he had stressed the Army's dominant role—an assurance which could not fail to flatter the Army officers, of whom Hossbach himself was one.

"Should I prepare any papers for the meeting?" asked Hossbach. He knew the answer before he spoke. Hitler had a phenomenal memory and a fondness for springing grand surprises. Information converged on him from a variety of sources to which he alone had access, and he liked to catch his listeners off balance by unveiling it at the psychological moment.

"My sole purpose," he said, shrewdly avoiding a straight negative, "is a further improvement in the Army's combat readiness. General von Fritsch, who commands my highest respect, is a first-class strategist. We're fortunate to have him. Personally, I consider it advisable to make the fullest use of his unique talents—in other words, allow him wide discretionary powers. I'm sure you agree."

Colonel Hossbach was quick to do just that, but the only effect of all these fine words was a fleeting sense of unease. For quite some time now, he had been haunted by an agonizing question. Was this man—his head of state—a person to be trusted?

The Police Commissioner of Berlin, Count Wolf von Helldorf, had just been assigned a new deputy—a fellow count named Fritz-Dietlof von der Schulenburg. Events were to prove him an enterprising but unfathomable character.

Mutual uncertainty reigned at first. Each man gingerly probed the other's defences. At one of their earliest interviews, the new Deputy Commissioner displayed his inquisitive turn of mind by referring to a directive circulated by the Prussian Minister of the Interior. Its main provision: "Establishment of a central card index listing such morally subversive elements as prostitutes, pimps, homosexuals, and similar degenerates. All information received will now be forwarded monthly, in a form suitable for filing, to the newly created records department."

Schulenburg regarded his superior quizzically. "This remarkable document has been lying on your desk for the past three weeks," he said. "So far, you haven't complied with the Minister's urgent request or issued any instructions on the subject. What's the idea, trying to stall for as long as you decently can?"

"Does it bother you?" Count Helldorf's sleekly handsome face had tautened. "Thinking of putting in a complaint?"

"Not at all," his deputy replied with a faint smile. "I'm merely pointing out that someone in higher authority may get wise to your delaying tactics and feel they're inconsistent with the Party line."

"Oh yes, I suppose they could be interpreted as negligence—certainly by as staunch a National Socialist as you are, to judge by your personal record." It had taken Schulenburg only two minutes to lure Helldorf into dropping his guard entirely. The Commissioner's voice became a growl. "Have you been sent here to spy on me? Are you going to take over my job unless I prove I'm a hundred per cent loyal to the régime? Well, I can't. Everybody flunks that test if the examiner wants him to, and I wouldn't put it past you to fail me—you or anyone. All right, you can have my job. There's no need to pussyfoot around."

Count von der Schulenburg was clearly amused. "I've a pretty fair idea how much you know about me, or think you do. I ran Party headquarters at Königsberg before and after 1933. I did such a good job there that the Gauleiter, that cretin Erich Koch, was able to bask in my reflected glory. Then I was appointed a district administrator in East Prussia, where I was just as successful. After that, I became right-hand man to another deadbeat, the Gauleiter of Silesia. His prestige soared, thanks to me."

"And now you've landed on *my* doorstep, Schulenburg. Why?"

"I suppose it's because I've always been one size too big for my job, if not several sizes. People find me a nuisance. I stir up trouble and ask difficult questions. It's the way I'm made."

"And you intend to go on making a nuisance of yourself?"

"Of course—and with a vengeance, mainly because I know a lot more about you than you do about me. For instance, I know you're listed as an anti-Nazi prospect by Admiral Canaris of Military Intelligence and that sidekick of his, Colonel Oster. So don't expect me to regard you as a devotee of the National Socialist system."

"What about you, Schulenburg—what are you?"

"Me? Something far worse. I'm a public enemy. That megalomaniac Hitler and his lower-middle-class fascists make me want to puke. I saw through those fake revolutionaries long ago. Schulenburg, I said to myself one fine day, if you can't kill the bastard, the least you can do is become his Fouché."

"I hope I misunderstood you, Schulenburg. If you're referring to Napoleon's minister of police, he stabbed his emperor in the back a couple of times. Is that what you're planning to do to Hitler?"

"With luck—and your help, of course."

"And you're telling me this openly?" Helldorf looked aghast. "What are you trying to do, provoke me? You've put yourself at my mercy, don't you see?"

"What gives you that idea?" Schulenburg chuckled. "It'd be your word against mine, so there's no problem there. All that worries me is your reluctance to take the plunge. You make an occasional joke about the Nazis and feed their opponents with useful information. That's worth something, but it doesn't make you an activist. Why don't we team up?"

Helldorf assumed a semiofficial tone, as if oblivious of all that had been said so far. "Shall we get back to the agenda?"

"If you mean this ministerial request for a blackmailer's list of sexual peccadilloes, by all means. One thing's for sure: the people who get their hands on this information plan to use it in the so-called public interest. I know we can't lend ourselves to such a scheme, Commissioner, but your halfhearted attempts to stall won't work forever."

"There's an easy way out. I formally delegate the job to my deputy, i.e. you. How do you propose to handle it?"

"In a businesslike and regulation manner, Commissioner. I'll confine my reports to known criminals and refrain from listing anyone temporarily or coincidentally involved with them."

"You do that, my dear fellow." Helldorf looked relieved but skeptical. "Commercialized sex is a grey area, but try to distinguish between the exploiters and the exploited—that's the best rule of thumb. I presume you realize who's behind this new central index?"

"State Security, I imagine. It smells like Heydrich and the Gestapo. They go digging anywhere, even beneath the sheets, but we won't make it easy for them."

"Just be careful, Schulenburg, and don't count on me to play guardian angel. If I ever had any wings, they were clipped long ago. Remember: one little slip—one hint that you're conducting an illicit cover-up—and we'll both be finished."

Punctual to the minute, Field Marshal von Blomberg and General von Fritsch presented themselves at the Chancellery. Colonel Hossbach conducted them to the Führer, who strode briskly towards them with his hands out-stretched. The rich brown of his Party uniform contrasted handsomely with their sober field-grey tunics.

He began by welcoming Blomberg, who was half a head taller but tactful enough to bow from the waist. This enabled Hitler to look down on the field marshal before grasping both his hands and drawing him gently erect.

"Delighted to see you, gentlemen."

He turned to General von Fritsch. The dictator and his Army chief were roughly the same height and thus stood eye to eye, except that one of Fritsch's eyes—the left one—was shielded by a glass disc. Although it gave him a look of aristocratic disdain, this monocle was merely worn to correct a lifelong defect. He was later credited with the apocryphal remark: "I wear it," meaning the monocle, "to keep my face as still as possible, especially in the presence of that man"—meaning Hitler.

General Baron Werner von Fritsch looked and behaved like an archetypal Prussian officer, although his father came from Saxony and his mother from the Rhineland. He was a military ascetic, a soldier of monastically frugal habits. He had never been known to utter a jocular remark, far less a flippant one.

Field Marshal Werner von Blomberg, on the other hand, was universally accounted a man of the world. He had a slim, supple figure and a cheerful disposition, though some who saw him just before the scandal broke described his manner as "woebegone" and claimed his eyes looked swollen with tears.

Hitler played the perfect host. He ushered his visitors to a group of chairs near the window beside his desk. Having treated his War Minister to an encouraging smile, he focused his attention on Fritsch. His tone was casual—almost amused.

"General," he began, "I've just received a report to the

effect that some of your officers referred to me as a house painter. Is that true?"

"It is," Fritsch said curtly.

"Is it also true that you instructed them to keep their voices down in future?"

"Yessir." Fritsch underlined this typically terse response by staring Hitler full in the face.

Hitler turned to Blomberg with an unmistakable look of inquiry. The field marshal reacted at once.

"According to my information, the men concerned were drunk. I feel—and I'm sure the general agrees—that it would be impolitic to exaggerate the importance of their remarks. When Frederick the Great caught sight of a caricature of himself on a wall—you know the old story, my Führer—his sole response was a lofty injunction to hang it lower. No one would expect you to react any differently."

"Quite so," said Fritsch.

Hitler, who was immensely gratified by any comparison between himself and Prussia's greatest monarch, seemed to accept this. Almost brightly, he changed the subject.

"It has also been reported to me that fighting broke out in our own ranks during some recent manoeuvres, and that several men were seriously injured. The parties concerned were an Army regiment and the Leibstandarte SS—my personal bodyguard."

"These things happen," Fritsch said simply.

"Yes, General, but did you issue an immediate call for the Leibstandarte's disbandment?"

"I suggested it, sir. I would remind you of the basic principle agreed between us. The Wehrmacht is the only body of men entitled to bear arms on behalf of the German nation."

"And so it shall remain," Hitler assured him, solemnly

now, with an expression that conveyed how deeply he deplored their misunderstanding. Then, expectantly, he turned to his field marshal.

"My Führer," Blomberg blurted out, "everything possible has already been said and done in this respect. The matter was settled long ago—Herr Röhm's removal saw to that."

He was referring to the massacre at Tegernsee, near Munich, on 30 June 1934, when Hitler had the SA chief of staff and many of his senior officers executed because of their alleged plan to convert the SA into a "people's army" and launch a revolution—not least against the regular armed forces.

"The basis of our working relationship is mutual trust," Fritsch declared. He obviously meant every word.

"Is and must remain so," Hitler agreed. "On the other hand, mutual trust entails a profound and wide-ranging obligation. Our resolve must be to make the Wehrmacht, and the Army in particular, a fighting force of unique and unparalleled efficiency."

"Are you dissatisfied with my efforts, Herr Chancellor?" General Baron Werner von Fritsch put this barbed question calmly. "If you ever lose faith in me and my competence, you need only say the word and I'll resign."

Blomberg frowned. "Don't even mention it!" he exclaimed. "I'm quite sure no one wants your resignation."

"Least of all me," Hitler assured him in a voice throbbing with sincerity. "Your outstanding services to the Army and the nation cannot be overestimated, General."

"My readiness to serve you, Herr Chancellor, is unqualified." It sounded like a profession of faith. Fritsch was a true soldier with all the loyalty and obedience of his breed. He would have been one in any age and under any auspices.

"Excellent, excellent," Blomberg boomed approvingly.

"Thank you," said Hitler. He bowed his head as though gracefully accepting this tribute but did not transfer his attention to the War Minister. Still concentrating on the Army Commander-in-Chief and choosing his words with care, he warmed to his theme.

"Your services, General, have been exceptional. On the other hand, even you must admit there's plenty of room for improvement. After all, we're still in the throes of a unique process of national resurgence."

Fritsch was unmoved. "My task is to expand the Army and bring it to a peak of efficiency. However resolutely we pursue such a policy, this will take time."

"But it mustn't drag on forever, General. To quote only one example, what about the Army's personnel policy? Its ranks have yet to become sufficiently imbued with the new spirit. Judging by its adherence to dusty traditions, the officer corps seems wholly unenlightened." Hitler turned to Blomberg. "Or am I being unfair?"

"No, my Führer, not altogether." The War Minister balanced this assurance by veering cautiously in Fritsch's direction. "However, there's something in what the general says. These things do take time. People are being slow to realize what the new Germany demands of them."

Hitler rose somewhat abruptly but favoured both his visitors with a cordial handshake. "Gentlemen, thank you for being so frank. I have found our discussion most informative."

Just how informative he had really found it the Führer and Chancellor conveyed that evening to Hermann Göring, whose many functions and appointments included overall command of the Air Force. Göring listened with grim but gleeful satisfaction.

"I made yet another attempt," Hitler told him, lolling back in his leather armchair and gazing heavenwards, "to sound out Blomberg and Fritsch. They simply don't have what it takes. Not enough guts and determination to equip them for our great national crusade."

"That's no news to me, my Führer. Fritsch is a military bureaucrat at heart. As for Blomberg, he's a yes-man. He compromises because he likes a quiet life. Lethargy, that's his trouble."

Göring could afford such effronteries whenever he and the Führer were alone or in conclave with their immediate circle. Hitler had a taste for these mudslinging sessions because Göring balked at nothing and no one—certainly not when he smelt intrigue. There was only one clearly discernible exception to this rule, Hitler himself. The Führer was not a man to be trifled with.

Göring knew this. So did Hitler, and Göring knew that he knew. His technique consisted in waiting for the ball to be thrown him. He would then catch it, juggle it more or less adroitly but always with panache, and toss it back.

"I did my best," Hitler purred encouragingly, "to convince Fritsch that he must speed up the Army's expansion and adapt his personnel policy to current requirements—in other words, pay careful attention to the importance of constructive links with our government and Party agencies—but he didn't take it in. Not at all. These things take time ... That was his only response to my criticism."

"Sounds just like him, the old Prussian war-horse." Göring laughed maliciously. "Fritsch can't see beyond the barracks gates. He's looking senile these days. Besides, they say he's a sick man. Shortness of breath, prostate trouble, hemorrhoids—that sort of thing."

"Who says so?" The Führer was all ears. "Do you have

any details—anything on paper? This is very disturbing news, Göring. I mean, I can't afford to leave an invalid in charge of the Army."

"I can drum up all the documentary evidence you need," Göring said gleefully. A sudden thought struck him. "Perhaps you'd like some similar information about Blomberg? It ought to be possible."

Hitler eyed him ambiguously. "Whatever you do," he warned, "don't attract any unnecessary attention. My motives are purely charitable, especially where Blomberg's concerned. We owe the man something, though I must confess I wasn't particularly pleased by his pro-Fritsch line. I made my position perfectly clear, and he failed to back me up. Obviously, he's another whose commitment to our cause falls short of perfection."

"I saw this coming!" Göring said delightedly. "Blomberg's too damned easygoing, it's as simple as that. He's a *bon viveur*. He eats like a pig, drinks too much, and shoots his mouth off."

Not content to have credited the War Minister with all his own most salient characteristics, Göring proceeded to revenge himself for a remark he found particularly offensive because it could only have been aimed at him in his capacity as Reich Huntsman-in-Chief.

"Besides, he's a pretty flabby specimen. I've even heard it said that he opposes stag hunting. And another thing: he prefers foreign liquor, gets his suits made in London, and reads American novels—in the original! Rather un-German, wouldn't you say?"

Not that he even hinted at it, Hitler was relishing this conversation. "For all that," he brooded, "we *are* talking about the two most senior members of the armed forces."

"Senior but not indispensable," Göring responded. "Under the circumstances, serious consideration must be given to their replacement—am I right, my Führer?"

Hitler's gaze seemed focused on some far horizon. Although he said nothing, Göring interpreted his silence as approval. Once again, the Führer had resorted to an invariably successful technique: anything not expressly forbidden to his personal entourage could be taken as sanctioned.

That was good enough for a man like Göring. He was a hunter, in politics as elsewhere. Once a living creature had been declared fair game, his predatory instincts always told hom how to track and dispatch it.

Another passage from Counsellor Meller's notes—

There was nothing particularly exceptional about the concoction of this devil's brew. On the contrary, it was reminiscent of a technique which ruthless adepts in the art of power politics have successfully employed for thousands of years: if you can't win the heart and mind of an unwelcome opponent, kick him in the balls.

By contrast, those who show no signs of disrupting or imperilling the authority of criminals in high places, be they Nero or Hitler, are subject to no moral prohibitions or taboos. As long as they prove "reliable," they can please themselves in almost every respect.

This was how Ernst Röhm, the SA chief of staff (not to mention numerous other Nazi notables, including a cabinet minister), could afford to remain an active homosexual until the precise moment in time when he became a threat to his Führer. For as long as Röhm and his cronies were seen to be loyal, they enjoyed free rein—or almost. As soon as they were even suspected of treachery, they were unblushingly denounced before the entire nation as "degenerate and swinish moral perverts" and thrown to the wolves—in other words, the shocked but essentially prurient masses.

The Eva Gruhn affair was peculiarly and disastrously suitable for use in this context. A woman whose one desire was to love and be loved, Eva felt that her affections had at last been returned—wholeheartedly. That was just what made her such a perfect target.

Second essay in dramatic reconstruction . . . Subject:
a false friend—

"Eva, darling, why have you been avoiding me? Can't you see how much you mean to me? I'm crazy about you!"

Thus Volker Vogelsang, alias Informant No. 134, who had arrived at Eva Gruhn's apartment and was sitting beside her on the sofa. The glass-topped coffee table in front of them bore a tempting assortment of delicacies: one terrine of genuine Strasbourg *pâté de fois gras*, one jar of caviar, Russian, and one bottle of champagne, French. All these offerings had been expectantly procured from Vogelsang's delicatessen in the Kurfürstendamm.

"But you, Eva—you don't feel the same way about me!"

It was a combined lament and accusation, accompanied by much heavy breathing. Eva gave her suitor a pitying smile and sighed. "I don't like people trying to own me," she said with surprising gentleness. "I've told you that time and again. Why keep pestering me?"

"Because I want to make you happy."

"Meaning what, exactly?"

"Look, Eva," he said, leaning towards her, "I'd even be prepared to marry you—on certain conditions."

"I don't accept conditions," she said with dignity. "What I expect from a man is absolute and unselfish devotion. That's what I call love, and I don't think you're capable of it."

This offhand assertion stung Vogelsang into candour. "I saw through you ages ago!" he snarled. "You're just a good-time girl—you're out to enjoy yourself, and you don't give a damn who with."

"That's not true. I've never wanted anything out of life except a man who'll respect me the way I respect him. You obviously can't understand that."

"A fairy prince, eh?" Vogelsang's tone was menacing rather than derisive. "So that's who you've been working on!"

Eva stared at him sadly. "Have you been spying on me, Volker? I wouldn't advise you to, not if you want us to remain friends."

"I want to be friends all right, but it's getting harder all the time. Who the hell is this boy Heersdorf, anyway? Oh, yes, I know his name! Herbert Heersdorf, import-export merchant. What do you expect out of him?"

"Very little," Eva said truthfully. "I told you, I'm looking for a man who'll love me for myself."

"Very smart of you," sneered Vogelsang. "You're trying to pressure me—trying to con me into proposing, aren't you? Well, I don't fall for that sort of trick."

Report submitted by Volker Vogelsang, Informant No. 134, immediately after the above conversation. Reference: Eva Gruhn—

The subject has been closely watched, as instructed. Activities have come to light which are bound to bring her into conflict with the authorities and cast serious doubt on her morals. For particulars, see below.

Subject is employed as a part-time photographic

model. Claims to be a mannequin but generally poses in
lingerie and beachwear. Works all hours.

Other instances of immoral behavior may be taken for
granted. I enclose a list of addresses, including that of a
man named Herbert Heersdorf. Calls himself an export-
import merchant but makes an extremely suspicious
impression. His activities could bear checking.

From hints dropped by the subject, her current friend is
a person of some importance. I have yet to discover his
identity. Another report will be submitted as soon as any
details become known. Am keeping subject under close
surveillance.

Otto Schmidt was handed over to the Gestapo in spring
1936. He had just been sentenced to seven years'
imprisonment but offered a conditional reprieve.

Why? Because Otto was a canary. As soon as he came
under pressure, for instance, when faced with a seven-year
stretch, he started to sing his way out of trouble. His status
as an expert on the Berlin homosexual scene gave him
plenty of names, addresses, and tips to impart.

Principal responsibility for this category of offences
had lately been transferred from the Vice Squad to a new
department resoundingly entitled the Reich Centre for the
Control of Homosexuality. This functioned as Section
II-H of the Central State Security Bureau, which put it
right inside the Gestapo's sphere of operations.

Here Otto unburdened himself in a series of interviews
lasting days on end. He delivered the goods. By the time he
was through, his list contained nearly a hundred names.
One of them was "Frisch" or "von Frisch"—"a senior
Army officer, very old family," so Otto claimed.

Otto wasn't too particular when it came to details like
that. They were just window dressing.

His interrogator, a man named Herbert or Hubert (at all events, he signed his reports "H-t"), did not seem dissatisfied.

"I see you've been busy, you dirty little rat."

Otto took this as a compliment, which it was. "I've done my best," he said smugly. "That should be enough, shouldn't it?" He had every hope that his revelations would earn him a substantial remission, if not a suspended sentence.

"I'll have to see what the chief thinks," said Herbert or Hubert. He sounded quite hopeful himself.

The new boss of the Reich Centre for the Control of Homosexuality was Detective Chief Superintendent Meisinger, who had now joined the Gestapo from Police HQ Berlin, bringing along several suitcases of files. Meisinger favored brutal, corrupt, and insidious police methods. He made a point of terrorizing subordinates from the outset because there was nothing he wouldn't do to ingratiate himself with higher authority. His first reaction on glancing at Otto's list was characteristic.

"This should keep the concentration camps busy." He prodded the list with a stubby forefinger. "Start by weeding out anyone with any kind of influence—anyone with money or official connections. Party members too, of course. We'll process them separately."

Peering more closely at Otto's list of names, he turned thoughtful and muttered something under his breath. Meisinger considered himself a brilliant detective, and prided himself on his "flair."

"Something's just struck me," he said.

"Anything special?" asked Herbert/Hubert, the interrogating officer, who was never slow to register awe and admiration.

"Could be," mused his boss. "This Schmidt—what's he like?"

"A rat, but a prize rat."

"Reliable?"

"One hundred per cent, as long as it pays him to be."

"I want a word with him," Meisinger commanded.

Half an hour later, he saw Otto in private. The two men exchanged a long look of bold appraisal. When Meisinger finally spoke, his tone was perceptibly encouraging.

"Can I depend on you, Schmidt?"

"All the way, chief. Just tell me what you're after, and I'll give it to you."

Meisinger leafed idly through the transcript of Otto's latest interrogation. He ran his finger down the list of names and paused at the one that had caught his eye—the eye of an ace detective and licensed custodian of German moral purity.

"Frisch, it says here."

"That's right."

"Senior Army officer, very old family, eh? Could he by any chance be a general?"

Otto's nimble brain told him something out of the ordinary was expected of him. Something of potential value.

"Well?"

"A general . . . Yes, he could be. It's quite possible."

"So it's also possible you got his name wrong. Only a little, I mean."

"Anyone can make a mistake, chief. What sort of mistake did you have in mind?"

"Is it conceivable, Schmidt, that his name wasn't Frisch but Fritsch—von Fritsch, to be exact?"

Otto could see light at the end of the tunnel. His services were obviously in demand and might even earn him a suspended sentence. He could already visualize himself as a prosecution witness.

"Sure! Fritsch, von Fritsch—a general. You could be right, chief."

Meisinger then resorted to a step which observers of his methods were later to describe as reprehensible, even in a "seeker after truth." He pushed a photograph across the desk—one photograph only.

This picture, taken at a military parade, showed a German general in full-dress uniform. Hair parted in the centre and combed austerely back, face dominated by a high forehead, two keen eyes with a monocle clamped into the left one, straight nose, chiselled lips, a neatly trimmed moustache. A sternly paternal-looking figure. The left-hand side of his tunic was almost obscured by a broad swath of orders, decorations, and medals. The Iron Cross First Class dangled at his throat.

"Could it have been him?" prompted Meisinger.

Usually cool, Otto Schmidt stared in consternation at the proffered photograph. It dawned on him that he was entering waters far more hazardous than even his imagination could have conceived of.

"Well, Schmidt?" The supreme scourge of the Third Reich's homosexuals watched him intently.

Otto cleared his throat. "Well, er—he certainly didn't look like that when I saw him at Wannsee Station."

"Of course he didn't." Meisinger laughed heartily. "You don't think I'd try and talk you into claiming that he waltzed into the men's room in full-dress uniform, medals and all, looking for a piece of ass? Forget the hardware and the monocle. Imagine him in plain clothes. Well?"

"Yeees—yes, when you put it like that . . ." Otto gulped. "It *could* have been him."

"Yes or no? Don't play the reluctant virgin with me, you scum."

"And if I really could swear to it . . ." Otto gave his

inquisitor a look of artless entreaty. "What then?"

"If you tell the kind of truth I want and stick to it, we'll put you on ice till the time comes."

"You mean I can take a sort of vacation till the case comes up?"

"At the taxpayers' expense," Meisinger said graciously. "It's up to you. If you cooperate, you're my man. Otherwise, you go to jail for the next seven years. Make up your mind, I'm waiting."

"Of course I'm your man." Otto Schmidt had opted for freedom as he understood it. Almost solemnly, he added, "You're right, chief, it was him."

From the Meller report—

The product of this unsavoury deal was a reasonably tight case. Meisinger used it to spring a pleasant surprise on my boyhood friend Heydrich. By 1936, therefore, or well over a year before final disaster struck with such speed, the Central State Security Bureau had opened its first "Fritsch file."

For some time, it remained one of the best-kept secrets in that death-and-destruction factory known as 8 Prinz-Albrecht-Strasse. Police Headquarters and Military Intelligence were unaware of it, nor was any of the Fritsch stock peddled in my own corner of the intelligence market. I doubt if even Himmler was notified.

But one man outside the RSHA was, and promptly. Heydrich submitted the file to Hitler with a great show of official secrecy, but the Führer merely flicked through it in silence, feigning boredom. "I'm not interested," he said eventually, and pushed it aside. In other words, not interested in the matter as it stands—not interested *yet*.

My "boyhood friend" was keenly alive to these subtle

distinctions. The inference he drew was that Fritsch still had his uses and enjoyed official protection. Hitler had yet to pronounce him fair game.

So the file disappeared into one of Heydrich's safes and remained there for several months.

3

Enter
the Mighty

Further extract from notes compiled by Counsellor Erich Meller of the Prussian Ministry of the Interior, Berlin—

The precise moment at which disaster finally struck is a matter of record. Date: 3 November 1937. Place: the Chancellery. Time: between 4:15 and 8:30 P.M. Occasion: a conference on the current political and military situation. Those present, apart from Hitler himself, included:

Field Marshal Werner von Blomberg, Reich War Minister and Commander-in-Chief of the Wehrmacht, who sat on the Führer's right; Reich Foreign Minister Baron Konstantin von Neurath, seated on his left; the commanders-in-chief of the three armed services: General Baron Werner von Fritsch, Commander-in-Chief Army, General Hermann Göring, Commander-in-chief Luftwaffe, and Admiral Erich Raeder, Commander-in-Chief Navy; finally, ensconced at the far end of the long shiny table, Hitler's Wehrmacht adjutant, Colonel Friedrich Hossbach.

Substantial sections of my report are based on Hossbach's personal impressions and notes. An increasingly skeptical observer of the Greater German scene, he kept a detailed record of these proceedings, which are of manifest historical importance. This record he circulated among a few of his trusted friends. I was included in their number—rightly so, I believe.

Adolph Hitler led off with the polished courtesy he could always muster when he chose—and he chose to on this occasion. He thanked his visitors for coming, assured them how delighted he was to see them, and hoped that their cooperation would prove as fruitful as it always had in the past.

He knew precisely why his War Minister had requested this meeting. Doubtless prompted by Fritsch, Blomberg was anxious to secure a more balanced and equitable distribution of the raw materials needed for armaments. This demand was an obvious dig at Göring, who had been in charge of Germany's four-year economic-development plan since 1936 and was not unreasonably suspected of favoring his personal enthusiasm, the Luftwaffe. "No money worries in our outfit" was the current Air Force boast. "There isn't much we can't afford, thanks to Hermann. It's his responsibility."

It wasn't that Hitler had any intention of leaping to his

lieutenant's defence—he never begrudged Göring a few problems of his own. The one thing he wanted to avoid was an open clash between the three Commanders-in-Chief. That was why he had decided to focus their attention on some desirable objectives of supreme and overriding importance. And that, in turn, was why he had invited his Foreign Minister to attend as well.

The Führer embarked on one of his classic monologues, which had been known to last for hours. This time, according to Colonel Hossbach's notes, he concentrated on three main points.

First, it was vitally important not only to be in tune with the times but to remain one jump ahead of them. Anyone who limped along in their wake was lost. The signs of the times were clearly discernible, claimed Hitler. Europe was in the throes of an incipient upheaval. Germany could count on Italy, where the Duce was doing his utmost to foster a mood of understanding. France was morally bankrupt and on the verge of collapse. As for the British, they would have to be jolted into an awareness of their true national values and international standing.

Next, Soviet Russia might well develop into a first-class power within a few years at most. Germany could not afford to wait that long. The Americans would probably take years to digest the political developments which Germany was hastening along. They were not only infected with the Jewish contagion but would first have to deal with their immense financial and economic problems. "We, on the other hand, have everything to gain and nothing to lose."

What followed, third, was to clear up the European mess as fast as possible. "France must be dealt with, Britain won over, and the Eastern situation clarified. As in Czechoslovakia, so in Poland—even in Russia. These backward and obstructive elements will be steamrollered into submission and brought under German control. This can only be done with speed and determination, so we shall have to prepare ourselves accordingly."

The Führer was glowing with an inward sense of his mission.

"We shall have a comparatively free hand in Europe until 1945, but not thereafter. By then, we must have Germanized our continent—welded it into a self-contained unit under our leadership. If we haven't succeeded by then, we never will, because we shall then be exposed to the destructive pressure of two world powers, the Jewish United States and the Bolshevik Soviet Union. And that must never, never be allowed to happen!"

Having proclaimed this like an Old Testament prophet, Hitler gazed searchingly round the table. Everyone seemed to have been overwhelmed by such an epoch-making series of revelations. The Foreign Minister, Baron von Neurath, was so visibly affected he had shut his eyes and was panting with both hands clasped to his chest. Even Göring was staring into space, rapt in thoughts, and Navy chief Raeder kept shaking his head as though in the grip of a sudden fever. Colonel Hossbach continued to scribble away, but Blomberg preserved his usual air of lofty and unassailable composure.

The Commander-in-Chief of the Army too seemed immune to emotional infection. As sternly dispassionate as ever, Fritsch ventured some comments.

"Herr Chancellor, no one could describe your remarks as other than extremely wide-ranging. I would not presume to assess their merits, let alone dispute them. Being a soldier, however, I favour a practical approach. My sole duty is to see things as they are—as they are *now*—and what I see is this. Our Army requires far greater

material and financial resources than ever before. I'm
bound to say, with regret, that we've been neglected if not
systematically discriminated against. At least, such is my
recent impression."

After a Hitlerian monologue lasting nearly two hours,
Fritsch had brought the conference abruptly down to
earth. His charges, which were clearly levelled at the
overweight administrator of the Four-Year Plan, drew
swift support from Admiral Raeder. Together they
launched a combined assault on Göring, frankly censuring
his methods and trying to block his proposals. Göring
conducted a no less spirited defence.

Hitler listened in silence, ready to play umpire at any
time, but he had no great urge to step in. Even this
development had its welcome side. As always on such
occasions, what mattered was to make the very most of
what the moment offered, and for that the Führer
possessed a sure and deadly instinct.

Driven into several corners at once, Göring gave a
positive wail of self-pity. "Surely I've got a right to be
heard too?" was how Colonel Hossbach recorded it in his
notes. Several of those present seemed to have banished
Hitler's visionary plans for world upheaval from their
minds. They were busy grinding their departmental axes.

Göring turned on his attackers. "Listening to all this," he
said heatedly, "having to sit here and listen to it—I'm
beginning to wonder whether somebody's gunning for
me. I can't believe you'd dare, any of you!"

Blomberg looked perturbed. "Please don't misunderstand us," he said. "It would never occur to anyone here to
call your abilities or achievements in question."

"I wouldn't recommend it either," Göring growled.
"Nobody does that to me—not to *me*."

"Speaking for myself," the field marshal said brazenly,

"I hold you in the highest regard." He was desperately anxious not to make an enemy of Göring, because he needed his good offices in a very personal matter. "I mean, we all regard you as one of the pillars of the state."

"Except," said Fritsch, completely undeterred, "that any pillar of the state has a duty to ensure the absolutely fair and even-handed distribution of our national resources. And the logical corollary of that, Herr Göring, is that your grossly preferential treatment of the Luftwaffe has got to stop."

Hitler summoned Göring to the Chancellery the same evening, officially for dinner. Anything could be discussed at table, with the exception of politics.

Immediately after the meal, Hitler and his lieutenant withdrew to the terrace room, where the Führer customarily studied newspapers and official documents. Once there, Göring spoke without waiting to be invited.

"They don't have a spark of greatness in them," he said, meaning Blomberg, Neurath, and the two other service chiefs. "They're blind to your vision of the future."

"I also deplore their lack of comprehension," Hitler said, eying Göring expectantly. "However, we mustn't move too quickly. Every avenue must be explored, thoroughly but cautiously. Martyrs are the last thing we need."

"Quite so, my Führer. Blomberg and his friends must be brought up to scratch as quickly and unobtrusively as possible—either that or torpedoed. I'm speaking metaphorically, of course."

"As long as it looks convincing to the outside world.... There must be some way out, but..." Hitler paused. "This is a delicate matter. I wonder who can be trusted to handle it."

"Me!" Göring said instantly. "Leave it to me, my Führer. It'll be a pleasure."

Hitler's smile was radiant with confidence. Göring seemed very sure of himself. "You can always rely on me," he added.

Which was true, but only when personal advantage beckoned. This, Göring firmly believed, was a case in point.

From the Meller report—

Anyone who plans to step into someone else's shoes must empty them first—or get them emptied. Ever faithful to this political infighter's precept, Göring probably reasoned as follows:

Discounting his numerous other posts, he was Commander-in-Chief Luftwaffe. This made him one of three equal-ranking service chiefs. In charge of the Navy was Admiral Raeder, who combined professionalism with a conciliatory and accommodating approach to his colleagues. The Army, on the other hand, was headed by Fritsch, whom Göring considered a stubborn idiot with an irritatingly patronizing manner.

But senior to all three of them, Göring included, was Field Marshal Werner von Blomberg, War Minister and Commander-in-Chief of the Wehrmacht. Blomberg's days were numbered—Hitler thought so too now—but as soon as he could be induced to retire a successor would have to be found. Long-standing tradition, together with the ascendancy still enjoyed by Germany's Army generals, prescribed that the top job would automatically pass to

Commander-in-Chief Army—in other words, Göring's pet aversion. The obvious step was to remove Fritsch in good time and leave the way clear for himself.

Baron von Neurath, Hitler's Foreign Minister, suffered several heart attacks immediately after the Chancellery conference. He confided to a few close friends that he was unable and unwilling to associate himself with such a perilously irresponsible ideological crusade, and that he was contemplating retirement.

Admiral Raeder oscillated between gloomy resignation and carefully nurtured optimism. "I don't know what to think," the Navy chief was heard to say. "Perhaps it's all one big misunderstanding." From now on, official policy was taboo. He abstained from unfavourable comment, let alone spontaneous criticism. However much this may have cost him in the way of self-control, his very silence spoke volumes to those who knew him well.

Field Marshal von Blomberg remained firmly aloof and viewed matters in a hopeful light, even at this late stage. "Nothing's final," was his verdict. "We'll have to wait and see. Steady nerves and a cool head, that's what we need. Sometime, somehow, everything will sort itself out."

The Commander-in-Chief of the Army, General Baron Werner von Fritsch, betrayed no emotion at all. All he said was "I do my duty." He also said, "The Chancellor knows what he wants, but so do I."

Probably the only person with an unflinching determination to obey the dictates of his conscience, both as an individual and as a soldier, was Colonel Friedrich Hossbach. Hitler's Wehrmacht adjutant felt his only course was to oppose the man he served, a decision which led to his speedy dismissal.

To crown everything, Hossbach crossed swords with

Göring as well. "Göring," he declared, "is a gigantic abomination. He tips the scales at three hundred pounds in that gaudy uniform of his, but he doesn't have an ounce of soldierly integrity."

You could despise Göring, but you had to respect him too. To provoke the man recklessly was suicidal, especially when he thought the Führer had given him a free hand.

Third essay in dramatic reconstruction ... Subject: a proposal of marriage—

"I love you very much." Werner von Blomberg spoke the words with undisguised tenderness. He reached for Eva's hand. "Knowing you has been a joy to me."

"Please don't say things like that." She tried to pull her hand away, then surrendered it. "I'm fond of you too. You mean a lot to me. Knowing you has made me just as happy, but ..."

"There can't be any buts if you really mean that."

Her face clouded. "You know what I'm getting at, Werner. Some people would say I'm not good enough for you."

"But you are!"

"You're all I've ever wanted, Werner. Being with you is like a dream come true, but I wouldn't want you to risk everything for my sake. You deserve better than that."

She nestled against him. Gently but ardently, he put his arms round her. "You aren't trying to break it off, are you?"

"I'd never do that. I'm your girl, Werner, and happy to be—happy deep down inside, now that I've found you at last."

"It's heaven to hear you say that. I've known nothing but happiness since the first day we met, and I don't intend to lose it. Stay with me."

"Of course I will, for as long as you want."

"For always!"

"I'll always be yours, believe me."

"Then be mine in every sense of the word, darling. Share your life with me."

"I'll do anything you say, Werner, but I refuse to become a burden to you—ever. That's part of the way I feel about you. You don't have to tie yourself down, not with me."

"But I want to," he said firmly.

She stared at him in disbelief. "You don't mean..."

"That's just what I do mean. I'm asking you to marry me."

"Me?" Eva shook her head wonderingly. "*Me,* of all people?"

"You and only you," he said, drawing her close. "I don't care what the problems are. We'll face them together."

"You're very brave, Werner," she said, "but I'm not. I'm scared. Nobody could be that lucky—nobody with my background."

Blomberg gazed deep into her eyes. "Who's the lucky one?" he said. "No man of my age could wish for more than to feel wanted—genuinely wanted—by a woman as wonderful as you. There's only one thing that can make my happiness complete. Love me, live with me—marry me!"

From the Meller report—
Werner von Blomberg's blind and selfless devotion

to Eva Gruhn may be assumed to have originated in mid-1936, because their first encounter probably took place in June of that year. Although extant documents are not in full agreement on this point and provide no detailed evidence, the discrepancies are only minor.

The crucial and inescapable fact was that a man aged just over sixty had become emotionally entangled with a woman nearly thirty years his junior. These things happen, and there is nothing reprehensible about them. A widower of many years' standing, Blomberg was still a fine figure of a man but not a reckless lady killer—far from it. He had charm, refinement, and an engaging manner which doubtless appealed to the opposite sex.

The other party, whom I was to meet at Huber's insistence, was a handsome young woman with a full figure and a strongly feminine aura. She did not strike me as a calculating or demanding person. On the contrary, I felt that she was possessed by a naïve and ungovernable yearning for "true love."

Everything would have been quite straightforward had the object of her affections been an ordinary mortal. Werner von Blomberg would, I imagine, have welcomed a less exalted status in this respect, but he happened to be a field marshal and his country's War Minister.

Berlin CID records still contain a few obviously doctored reports on the origins of this love affair, together with some effusions composed by Volker Vogelsang, alias Informant No. 134, whom a police memo described as "an obligingly versatile liar."

"The first meeting between Eva Gruhn and Herr von Blomberg," he reported, "probably occurred at the White Hart, a restaurant just off Steinstrasse. The subject was employed there as a waitress, though in a superior capacity roughly equivalent to that of a headwaiter. She gave full satisfaction in every respect, or so I am reliably informed.

"The subject attracted Herr von Blomberg's attention the very first evening, presumably by an artful display of maidenly reserve. She waited on him hand and foot and was rewarded with an extravagant tip. His words were as follows: 'Kindly permit me to express my admiration of your personal charms. I should very much like—again with your permission—to renew our acquaintance.'

"They met only two or three days later in the tearoom of the Adlon Hotel. Then they went to a variety show at the Wintergarten. Two weeks later, a meeting took place at the subject's apartment in the building where I happen to live. Herr von Blomberg brought some cakes along, probably from the Café Kranzler, also a bottle of wine and some flowers. They were red roses—two or three dozen of them."

So much for the shady Herr Vogelsang's report. Its accuracy was disputed even at the time, and not only by Huber.

"Morning, Maier," said General von Fritsch.

"Morning, General," said Sergeant Maier.

These were just about the only words the two men exchanged, day in, day out. The Commander-in-Chief's voice was always friendly. It never sounded patronizing, condescending, or blasé—in fact, it sometimes carried a trace of austere warmth. The sergeant's manner was neither heel-clickingly formal nor crudely familiar. A decorous and businesslike atmosphere prevailed in Fritsch's entourage.

Sergeant Maier groomed several senior officers' horses,

one of which belonged to the general. He always had it ready for him on the dot because the Commander-in-Chief's punctuality was legendary.

Like his trusty sergeant, Fritsch looked upon horses as travelling companions rather than objects of convenience. That was why he followed the same procedure day after day. Instead of mounting his charger in an abrupt and possessive fashion, he began by running a gentle hand along the animal's velvety, well-groomed flanks. Then he stationed himself in front of it—face to face, as it were—and bent from the waist until man and beast brushed heads.

Then the general would give his groom a curt and unspeaking nod. Once this accolade had been bestowed, his daily ride in the Tiergarten could begin.

Today, however, there was a delay. From the look in the sergeant's eye, Fritsch guessed he had something on his mind.

"Anything wrong, Maier?"

"Nothing much, General—nothing important, but I still don't like the look of it." Maier intercepted a sidelong glance. "It isn't the horse."

"What, then?"

"I could be mistaken." The sergeant sounded rather sheepish. "There are some things I don't know much about."

"Things apart from me and horses, eh?" Fritsch smiled faintly. Coming from him, the mild jest and the attempted smile had great rarity value. "All right, what's the trouble? I know you trust me, Maier, and I'm sure you know I return the compliment. Out with it, man!"

Maier unburdened himself at last—hurriedly, as though he couldn't wait to get the subject off his chest. "Some fellow in civvies turned up here yesterday afternoon. He tried to pump me, General. Asked a lot of questions about the horses, my daily schedule, what I do with myself off duty, who I look after, when, how often—that sort of thing."

"Did you tell him what he wanted to know?"

"Of course not, sir. I told him to take a running jump at himself, but it didn't put him off."

"What sort of person was he?"

"He flashed his ID before I had a chance to kick him out. He was from the police—the Gestapo, I think."

Maier looked at the horse, not the general, because he knew Fritsch would not move a muscle at this disclosure, whereas the animal would sense the slightest flicker of agitation in a person whose hands were gently fondling its head. The horse stood stock still.

"Is it a bad sign, General?" Maier asked. "I mean, him turning up here like that?"

"My dear Maier," Fritsch said, and his tone was that of a comrade-in-arms, "are you in some kind of trouble? It can happen to the best of us. Problems are there to be spotted in time and tackled head on. Anything I can do to help?"

Maier was so taken aback that he started stammering and lapsed into the third person, a mode of address now banned as obsolete. "Does the General mean he'd—I mean, if I . . ."

"But of course," said Fritsch. He had known the sergeant for years. Maier was the best and most faithful custodian of horse and rider he had ever met—honest, straightforward, and utterly dependable. He could not believe him guilty of anything serious. "If you've landed yourself in a mess, Maier, tell me, and we'll sort it out together."

"Thank you, General." The sergeant was touched by this unmistakable expression of trust but astonished at

Fritsch's almost incredible naïveté. Had he purposely misunderstood him? If so, what was his game? Maier gave an embarrassed grin.

"Thank you, sir," he repeated, "but it isn't that. Who am I, after all? Just a person who looks after horses and enjoys his work. My private life's an open book. I don't play cards, never drink more than a couple of beers, and steer clear of other woman—I'm well and truly married, General, as you know. I've got a good wife and two kids. There's nothing wrong with my family life. It's as normal as two and two makes four. No, it isn't me they're after, I'd take a bet on it."

"In that case, who?"

"Well, sir, I reckon it must be you." Maier looked even more sheepish. "That secret policeman—he asked a load of questions about you. Impertinence, I call it."

"My dear Maier, there's nothing so extraordinary about that." Fritsch could always muster an air of martial superiority. He did so now, still holding his horse's head. The animal's limpid eyes seemed to regard him sympathetically. "This is a well-disciplined country—the police help to keep it so."

"Maybe, General, but why should they be so interested in what you do or don't do? That fellow had a nerve, the questions he asked about you. When and where you go riding and how often, who goes with you and whom you meet, whether you turn up in riding gear or change at the stables, whether you change on your own or have someone to help you, whether you're armed and escorted—that sort of thing. If that isn't a barefaced liberty, what is?"

Werner von Fritsch continued to smile, but only faintly. He seemed, even now, to be striving for a better comprehension of the new Germany.

"You're forgetting something, Sergeant. Rightly or

wrongly, I'm regarded as a person of national importance. As such, I have to put up with certain things, one being the close surveillance essential to my personal protection. That's all there is to it."

"I see," Maier said slowly. He sounded dubious but relieved. "If that's the way you look at it, I must be barking up the wrong tree. Sorry to have kept you—and the horse. He's getting fidgety. Enjoy your ride, sir."

Fourth essay in dramatic reconstruction ... Subject: Eva's reservations—

"I'm so happy," Eva confided softly, snuggling up to her lover. "And yet ... Sometimes I feel just the opposite."

Blomberg looked dismayed. "Don't say that, Eva! Please don't ever say that again. You belong to me now."

"I've always longed for someone to love me just the way I am."

"But I do, darling!"

She smiled at him through a mist of tears, happy once more. At long last, a man had entered her life who actually wanted to marry her. She realized, even so, that their love might prove a threat to his career.

Eva was often haunted these days by a claustrophobic dread of losing what she had found. There was an ever-present danger that Werner might hear some malicious gossip about her from a third party, so she had decided to leave nothing unsaid which could blight their relationship.

"You aren't the first man in my life, Werner," she began tentatively. "I've never made any secret of that."

He dismissed this with a magnanimous shrug. "You aren't a child, you're a grown woman. No need to go into details. Let's concentrate on the future—*our* future."

They had recently been meeting twice a week with no particular attempt at secrecy. Their favourite rendezvous was Eva's cramped little apartment, where Blomberg felt infinitely at ease.

The apartment was in Eisenacher Strasse in the Schöneberg quarter of Berlin. The décor was haphazard, with its hodgepodge of art-nouveau furniture and red-brown colour scheme. Light was provided by a few candles, most burning in the minuscule bedroom beside a dressing table with a mirror the size of a pocket handkerchief.

Though normally accustomed to large and spacious rooms, Werner von Blomberg felt thoroughly at home here. He was simultaneously exhilarated, intoxicated, and relaxed by Eva's physical nearness—by the knowledge that he could reach out and touch her whenever he chose. He loved and was loved in return. No man could ask for more.

It was a sensation he had not experienced for decades. He had to think back very, very far, to the days when he was still a lieutenant, before he could recall anything similar, but even that paled beside the happiness he felt now. To him, Eva represented a grand, glorious, and unexpected gift bestowed on him at an age when most men felt old and played out. He had had to wait until now for the great fulfilment of a genuine passion. It was the first and last in his life.

He had spoken of their future together. The past didn't interest him, he said, but Eva's doubts were not so easily allayed. A note of desperation crept into her voice.

"My God, Werner, think of my family background—think of my childhood! There was nothing nice and refined about that."

"Forget it," he urged her. "All that matters is

here and now—and what lies ahead of us."

His spontaneous generosity made her burst into tears. He lent her a handkerchief and folded her in his arms. She sobbed and clung to him, feeling more than ever like the heroine of a romantic novel.

In vain, she tried to disengage herself from his embrace. "I don't want to saddle you with my past—I can't and I mustn't. It was all so sordid. The same questions keep going round and round in my head, Werner. What are we doing together, the two of us? What have I done to deserve a wonderful man like you?"

"Trust me, my darling girl," he said. "Everything's going to be all right."

From the Meller report—

My growing concern was only intensified by a close study of other relevant documents made available by Huber. It was like sniffing an accumulation of sewage.

"Please spare me the unsavoury details," I told him. "They're not our business. Unless, of course, the Gestapo are already keeping tabs on Blomberg. Are they?"

"I can't say for sure, but they're definitely collecting all the dirt they can find. Indiscriminately, from the look of it."

"How indiscriminately?"

"They're building up a mountain of files on suspected homosexuals, prostitutes, and crooks. Likewise on any generals and Party bosses who may be linked with them."

"And Blomberg isn't on their list?"

"Not yet, but they're already working on the Gruhn woman. With obvious relish, I might add. She's an attractive creature—quite tasty enough to whet the appetite of those dusty, deskbound sleuths in the Gestapo records department. Whoever's working on her and for whatever reason, they're bound to trip over the field marshal sooner or later. Then what happens?"

"How much have they got on her so far?" I asked.

"Any amount of dirt if they care to use it, and why shouldn't they? It's their idea of fun." Huber shrugged. "For instance, they've turned up some photographs showing the girl in various poses. Like admiring herself in a mirror with her hands on her breasts or bending over a washbasin or lying on the hearth rug..."

"So what? You can find pictures like that in the best-regulated families. Why, I've even got some snaps of myself and a girlfriend pawing each other in bathing costumes. She reserved her passion for the camera, worse luck."

"All the same, some items in the Gestapo's collection do err on the pornographic side. They've been circulating some pictures showing the lady in action with a male partner."

"That *is* bad."

"Not necessarily. I managed to get a closer look at the pictures, and guess what? They're fakes—photomontages, every one! The Gestapo have a fully equipped forger's laboratory, don't forget."

"Can you prove they're fakes?"

"Yes, pretty conclusively, but only if they're officially produced in evidence."

"Then you'd better get ready to do so."

Huber grinned broadly. "My dear Counsellor, your concern for the field marshal and his lady friend does you credit. I'm not saying it's unjustified, but it does seem premature. There's something else you should know— something just as important. The Gestapo have lately been turning their attention to General von Fritsch."

"What!" I said. "Come off it, Huber. I don't care what these people unearth or who they try to frame. If there's one paragon of unblemished and unimpeachable integrity in this degenerate age of ours, it's General Fritsch."

"I wouldn't say no to another straight Scotch and another Havana," Huber said. "The cigar'll help soothe my nerves and the Scotch I'll drink to your spiritual enlightenment. You'd better get something straight, Counsellor. If the authorities need a whipping boy, the Gestapo will supply one, even if he happens to be the last Prussian officer and gentleman left in Germany. Cheers!"

Detective Chief Superintendent Joseph Meisinger had been summoned to the office of Reinhard Heydrich, head of the Central State Security Bureau. Object of interview: the "F File," which was now pronounced ripe for discussion and ready to receive its finishing touches.

Heydrich awaited the arrival of his subordinate, who presided over Section II-H (Control of Homosexuality), with some degree of optimism. Even if he privately regarded Meisinger as a muckraker—who wouldn't be, in his line of work?—the man was a persevering sleuth. He was also a staunch Party-liner.

"You know a bit about me, Meisinger," Heydrich said by way of introduction. His voice took on a crudely menacing note. "That's why I don't expect you to present me with a measly little turd like the last one. This time I want a great big steaming pile of shit."

"That's just what I've brought you, Gruppenführer."

"All right, let's see it."

Meisinger, who had been hugging a red folder to his chest, deposited it in front of his chief. It bore the words "Otto Schmidt—Information re H incidents" and contained an expanded version of the so-called Fritsch file.

Heydrich regarded the bulky folder with a faint scowl of distaste, which he then transferred to its author. "You don't expect me to wade through all that filth, do you? Give me the bare bones, and make it quick."

The Gruppenführer liked to instil respect in his subordinates by jolting them hard. Duly chastened, Meisinger delivered his report with the requisite brevity, concentrating on essentials. Otto Schmidt, a veteran police informer who specialized in homosexual activities and had recently supplied details of some hundred relevant cases, was now prepared to testify that one of them involved von Fritsch.

"He'll even swear to it if necessary, in front of any court in the land—and I mean any!"

Heydrich pushed the folder aside unopened. Only his arms moved, leaving the upper part of his torso stiff as a poker. There were no creases in his uniform, which was elegantly tailored and always looked brand new—a point he set great store by. He did not take exception to Meisinger's worn and shabby suit. On the contrary, it helped underline their difference in status.

Then came his instructions. Although they carried an undertone of menace, or at least of admonition, Meisinger found them almost encouraging.

"Point number one, this informant of yours—this Schmidt. I want his statements checked down to the last detail, checked and double-checked. Everything's got to tie up. Or be made to.

"Number two, Fritsch. One prosecution witness won't be enough, not for him. Put his private life under the microscope, go through his service record with a fine-tooth comb, screen his family and friends. Oh yes, and talk to his subordinates, past and present—ADCs, batmen, grooms, et cetera. Find out if he's made any enemies. Everyone has those, and they're always the first to deliver.

"Last but not least, full access to the contents of this file is restricted to you and me. If you think it necessary to bring in somebody else, do so only with my personal consent. The men you assign to this case will cover individual sectors only. They won't be given an overall picture of the operation, is that clear?"

"Absolutely, Gruppenführer." Meisinger was dominated by the certainty that his hour had come at last. This unique assignment could only be a prelude to the career he had always dreamed of. "Leave it to me," he added confidently.

But Heydrich, who had been quick to detect the elation on his homo-hunter's face, quelled it at once. He didn't like self-esteem in others.

"Just one thing, Meisinger. I hope you realize what a hot potato this is. It'll burn your fingers if you don't watch out. Fall down on the job and you're finished. And now, get back to work."

More extracts from the Meller report—
Field Marshal Werner von Blomberg, War Minister and Commander-in-Chief of the Wehrmacht, was an extremely controversial figure, and not only during his lifetime. He remained so for years after his lonely and lamentable demise in a British POW camp. Not that it pained him unduly, Blomberg felt permanently misunderstood.

He sometimes broached the subject, though always with that characteristically urbane and indulgent smile of his. One such occasion was a dinner I attended at Rollenhagen's in May 1937.

"Some people," he said, "see me as the Führer's head cook and bottle washer. They claim I handed him the armed forces on a platter. There's something in what they say, discounting their crude phraseology, but I'd prefer to put it another way. I helped, partly at the request of President von Hindenburg, to prevent our Army from becoming infected with the biased, nationally injurious views and activities of the SA and SS."

He really seemed to believe this. In fact I wasn't alone at the time in regarding Werner von Blomberg, unlike some other generals, as a reasonably principles man. To me, he always seemed sympathetic, accommodating, and magnanimous. Colonel Oster of Military Intelligence placed a different interpretation on his attitude. "He can afford to be loftily magnanimous—or so he thinks. After all, he's achieved everything a peacetime soldier can achieve: the highest rank and the trappings of supreme authority. His problem, which he probably hasn't spotted yet, is how to hang on to what he's got for as long as he can."

It may be appropriate at this stage to venture an explanation of how I came to enjoy such easy access to these exalted circles. Like the quirk of fate that allotted me a boyhood friend of Heydrich's calibre, none of my privileges was due to personal merit. Being the only son of Maximilian Meller, born at Königsberg on 1 January 1900, I inherited them. Father was a respected lawyer, not only during the imperial era but later on, under the Weimar Republic. He also had two brothers, both of them Prussian to their fingertips.

One was Uncle Adalbert, known in the ranks as "Old

Blood-and-Guts." He had served as a colonel and
regimental commander at Verdun, where his unit chalked
up the heaviest casualties on record. That made him a war
hero. From then on, anyone who mattered spoke his name
with awe.

The other was Uncle Erich, commonly referred to as
"Last Rites" Meller. Although he liked to call himself a
plain Army chaplain, this studious understatement concealed his true status, which was that of a Protestant
bishop. Uncle Erich blessed many a dying man on the
battlefields of Flanders and spent some time officiating at
supreme headquarters. He was reputed to have prayed in
devout communion with Emperor William II, Field
Marshal Hindenburg, and General Ludendorff. For
victory, of course.

To sum up, my elders were made of the finest German
material, and their trademark covered me as well. It did so
on the long-established "like father like son" principle. As a
result, I too was welcomed into the officers' mess set, the
exclusive clubs frequented by aristocrats, diplomats, and
senior civil servants—even into the exalted trade union of
generals. Few of these gentlemen harboured doubts about
the wisdom of their membership policy, nor did they do so
in my case. I enjoyed consorting with my distinguished
friends and patrons, though not, perhaps, in quite the way
they thought.

But to return to Werner von Blomberg. There were
times when he looked immeasurably sad, like a man
haunted by the fear that his sands have finally run out. His
first wife, whom he always spoke of with the deepest
respect, had died in 1929 after a grave and protracted
illness, probably cancer. The children of this marriage had
since grown up, married, and left home. Even though their

ties of affection seemed close and continued to endure—at least until the events related here—Werner von Blomberg often made a lonely and forlorn impression, professionally as well as privately.

One noteworthy feature of the situation—and one whose "fortuitous" nature was soon to prove an embarrassment—was that Blomberg's eldest daughter had married the son of a certain Wilhelm Keitel. Keitel had also attained senior rank—not, one surmises, without some assistance from his new connection by marriage, whose right-hand man he soon became. He was destined, only a little later, to become Hitler's right-hand man in the Wehrmacht domain, but not before he had disposed of certain obstacles. One of them was the father of the girl his son had married.

Very characteristic of Werner von Blomberg was a remark he happened to make in my presence while conversing with the military attaché on the staff of our embassy in London. The latter was telling him about the extremely awkward relationship that had blossomed between King Edward VIII and an American divorcée whom the British government and public regarded with some suspicion, one Mrs. Simpson.

"I've seen her at close quarters," the military attaché reported, sounding genuinely puzzled. "With the best will in the world, sir, I really don't know what's so special about her. She looks as dull as ditchwater to me. Apart from that, she's encrusted with makeup."

Werner von Blomberg nodded absently. He seemed to be smiling—smiling to, or at, himself. Then he spread his arms in a rather Gallic gesture.

"There you are," he said, "that's love for you."

Only a few months after these words were uttered, they

fitted Blomberg's own predicament to a T, though the
Gestapo's false testimony, doctored records, and forged
papers put a different complexion on it. After that,
probably in mid-September 1937, something crucial
occurred. In an attempt to bind Blomberg even closer to
her—and even though the immediate effect seemed a
substantial stride towards the happiness she craved—Eva
Gruhn took one step too many.

**Fifth essay in dramatic reconstruction . . . Subject:
the patter of tiny feet—**

"Would you be very angry if I didn't see you the day
after tomorrow?"

"Of course not, my darling," Blomberg said quickly.
"You mustn't always be governed by me—your time's
your own. It'll give me a chance to fit in with your plans for
a change."

"You don't have to, really you don't." Eva sometimes
felt she could read his thoughts. "If anyone deserves
consideration, it's you."

This was just another version of her favourite theme,
probably inspired by her mother. Even though she always
knew how he would react, she couldn't resist savouring his
devotion yet again. His response was as predictable as
ever.

"Worried about something?" he asked. "My darling
girl, please stop brooding about your past—the shadows
you keep talking about. If they ever existed at all, they've
gone for good. I thought the subject was closed."

"It isn't that, Werner, not this time. This time it's
something quite different. If I'm right, it'll all be over in
seven months' time. But that's my affair—I don't want you
to worry about it."

"About what, darling? What are you trying to say?"

"Only that I'm the happiest girl in the world," she said. "I think I'm going to have a baby."

"My God, how marvellous! A baby . . . Our baby—my baby!" He hugged her fervently.

"You're wonderful," she breathed, melting into his arms, "but I don't want to be a burden to you. Besides, I'm not absolutely sure yet. If I do have a baby—our baby—I'll love it the way I love you, but you needn't feel committed in any way. I'd rather die than do anything to hurt you."

"Hurt me? I'll gladly lay claim to you in front of everyone—you *and* the baby." He was looking relieved and cheerful now. His smile already conveyed the pride of a father-to-be.

"Darling Werner, I'll be seeing my doctor the day after tomorrow. As I say, I'm not quite sure . . ."

"There's only one thing you must be absolutely sure of, my wonderful girl. We really belong together and nobody's going to come between us. Not now!"

The two heads of the Greater Berlin Police Department, Commissioner Count von Helldorf and his deputy Count von der Schulenburg, continued to engage in flights of fancy, many of them extremely audacious, without ever quite abandoning the caution appropriate to such a pastime.

This time, Schulenburg had brought his chief a list comprising four sheets and seventy-three names complete with some rather sketchy personal particulars. It was a documentary mine field.

"This is the Gestapo's latest piece of impudence. First, they insist on our keeping their records up to date with a regular flow of information, but that's not good enough for

them. Oh no! Now they request us to follow specific lines
of inquiry—the sort of thing a higher authority expects
from a department lower down the scale. Are you going to
stand for it?"

"What do you expect me to do, lock horns with the
Gestapo?" Helldorf made a dismissive gesture. "You've
evolved some very promising methods, Schulenburg, so
kindly stick to them. I don't care what the Gestapo request.
We—or, rather, you—will continue to supply them with
stuff that doesn't lend itself to mischief-making."

"They could make plenty of mischief with that list
alone," retorted Schulenburg, only moderately amused. "I
hit on the idea of getting a dozen of our men to work their
way through it without telling them where it came from.
The results were highly instructive. Want to hear them?"

"The hell I do but I suppose I'll have to. You're
determined to involve me, it's written all over your face.
Well?"

Schulenburg produced a sheet of paper covered with
notes. "Seventy-three names, of which sixty-one appear in
our records. Nineteen of those are insignificant—a
random list of minor suspects. Twenty-two are routine
cases, and the other twenty refer to habitual criminals."

"Is that all?" Helldorf gave a relieved chuckle. "Looks
as if the Gestapo are testing our efficiency—checking our
records and trying to trip us up in the process. Why worry?
You're ready for them."

"If that were all!" The Duputy Commissioner turned his
sheet of paper over. More notes were scrawled on the
back. "If that were all," he repeated, "we could relax.
Unfortunately, it isn't."

"What else did you turn up?"

"A booby trap, Commissioner. After careful cross-
checking, I discovered that two-thirds of all the names

listed are Vice Squad material. But here's the point: half of those are connected—directly connected, in most cases—with the armed forces. What do you say now?"

Helldorf tried hard to conceal his alarm. "It may be a coincidence. The Gestapo would hardly dare to tread on the Wehrmacht's toes—Hitler would never allow it."

"Of course not. Not if it were just a solo effort by Heydrich's hatchet men. But what if our great Leader authorized the operation himself, or at least inspired it?"

"Come, come!" Helldorf said loudly, as if sheer volume would drown his uneasiness. "Why should he do that? The man's no fool. He needs the Wehrmacht, and the Wehrmacht needs him."

Schulenburg was unmoved. "You can look at it another way. Just for argument's sake, assume that some of these war-horses are getting frisky and upsetting the whole stable. That means they'll have to be dealt with, and the two commonest methods in this noble land of ours are gelding or the glue factory."

"Even if you're right, Schulenburg, which I beg leave to doubt, what then?"

"Even then, Commissioner, there'd be no need for you to man the barricades or me to wet my pants. I propose to go on laying my smoke screen while you have a few confidential chats with your friends in Military Intelligence—Colonel Oster, for instance. Try to find out if they've any idea what's in store for the Wehrmacht and then let me know, preferably in the fullest detail. Then we'll see."

Joseph Meisinger had been privileged to pay another call on his lord and master, Reinhard Heydrich. He stood there with his shoulders bowed beneath an invisible burden.

Heydrich digested this pathetic spectacle at a glance and modulated his voice accordingly. It became harsh, imperious, and relentless.

"What's up, Meisinger? Cold feet?"

"Not exactly, Gruppenführer, but . . . To be quite frank, I don't feel altogether happy about this assignment."

Heydrich left his subordinate standing by the door, where Meisinger hovered with an expression of agonized subservience. The next question smote him like a sledgehammer.

"This key witness of yours, has he broken down?"

"No, Gruppenführer, it isn't that. Schmidt's rock-solid—I mean, it'd take a lot to shake him. However, we did come across some discrepancies when we checked out his statements. One or two details don't add up, like his description of the scene of the offence and his method of collecting hush money. The same applies to his personal description of Fritsch. It doesn't sound a hundred per cent convincing."

"I hope I misheard you, Meisinger." Heydrich leant back a couple of inches, taking care not to disturb the immaculate drape of his uniform. "First, you claim to have a first-class witness and assure me his evidence will stand up in court, and now, suddenly, you're scared he'll come apart at the seams. That's crazy, man! You'll have to work on him till he's fireproof, understand?"

"Yessir," Meisinger said eagerly. "The only trouble is, it can't be done overnight. I'm terribly sorry, Gruppen-führer, but I need more time."

"You can have it, as it happens." Heydrich's tone mellowed. "Your prime target is due for a long spell of leave in the Mediterranean. An aide will be accompanying him."

"An aide?" Meisinger had come to life again. "A young

man, you mean? That's perfect! I'll have them tailed during the trip and..."

"I'll handle that, Meisinger. Your job is to gather more information and concentrate on Otto Schmidt. When the time comes, I want to hear him sing like Caruso."

Information volunteered by ex-Corporal Schmiedinger, formerly batman to General von Fritsch in Berlin, now a janitor in Stuttgart—

Me, on intimate terms with the Commander-in-Chief? What gives you that idea? Nobody really knew old Fritsch. He was more like a marble statue of himself, put up while he was still in the land of the living. I worked for him only two or three years—1935 to early 1938, if my memory serves me. That's right, I was his batman—polished his boots, pressed his uniforms, and so on.

But as for getting close to him personally, no sir! I don't suppose he wasted more than a few dozen words on me all the time I was with him, though he was always friendly. He made his own bed. Often cleaned his own boots too, mostly alone but sometimes with me. I never recall seeing him out of uniform. He was a stickler for regulation dress. Is that the sort of thing you're interested in? Okay, if you say so.

The old man seemed to have a built-in clock. His daily schedule was mapped out down to the last minute. How did he sound when he talked? Dignified, always very clear and distinct, never loud. He treated me like a teenage son.

His housekeeper was some kind of baroness, I think. No chicken, but a very nice lady. She always looked worried. "You have to take him as he comes," she used to say, meaning Fritsch. "He's just a soldier." Which was grim but true.

Emotional peculiarities? Don't make me laugh! Old Fritsch was made of cast iron. Did he have any favourites? Not unless you count his horse, but he also had a soft spot for cats and dogs. It was funny, watching him with animals. You could have sworn he was trying to talk to them, as if they were his own kind.

Joking apart, though, I never felt sorrier for anyone in my life. He didn't have any friends—probably didn't know the meaning of the word. He didn't smoke, hardly touched a drop, and never went to parties. I doubt if he ever had a girlfriend, but he did go racing occasionally. People called him stuck-up, but he certainly wasn't that.

His housekeeper sometimes let her hair down to me. "He's not an easy man," I recall her saying once. "I've no idea what he earns, but he insists on living like a church mouse."

I heard later that he was very generous to his old mother, not to mention several relatives and members of his old regiment. He never spent more than five hundred marks a month on himself. He led a quiet life, all told. Pretty depressing by most people's standards, but it seemed to suit him.

Sixth essay in dramatic reconstruction . . . Subject: possible ways out—

Eva Gruhn nestled tenderly against her lover after one of their happiest moments together. "I think I know how to get round my problem—our problem, I mean. It's the baby I'm thinking of, mainly."

"But I'm going to claim paternity, darling, I told you that."

"You'd only complicate things and make a lot of trouble for yourself, maybe for no good reason." Eva not only

looked worried but really was, and all for his sake. "You're
an important man, Werner. You've got to remember your
position and let me do likewise. I'm just not good enough
for you—how many more times do I have to say it?"

"My dearest darling girl, why worry your head about
that? We aren't living in the Middle Ages, thank God. I've
been a widower for years. That makes me a completely
free agent—free to take on any commitment I choose.
Who's to stop me?"

"But you've got to be careful!"

"Of what or whom? This country's in the throes of a
national upheaval—a social revolution. The old rules don't
apply any longer."

"You're forgetting my background again. I'm not your
class. Besides, there's something else I should tell you. I'm
being pestered by someone."

"Pestered? By whom?"

"Someone who was chasing me before I met you. His
name's Herbert Heersdorf—he's a businessman. He keeps
on saying he won't give me up, and I keep on telling him I
don't want anything more to do with him."

Blomberg felt tempted to ask if the man was very much
younger or more attractive than himself, but he knew
Eva's answer in advance: she loved him and him alone,
precisely because he was what he was—the fulfilment of
all her dreams.

He simply said, "Sounds like a nuisance, but no real
problem—not to us. What sort of person is he?"

"It's like I said. He's been after me for ages, but not like
you, Werner. You're so unselfish and considerate. He's the
pushy type, very demanding and possessive, but he loves
me in his own way."

"And you're finding it difficult to break with him?"

"Of course not. He's the one who's being difficult. He

wants me on any terms, he says, including the fact that I've
been having an affair with you. He'd even be prepared to
take on the baby."

Blomberg drew her close. She clung to him like a child
seeking warmth and security.

"All that matters is this, Eva. If I asked you to make a
decision, a clear-cut decision between him and me, which
of us would you choose?"

"You, Werner! Only you! I don't have the faintest
shadow of a doubt about that."

"That settles it, then. We'll get married just as soon as I
can make the arrangements."

He spoke as if the die was cast, which it was.

Towards the end of November 1937, one of Field Marshal
von Blomberg's aides telephoned his opposite number
on the staff of General Göring, Commander-in-Chief
Luftwaffe.

The Air Force officer who had taken this call hurried
off to inform Göring. He found him sitting over a
protracted breakfast at Karinhall, the country house
named after his first and adored wife Karin, who had died
young. Strongly infused with the Nordic and Germanic
spirit, this architectural extravaganza occupied a site not
far from Berlin, hemmed in by indigo waters of a lake.
Dominating the décor were rough-hewn stone and
seasoned oak, rawhide and damask, wrought iron and
crystal.

Göring's ADC waded ankle-deep through a sea of
carpet and clicked his heels at a respectful distance from
the Commander-in-Chief, who was swathed in a sort of
fur-trimmed bathrobe. He waited until the jewels on
Göring's left hand had flashed a brief signal to proceed.

"Message from the field marshal, sir." The ADC's stance was ramrod-stiff but combined with a permanent bow of submission.

"From Blomberg? What does he want?" It was one of Göring's principles to pour scorn and suspicion on any communication that did not come straight from the Führer, a technique designed to persuade his entourage that no person or thing could be other than secondary compared to himself. "I've got better things to do than make phone calls."

"The field marshal sends his very best regards," the ADC continued deferentially.

Hermann Göring gave a thin smile. Greater Germany boasted only one peacetime field marshal, and it wasn't him—a definite flaw, in his opinion. He alone should have been entitled to that unique rank.

"Herr von Blomberg," the ADC went on, "would like to fix a meeting. A very private and informal meeting, so I was given to understand."

Göring's somnolent expression had vanished. He rose abruptly with a rustle of silk, like a latter-day Louis XIV.

"A private matter, you say?"

"Yes, General. Private and confidential."

"That sounds promising," drawled Hitler's lieutenant, conveying yet again what an influential and sought-after figure he was. "If he really wants a word with me, let him come. I'll see him here—today."

Corporal Schmiedinger, the Army Commander-in-Chief's batman, clicked his heels. "That Hitler boy's here, General," he announced brightly. "Knees scrubbed, hair combed, nails clean. I don't know about his pants, but he's probably wetting them."

Fritsch wagged his bullet head, looking faintly amused. Schmiedinger enjoyed the privileges of a court jester, though only when they were alone. He obeyed this rule to the letter but blithely took advantage of it in private.

"Do be a little more careful in your choice of words, Corporal," Fritsch corrected him. "The Chancellor has no son and heir, as your use of the term 'Hitler boy' seems to suggest. He's a member of the Hitler Youth. As for wetting his pants, I take it you mean he cherishes a certain respect for my paternal authority."

This particular member of the Hitler Youth, Heinz by name, was one of three youngsters who visited the general at regular intervals. In accordance with an official suggestion made by Hitler himself, bachelors of senior rank were encouraged to devote a certain amount of time to orphaned members of the Führer's youth movement and provide them with the rudiments of a father-son relationship. Fritsch had willingly supported the scheme.

"I'll take him off your hands if you like, General," Schmiedinger suggested. "There's always the zoo or the movies. Afterwards, I can stuff him full of sandwiches, and that'll be that till next time. He wouldn't enjoy himself as much with you, sir, believe me."

"My dear Schmiedinger, it isn't a question of giving the boy a good time. I've volunteered to help with his upbringing—I'm in loco parentis, so to speak."

Heinz was duly admitted to the general's table and shared his frugal midday repast. This was accompanied by a crash course in table manners and followed by lectures on a variety of subjects, including Prussian history—notably military history—and the martial arts. Special emphasis was laid on fieldcraft, map reading, and land warfare.

Heinz was looking worn out when Fritsch handed him

over to Schmiedinger for redelivery to the hostel where he lived. The general slipped two marks into his batman's hand and murmured, "One beer for you, two sandwiches for the boy."

"Well," Schmiedinger said boldly as he and Heinz made tracks for the nearest place of refreshment, "what did the Old Man do with you today?"

"He hit me."

"You don't say!" The corporal was slightly disconcerted by this statement. "Tanned your hide for stepping out of line, did he?"

Heinz denied this with a scowl which conveyed that no member of the Hitler Youth was ever guilty of indiscipline. "He hit me with his ruler. Only a little tap—it didn't hurt a bit. It was during map reading. I can't understand the grid system."

"Is that all?" said Schmiedinger, looking relieved. "So he played the heavy father, eh? Fathers are like that, my lad. They lay it on you just to prove how tough they are. My old man used a leather strap."

"Really?" Heinz frowned thoughtfully. "In that case, I suppose I ought to be glad I don't have a father, or not a permanent one."

"Still, one day you'll be able to look back and tell yourself: A great man—a really top-notch general—spent hours of his precious time on me. You ought to think yourself lucky. Make sure you're a credit to the old bugger, that's all."

Blomberg turned up at Karinhall the same day, after another exchange of preparatory telephone calls between his ADC and Göring's. He was wearing a discreet grey Savile Row suit.

Göring welcomed Blomberg in the baronial hall which served as his drawing room. He waddled towards him like a dancing bear, comfortably attired in a voluminous hunting outfit of medievally Nordic appearance: buckskin waistcoat, silk shirt, leather breeches, and chain adorned with marksman's medals. He spread his arms wide—very wide—before shaking Blomberg's hand with the insouciance affected by members of the same officers' mess.

After all, it was Blomberg who had requested this audience and he, Göring, who had given his gracious assent. It always paid to observe such fine distinctions among the great. Differences in pecking order could develop automatically during encounters of this kind.

They sat down facing each other in a pair of outsize leopard-skin armchairs. As they did so, Göring's alert eye detected that the field marshal was wearing a faintly sheepish expression. The sight of it whetted his curiosity still further.

"You're looking well, Herr von Blomberg."

"And feeling well too, General—well in myself, so to speak. Life has been good to me lately, and I'd like it to remain so. That's why I need your help, to be honest. I'm pinning a lot of my hopes on you."

"Then you've come to the right place," boomed Göring. "I always try to do my best, especially for brother officers."

He sat back, never taking his eyes off Blomberg's face, and lovingly massaged his huge convex paunch with both pudgy hands. Göring was a mighty man in every sense of the word.

"I have the highest regard for you, Herr von Blomberg," he said, beaming at his visitor. "I not only welcomed your promotion to field marshal but actively sponsored it. A matter of course, my dear sir—no obligation on your side.

However, since we're being absolutely honest with each other, I had hoped you might show rather more understanding of my special problems—for instance at that meeting with the Führer on 3 November. You hardly backed me up, to say the least."

"If you really formed that impression, my dear General, it can only have been a regrettable misunderstanding. I took the liberty of writing you a letter immediately afterwards, assuring you how much importance I attached to mutual trust and close cooperation. With you in particular."

"I was delighted to hear it—delighted!" The master of Karinhall was smiling now, half jovially, half confidentially. The conversation had got off to a good start. His visitor's attitude seemed markedly cooperative. He must have some ulterior motive, of course, but what was it?

Göring leant forward and gave Blomberg a comradely pat on the arm. The field marshal did not recoil. He made an effort to radiate good-fellowship, breathing with some restraint because his suspiciously affable host was wreathed in a rich and cloying effluvium of scent. This distant reminder of his beloved Eva had a mollifying effect on him.

"Personally," Göring cooed, "I'm quite prepared to forget our little misunderstanding."

"Nothing could please me more."

"I don't hold it against you. That would be petty, which I'm not. Especially not now, when you're proposing to honour me by taking me into your confidence—or so I gather. Very well, fire away. I guarantee you a sympathetic hearing and all the help I can give."

"It's an extremely personal matter, General. I'm not sure I should burden you with it."

Göring immediately grasped the delicacy of the

situation. He also sensed Blomberg's reluctance to disclose the full extent of what was troubling him, so he switched to a note of jovial and sympathetic encouragement.

"Anyone can tell me anything, man to man. Absolute discretion is my watchword, so what can I do for you? Money worries? If so, never mind how much. I'll gladly let you have it right away."

"Very kind—extremely good of you to offer. No, many thanks, but it isn't that."

"Let me try another guess. An enemy? Somebody you want disposed of? A favour for a friend or relation? Not that either? What, then?"

"I'm a widower, as you know." Blomberg had made up his mind to confide in Göring. "My dear wife died nearly ten years ago. I can't forget her, of course—I don't suppose I ever shall, but life must go on."

"How right you are! Much the same thing happened to me, which is yet another reason why we ought to help each other out. You want to get married again, correct?"

"Precisely, General, and you're the first person I've taken into my confidence—officially, as it were."

Göring's nostrils twitched. There was something fishy about Blomberg's story, some hint of a development so explosive it might be turned to good use. "So what's your problem?" he asked eagerly. "Is the lady married? If she is, we'll unmarry her. Is that the trouble."

"Not at all," said Blomberg, visibly impressed by all this comradely concern. "It's just that the woman of my choice is a very unpretentious person, socially speaking. She works in a restaurant—a good one, though, and she occupies a semimanagerial position. Her name is Eva Gruhn."

"Splendid, splendid!" cried Göring, instinctively delighted. "A good deal younger than you, I suppose?"

"Nearly thirty years my junior."

"Bravo, well done! Please accept my heartiest congrat-ulations!" Göring was revelling in the news. "I couldn't be happier for you—or, just between friends, more envious!"

He then hit on a phrase which was to recur later on, though in a less felicitous context.

"I see," he mused, "so she's a daughter of the people..."

"That's just it," said Blomberg. "I can't help wondering how the Führer will react."

"Let me break it to him," Göring said quickly. "Why not? I'd be glad to—delighted to. Don't worry, my dear fellow. Put your faith in my persuasive powers—not to mention a fortunate coincidence which may have escaped you. With all due respect and no intention of trespassing on the Führer's privacy, permit me to whisper two little words: Eva Braun! See what I mean? Another Eva!"

"I can't thank you enough." Blomberg bowed. He felt immensely relieved—so relieved that his host's malicious glee was completely lost on him.

"No, no," Göring exclaimed, "I'm the one who must thank you for confiding in me. I consider it an honour and an exceedingly hopeful sign. You'll be amazed how helpful I can be when I try. Let's drink to that. For a decadent race, the French produce some very decent wine."

As soon as he had dealt with his second glass of Ruinart Dom 1933, a superb champagne served in one of the classic potbellied bottles, Göring blithely turned his attention to some practical problems confronting Blom-berg in the weeks ahead.

"Your fiancée works in a restaurant—a first-class one, I think you said. Very creditable. Nothing wrong with that, except—well, in view of her forthcoming marriage to a field marshal, it might be advisable to perform a little cosmetic surgery. On her professional status, I mean. You know how narrow-minded and class-conscious most of our brother officers are. I'm afraid you'll have to allow for that."

"In what way?"

"I've had a most effective idea—something which can be arranged with very little difficulty by someone like me. I control a wide variety of institutions, departments, and offices, don't forget. Fräulein Gruhn could find a temporary slot in one of them until the day of your wedding—which I insist on attending, by the way. That would absolve your fiancée—your daughter of the people—from working in a restaurant. She'd be a government employee instead. How does that appeal?"

Blomberg liked the idea. His gratitude to Göring grew by leaps and bounds.

"Do you have anything specific in mind?"

Göring refilled their glasses and toasted his visitor with gusto. Then he launched into a lengthy dissertation on his official capacities, the resources he controlled, and the benefits of unlimited mutual cooperation. His offers of help were bewildering in their profusion.

Göring's preserves included the Air Ministry, the Prussian Cabinet Office, the State Game and Forestry Department, a number of development and planning authorities, the so-called Research Bureau—which tapped phones and intercepted telegrams—and various bodies supervised by him in his capacity as chief administrator of the Four-Year Plan. Among these were the Crop Coordination Office, the River Purification Authority, the State Beef Unit, the State Butter Centre, and the State Egg Marketing Board.

"The Egg Board's a new baby of mine," he said. "I'm expecting great things of it. The director's a highly qualified man, but he's short-staffed, or so I gather from his latest report. I'm sure he could find a comfortable niche for your fiancée. Would that suit you?"

"Perfectly," Blomberg assured him.

Göring gave the field marshal an encouraging grin. "Fine. A nice harmonious public image, that's what we need. I'm sure the Führer would agree. No matter what happens, he likes to feel it's in the national interest—always remember that. Any other problems?"

"Well, er..."

"I thought so! I've got a nose for these things. What's the trouble?"

"It's only a minor problem. There's someone else—an unpleasant type, considerably younger than me. The truth is, he's making a nuisance of himself."

"Really?" said Göring in high delight. This might prove useful if properly exploited. "Competition, eh? You're talking to an expert, my dear fellow. Emmy—my second wife—was an actress, as you know. They used to swarm round her like bees round a honeypot—actors, journalists, critics, producers who thought they were God's gift to women... Well, I saw them off, and I'll gladly do the same for you. Who's the fly in the ointment?"

"Someone called Heersdorf, Herbert Heersdorf. An important merchant, or so he says."

"Who cares what he does? I've made a note of the name. Just give me his address, and I'll deal with the problem—discreetly but thoroughly. You'll be amazed, believe me."

4

Plans and Coincidences

From the Meller report—

I came across a number of puzzling features while following this course of events.

One thing that struck me as disgraceful was how quick certain people were to brand Eva Gruhn a prostitute, and not just Hitler and his Gestapo. Several of Blomberg's brother officers used the same opprobrious term. "You don't marry creatures like that!" was their mildest comment. *Very well*, they thought, *let him make a fool of himself. If he goes, all the more room for us.*

No less outrageous was the attitude of a substantial proportion of the generals' clique to the charges against

Fritsch. He was anything but a Nazi general, just a quiet and unassuming man with no taste or talent for intrigue. This prompted remarks such as "He must know what he's doing. If he's innocent, why doesn't he fight back?"

But what really astonished me was the brevity of this pernicious campaign. The ruthless tacticians who waged it took barely eleven days—from late January to early February 1938—to bring it to a successful conclusion. They eliminated every obstacle in their path, aided by an ideal combination of circumstances.

"You must go. You've no choice." General von Fritsch's doctor spoke with all the authority an eminent physician could bring to bear. "I consider it absolutely essential you take a long sick leave at once. At least two months, or I won't be answerable for the consequences."

Fritsch, who had just undergone a thorough physical checkup, shook his head. "Out of the question. I can't drop everything. My presence here is vital, now more than ever."

"Then your days are numbered, General," the doctor said flatly. "How can it benefit you or the Army to work yourself into an early grave? You're a danger to everyone and everything in your present state of health. Your constitution, your life, your professional efficiency—my reputation as your personal physician."

"Don't try to bully me, Doctor. I'm not just the patient of a distinguished medical man—I also have a job to do. That's as far as my sense of responsibility goes."

"A noble sentiment, but it leaves me cold. To me, you're simply a patient with respiratory trouble. You suffer from chronic fits of coughing and periodic vomiting. Your chest sounds like a pair of leaky bellows. One of these days, you'll die of asphyxia."

"How soon?"

"Very soon, if you aren't careful." Fritsch's obstinacy had an almost ritual quality, but the doctor was determined to prevail. "You're going on leave," he commanded. "Two months at the very least—I absolutely insist. Switzerland would do you good, but Egypt might be better in your particular case. Your lungs are in a frightful state. An immediate change of climate will give them a chance to recuperate."

"What if I reject your advice?"

"Then it won't be long before the Army gets a new Commander-in-Chief and I lose a patient—one who means a lot to me personally, General, if it's of any interest to you. That's all I have to say."

Probably on the same day, and for ostensibly gastronomic reasons, two men met for dinner. They were Count von der Schulenburg, Deputy Police Commissioner of Berlin, and Colonel Hans Oster of Military Intelligence, Admiral Canaris's right-hand man. Their rendezvous—Horcher's, a glossy restaurant in the Kurfürstendamm—could hardly have been more neutral territory.

Schulenburg stared quizzically at his table companion. "Who's paying?"

"You, of course. You invited me."

"I merely suggested a meeting—a confidential exchange of information. Besides, you know how stingy my department is when it comes to expenses. You Military Intelligence boys can afford to pick up tabs and no questions asked. Take this dinner. Establishing contact with the enemy—you can chalk it up to that."

Oster chuckled. "Always trying to steamroller me, aren't you? Well, please don't. It's hard to get used to your methods, Schulenburg, and I'm not the only one who finds them baffling. What are you after this time? Helldorf only dropped a few hints. How much do you actually know?"

"I'll tell you, but not until your department has stood me a broiled lobster and some saddle of lamb."

Schulenburg waited until they had both done justice to a superb dinner, then floored Oster with a direct question.

"Do you think it conceivable that General von Fritsch is homosexually inclined?"

Colonel Oster choked on a mouthful of wine and stared at him in horror. "My God, are you crazy? That question's out of court, Schulenburg. I'll forget you ever asked it."

Schulenburg was unmoved. He hadn't expected any other reaction. "Are you positive, Hans?" he drawled. "You certainly sound it. May I ask why?"

"Because I've known the man for years, that's why."

"Precisely. He was your commanding officer, or I wouldn't have asked you in the first place. But do you really know him well enough to be sure—well enough to pronounce on his private life?"

"He doesn't have one, so get that straight from the start." Oster was indignant. In a restaurant as select as Horcher's, his raised voice threatened to attract unwelcome attention. "Fritsch is above suspicion. There are only three things in this world he values, apart from God, and those are his mother, his job, and his horse."

"I hope you're right."

"I'd stand bail for that man," Oster said solemnly. "I spent a lot of time with him in the old days, on duty and off. It wasn't a particularly exhilarating experience, but one thing's for sure. Boring he may be, God knows, but he's straight as they come."

"You're forgetting something. As the law stands today, even a saint can end up behind bars."

Oster gave Schulenburg a level stare. "Look," he said, "what's behind all this? How did you arrive at such a dangerous theory about the old man?"

Schulenburg deputized for the wine waiter and refilled their glasses. "One or two Gestapo inquiries point straight in that direction. Prinz-Albrecht-Strasse seems to be taking a keen interest in his private life, and the focus of that interest is unmistakably sexual."

"But it can't be anything more than a semiofficial probe by Meisinger and his snoopers. They're trying to justify their existence, that's all."

"Maybe, maybe not. If not, what do you and Military Intelligence propose to do about it?"

"So that's it!" Oster slapped the table. "*That's* what you're after, Monsieur Fouché. You're trying to engineer a clash between my department and the Gestapo. Military Intelligence versus the SS, isn't that your game?"

"Of course, what could be more natural?" Schulenburg busied himself with some slices of pineapple steeped in Black Forest Kirschwasser. "The SS have been moving in on you for quite a while now. They're making life difficult for your department with a view to absorbing it."

"I'd like to see them try!"

"They'll do it all right, but only if you go on acting with gentlemanly restraint and let them undermine your defences one by one. Damn it all, man, your outfit can also play dirty when it wants to."

"I know."

"Then give them a demonstration—unless, of course,

you intend to hand them Fritsch's head on a platter?"

"Of course not, but why should we launch an all-out campaign because a few Gestapo underlings make a minor nuisance of themselves?"

"You mean you're going to sit back and do nothing?"

"We'll keep them under routine observation, naturally. As for taking further action, it depends whether there's anything more to it than the Gestapo's usual love of bureaucratic meddling. What about Heydrich and Himmler? Any sign that they're masterminding the operation?"

"No," Schulenburg said frankly. "It's quite possible, but I can't give you a categorical assurance. Not yet."

"That's what we need. Try and find out for certain. Call it the price of your next gourmet dinner."

Meetings between the Commanders-in-Chief of the three armed services—Army, Navy, and Air Force—occurred sporadically. Apart from attending joint conferences with Hitler, the three service chiefs cultivated interdepartmental contacts whenever it seemed necessary.

In this particular instance, Hermann Göring had dropped in on General von Fritsch because he "happened to be passing." He was admitted at once and greeted with the civility, if not warmth, prescribed by the general's sense of decorum—and expediency.

The interview turned out to be brief and acrimonious. Göring was obviously looking for a fight.

"You're a constant source of trouble, Herr von Fritsch!"

"What am I supposed to have done this time, Herr Göring?"

"It's this so-called church parade order of yours, encouraging officers to attend services with their men."

"Precisely." Fritsch spoke with dignified restraint. "I

consider that a highly desirable practice. The Christian faith provides a firm foundation for the military concept of duty. It always has."

"Yes, yes, of course!" Göring became heavily confidential. "I'm fully aware of your feelings on the subject. I don't quarrel with them as such, but I insist on making my own position clear."

Fritsch felt slightly puzzled. He had inherited his religious beliefs from his mother, who belonged to one of the biggest and most influential Protestant families in Germany, but he couldn't see what they had to do with Göring. "Look," Göring went on, "you can give your Army chaplains all the latitude you like, but there are limits. Some of my Air Force padres have become infected by your bunch. They're spreading your half-baked ideas round the Luftwaffe, and I won't stand for it."

"That's hardly my fault. I had no intention of encroaching on your territory. Simply take my standing order and adapt it to your own sphere of command."

"I'll be damned if I will!" snapped Göring. "I don't take orders from you, nor do I act as a father confessor to Christians in uniform. You're way behind the times, certainly when it comes to religion."

Fritsch stood there like a gnarled oak stripped of leaves before its time. His face was rigid, but his voice remained courteous and businesslike, even now.

"It may become necessary to seek a ruling on the matter. The Chancellor ought to decide. I propose we jointly request that the item be included in our next conference agenda."

"Stop quibbling, General! We both know the Führer's attitude to religion. He's realistic—he knows it can't be abolished overnight. Any attempt to do so would only create bad blood, and none of us wants that."

"Of course not, Herr Göring. Which leaves me wondering what lies behind your visit. Please tell me, and be as frank as you know how."

"All right. You're not only a troublemaker. You've recently been making trouble for me—*me*! If you think you can get away with that, you're wrong."

Fritsch stared at his visitor, surprised and disconcerted. He silently adjusted his monocle.

"My God," Göring pursued fiercely, "how stubborn can you get! I extend the hand of friendship, and what happens? You spurn it!"

He waited for a moment but got no answer. Then, as though responding to a private word of command, he turned and stormed out.

An aide hurried in as soon as Göring had gone. He found Fritsch beside the window, which he had opened to its fullest extent.

He was leaning against the window-frame. He had removed his monocle and was breathing heavily with his eyes half-closed. His face was ashen.

"That was distasteful," he said, breaking the oppressive silence with an effort. "Most distasteful."

From the Meller report—

Many contemporary observers found General von Fritsch an "unfathomable" person. Even now, decades later, he seems to puzzle the most perceptive historians. One of them, an otherwise outstanding authority on the military resistance movement against Hitler, has called him "fundamentally helpless and childlike."

Fritsch, the man acknowledged by many to be "a military planning expert of the very highest order," a helpless child at heart? Even Hitler cherished a great and entirely justified regard for his unique qualities.

However, the quality that really constituted his special value to Hitler was defined for me by Colonel Hossbach, who had only to quote one of the Führer's pronouncements: "The general isn't an easy or unduly approachable man, but he enjoys my complete confidence because, when all's said and done, he can be trusted to the hilt. He still knows the meaning of an order."

The general himself provided me with a further insight into his philosophy while we were riding in the Tiergarten one day. "There's no doubt," he said, "that a soldier's paramount duty and cardinal virtue is the will to serve without question. Serve," he repeated almost inaudibly, "—yes, but whom?"

Fritsch was no "helpless child at heart." There were altogether different reasons underlying the grand tragedy associated with his name, one of them extremely human. Although many people respected the general, and some regarded him with boundless admiration, hardly anyone seems to have loved him except his mother, whom he always treated with touching solicitude.

Fritsch radiated self-confidence. His habitual manner was reserved and uncommunicative to the point of abruptness. One of his aides compared him to a man encased in glass, and his batman Corporal Schmiedinger, who was not easily impressed by the great, recalled that nobody could put anything over on him. "He saw through them all, but few people spotted it."

Like Werner von Blomberg, Fritsch was just another of those whom Göring tersely categorized during the Nuremberg war-crimes trials as "in our way."

Even at the time, however, this ruthless logic was not accepted without demur by all who had recognized the brutality of a regime founded on power politics. Among those who tried to mobilize its opponents, myself included, was that tireless conspirator Hans Oster. His appeal could hardly have been more explicit.

"We're counting on you, Meller," he told me. "It's time you started pulling a few strings. After all, you're virtually a friend of the general's."

"Nobody's a *friend* of his," I retorted, "not even virtually."

"All right, if you won't approach him direct, what about your old friend Heydrich? You ought to be able to do something through him."

"He's not my old friend," I said, politely but uneasily. "I make it my business to be his, which isn't the same thing. There were three of us—our parents were neighbours. I don't know what happened to the third member of the gang. Heydrich says he has no idea where he is. Nobody could have foreseen we'd meet again in Berlin, him as a security chief and me as a civil servant. For all I know, number three's in a concentration camp."

"Do you see a lot of him?"

"Heydrich? No, not these days."

"That's a mistake. You ought to remedy that as soon as you can."

"I agree, not that the idea appeals to me."

"It's essential, under the circumstances." A note of caution crept into Oster's voice. "Be careful, but I don't have to tell you that. In the future, avoid all contacts that can easily be traced—me, for instance. As soon as you bring Heydrich into the picture, things are bound to get tricky."

Even at this stage in his career, Reinhard Heydrich felt he had a friend or two left—or, if not two, one at least. The all-powerful head of the Central State Security Bureau savoured this thought as he sat ensconced behind the massive walls of his Prinz-Albrecht-Strasse headquarters, an elegant and determined young man whose lethal proclivities were strangely allied with a genuine appreciation of the arts.

He received few visits from civilians, most of whom were rated "unauthorized." The only one who always got the green light was Counsellor Erich Meller. Heydrich greeted him effusively.

"My dear Erich, this is a pleasant surprise! Pardon me for saying so, but you're quite a stranger these days."

"Ah," said Meller, dredging his memory for an obscure but apt quotation, "go not to thy prince unless he summons thee."

Heydrich's sallow face flushed with pleasure. He shook hands with his visitor, then gave him a companionable slap on the shoulder. Alone of all his acquaintances, Meller knew the meaning of tact. He was never intrusive, never tried to take advantage of their friendship. Now he had even compared him to royalty. That was a joke, of course, but still . . .

"Sit down, old friend. Make yourself at home. I've only got a few little chores to polish off. After that, I'm all yours."

Meller sat down at a table in one corner of the office. There were some files on it. Quite casually, as though to pass the time, he started to leaf through them.

Heydrich, not in the least disconcerted by Meller's presence, applied himself to his "chores." He initialed a list of suspects to be detained—a relatively small one of only eighteen names—and buzzed his outer office. An assistant hurried in. "See they're picked up tonight," he commanded.

Then he telephoned someone called Meisinger. "I've run through your latest reports," he snarled, "and they're pretty damned useless. It's time you got something straight, Meisinger. I don't care who's on our blacklist—I don't care if it's the Pope himself—there are dozens of skeletons in every cupboard, even a general's. Anyone who fouls his own doorstep gets his nose rubbed in it—by us, understand?"

Heydrich listened to the effect of this pep talk, looking faintly amused. He flashed Meller a conspiratorial wink before cutting the conversation short.

"Watertight evidence, Meisinger! That's all I want from you, so make a thorough job of it. Time's no problem. Our target won't be back from his foreign trip for seven or eight weeks. But *then*, Meisinger! That's when you deliver the goods."

Heydrich slammed the phone down and turned his attention to Meller. He sat down beside him and gave him another slap on the back. "Thank God you're still around, Erich. You're a refreshing sight in a world full of bootlickers."

"A world the Führer plans to rebuild with their help," Meller said drily.

"It's the only way." Heydrich gave an unembarrassed bark of laughter. "The more boots they lick, the more glorious the age we live in."

"You seem to get a kick out of the situation."

"Why not? They're animals, these people—and it's a lot of fun training them. I realized something long ago, Erich. I can get them to eat out of my hand if I want. They'll swallow anything they're given, even their own excrement."

"All that interests me at the moment," Meller said, "and the real reason for my visit, Reinhard, is a glass of your excellent champagne. I can't afford the stuff myself."

"I could always send you a few cases." The head of the Central State Security Bureau looked boyishly arch. "But then I'd see even less of you than I do now, and you know how I enjoy talking about our misspent youth."

Heydrich liked to recall his boyhood, but only in Meller's company. He mellowed visibly during these reminiscences, becoming almost exuberant. The three boys had been inseparable for years. It was a close but carefree relationship cemented by escapades typical of early adolescence—the snipping of girls' braids, the systematic persecution of cats and younger children, the smashing of windows, the theft and secret consumption of altar wine, the lacing of beer with schnapps before a patriotic rally which left their fathers inexplicably hung over, and so on.

One local attraction had been the presence of Russian prisoners in a camp near their village. The boys, who were fascinated by these victims of World War I, promptly started to pick up their language. They became quite fluent and could still communicate in Pidgin Russian to this day.

"We couldn't have guessed what would become of us," mused Heydrich.

"No," said Meller, "not in our wildest dreams."

Sergeant Maier, the general's groom, invited his batman, Corporal Schmiedinger, to join him for an exploratory beer at Aschinger's, near the Zoo subway station.

Aschinger's was a rendezvous popular with workmen, students, prostitutes, and soldiers. Popular mainly because of its modest prices. A meatball cost thirty pfennigs and a grilled chop one mark, but half that would buy a bowl of thick pea soup with a frankfurter floating in it. Crusty little rolls were available by the basketful—free of charge.

Maier and Schmiedinger ate and drank at considerable length, studying each other in silence. They seemed to like what they saw. Maier drained his second mug of Schultheiss-Patzenhofer and sighed with relief.

"Just shows how wrong a man can be," he said. "You look quite normal."

"Thanks. So do you, Sergeant."

"That gives us two things in common. We're both normal and we both work for the general. I look after his horse."

"And I look after his things. Clean his boots, keep his quarters tidy, and so on." Schmiedinger went on to describe how Fritsch always made his own bed—probably a hangover from his days in a Prussian military academy. "What's more, he rinses out his own socks, pants, and handkerchiefs before he lets me send them to the laundry."

"A little peculiar, isn't it?"

"Not when you know him. He likes to get rid of his own dirt, that's all. If you want to call that peculiar, you can. He's certainly no ordinary man."

Maier hesitated. "That could be just his trouble."

"Not from my point of view. He's a decent type."

"He sounds it." Maier hesitated again. "Tell me, Schmiedinger, are you married?"

"No."

"Don't you go out with girls?"

The corporal's eyes narrowed. "What are you driving at? If you think I'm that way inclined, you can damn well ..."

"All right, take it easy. I never said any such thing."

They fell silent for a while, Schmiedinger looking

thoroughly offended. Maier paid for the meal and rose.

"Yes, well—that's all I wanted to know."

"I can guess what you were getting at," Schmiedinger growled. "I've already been grilled by a couple of plainclothesmen. The bastards wanted to know if the general had ever made a pass at me."

"And has he?"

"Of *course* he hasn't. What a ridiculous question!"

"Could you swear to that?"

"Sure I could, but why should I? I just laughed in their faces."

"Have you told the general?"

"What do you think!" Schmiedinger looked genuinely outraged. "Could *you* go to a nice old man like Fritsch and tell him some shit of a secret policeman says he's a fairy? Sooner you than me!"

"All right, Schmiedinger, so you think a lot of the general. That makes two of us." The sergeant paused. "And that, my boy, is why we ought to figure out a way of helping him."

Counsellor Meller had decided to dine at Emil's in Uhlandstrasse that evening. Emil's was snug, solidly middle-class and resolutely unglamorous, all of which preserved it from unwelcome visits by senior members of the Party, government, and armed forces.

The restaurant's proprietor, Emil Labenske, made a point of knowing his patrons well—for safety's sake. Labenske was a former Red who claimed to have turned "brown," or Nazi, and had advertised his new beliefs loudly enough to convince some people of their authenticity. He valued this impression, as his friends were aware.

Labenske welcomed Meller warmly, with a familiarity

of several years' standing—seven, to be exact, because it was seven years since he had given him first aid after a brawl between members of the Republican "Reichsbanner" and a squad of SA rowdies.

"Anything I can do for you?" he asked.

Meller slipped him a scrap of paper. "Yes, would you mind calling this number?"

Labenske knew the number by heart. "You want to see him?"

"Right away, if possible."

"Leave it to me."

Labenske got through to Police Headquarters and asked for the Deputy Commissioner.

"Who's speaking, please?"

"The proprietor of Emil's in Uhlandstrasse. Labenske's my name."

"And you wish to speak to the Deputy Commissioner? In what connection?"

"I'm calling about a meal he ordered."

Labenske was put through, knowing from experience that everything he said would be monitored and probably recorded as well.

"Schulenburg here," the count said briskly. "What's the problem, Herr Labenske?"

"No problem, sir. You asked me to let you know when your favourite specialty was on, and we're serving it tonight."

"Thanks for telling me." Schulenburg sounded as offhand as Labenske had sounded every inch the obsequious restaurateur. "I'll be with you as soon as I can, so make sure you don't run out."

Schulenburg reached Emil's within half an hour, received an effusive welcome, and was conducted to a table in the far corner. Meller was already sitting there alone. They didn't speak or shake hands, merely exchanged a curt nod, like two diners seated together by chance.

Labenske remained equally silent while dispensing Berlin's most awe-inspiring specialty, knuckle of pork on sauerkraut. Almost overflowing the spacious platter, it was a dish capable of testing anyone's gastric staying power.

For the next half-hour, the two men seemed wholly engrossed in their meal. Although they exchanged an occasional glance, not a word passed between them until Labenske came up and reported the coast clear.

Then they appeared to the casual observer to assess the meal—presumably praising the creamy tenderness of the pork and the superb aroma emanating from those mountains of sauerkraut, which anaesthetized the stomach without numbing the brain.

Schulenburg opened. "Why all this cloak-and-dagger stuff, Meller? Is it really necessary?"

"It is now. I called on my old friend today, for the first time in months."

"I see what you mean." Schulenburg smiled politely and passed Meller the breadbasket. "A privileged visitor like you will probably be kept under surveillance as a matter of course—and so will all your contacts. Never mind, we'll have to allow for that. Oster thinks it's worth the risk. You must call on your friend more often in the future—you're bound to pick up something useful." He retrieved the breadbasket and helped himself. "Unless you already have..."

"If I told you that one of our top generals is going on a long trip abroad, could you hazard a guess at his identity?"

"You know perfectly well who he is." Schulenburg concealed an ironical grin by dabbing his lips with a napkin. "I suppose you're taking out insurance. If it comes to the crunch you want to be able to swear you never mentioned his name."

"Right first time. I've no intention of compromising either of us unnecessarily. In my experience, one can't be careful enough. You're welcome to mistrust me—I won't be offended."

"But *I* will be if you think I do."

There was a ring of sincerity to this simple statement. Count von der Schulenburg had a pretty fair idea of Erich Meller's reasons for coming out so strongly against the Nazis. No one acquainted with them could fail to take his loyalty for granted.

Many people suffered in the aftermath of the Nazi takeover on 30 January 1933. Among them were the Mellers, who had already moved to Berlin from Königsberg. A gang of Brownshirts broke into their home and burned it down after butchering three members of Erich Meller's family: his wife, his four-year-old daughter, and his lawyer father, a widower living in retirement. Erich himself had survived only because he was away on official business.

Heydrich was informed of this massacre shortly afterwards. He showed every sign of outrage, but not at the incident itself, which he described as "quite commonplace." His genuine anger was reserved for the inefficiency of the SA. Unfortunately, he said, blunders of this kind were not infrequent.

"My God, what a disaster!" Heydrich remarked to his grieving friend. "Just wait till I get my hands on those incompetent swine!"

He never did, because his lieutenants claimed to be unable to trace the particular SA men responsible for this heroic deed. That being so, he felt entitled to close the "case" on the following note:

"Damn sorry it had to happen to you, Erich old friend, but that's life—the innocent always suffer with the guilty. If I were you I'd regard the whole thing as an unfortunate accident. You'll be compensated financially, of course."

It never came to that. Erich Meller made no attempt to claim or extract any form of indemnity for the loss of his home and family. He never mentioned the "accident" again—but neither could he banish it from his mind.

Schulenburg, who knew all this, did his best to remain businesslike and unsentimental.

"Very well, Counsellor, I confirm that no reference to General von Fritsch has been made by either of us. For safety's sake, let's agree we met here by chance. Our conversation was limited to food. We discussed local specialties and compared them with those of East Prussia, all right?"

"Quite all right, and I apologize for dragging you here unnecessarily. I couldn't know you were so well informed."

"Informed, Counsellor, but not to this extent. All we'd gathered so far was that the Gestapo were nosing around, but when the chief steps in—well, that's a storm warning."

"What do you plan to do?"

"Pretty much what you expect, I imagine. And now please excuse me."

"By all means, Count. I take it you're going to call on a certain party. Please tell him I'd have liked to brief him myself, but it's better not. Too much personal contact might be risky at this stage."

Count Fritz-Dietlof von der Schulenburg, Deputy Police Commissioner of Berlin, called on his friend Colonel Oster the same night. He pounded the apartment door with his fist.

Lights went on, and slippered feet shuffled along the passage. "Who is it?" a resentful voice asked sleepily.

"Police," called Schulenburg. "Open up!"

The door opened at once. Oster had guessed who it was. He stood there in his blue-and-white striped pajamas and glared at Schulenburg.

"You and your perverse sense of humour," he grumbled. "All right, come in, but what's the point of shattering my nerves at this ungodly hour?"

Oster shuffled ahead of his visitor and flopped back on his bed. Every movement conveyed that he wasn't perpetually at his fellow conspirators' beck and call.

"This had better be important."

The count perched on the end of his bed. "I won't take up much of your time, but I can't guarantee you any sweet dreams afterwards."

"News?"

"More than that, Hans. You know that theory of yours —the one you were doubtful about? Well, it's a near certainty. They're gunning for Fritsch."

"I see." Oster did not look unduly surprised. "We were prepared for that. All that matters is who 'they' are. Have you found out?"

"Have I! Or rather, our friend Meller has—he sends his regards, by the way."

"Why didn't he come with you?"

"He's playing safe. Having a friend in high places can be dangerous."

Oster sat bolt upright. "Heydrich, you mean?"

"Yes, and he's personally involved."

"Are you sure?" Oster's face was filmed with sweat. "You realize what this means?"

"Obviously, or I wouldn't be disturbing your beauty sleep."

"Heydrich, by God! So the SS are spearheading an attack on the Commander-in-Chief and, indirectly, on Military Intelligence. Is that what you'd like us to believe, you and Meller?"

"It's a fact, and you'd better face it. If your outfit can't deal with this threat, nobody can."

"Take on Heydrich and the entire SS, you mean?" Oster blanched at the thought. "I'm not afraid of a fight, but look at the odds... State Security outnumbers us a hundred to one in manpower and financial resources. It also enjoys the Führer's personal blessing. You honestly expect us to tangle with *that*?"

"Not necessarily. Not if you don't mind throwing your Commander-in-Chief to the wolves. The Nazis are a voracious bunch. One general more or less won't spoil their appetite, but if you're really prepared to sacrifice him on the altar of the Fatherland..."

"My God, Schulenburg, what have we let ourselves in for?"

"If you still don't know, that's your funeral. I'm sure the state'll be happy to bury you at public expense."

Hermann Göring, who combined his incumbency of several dozen government and honorary posts with supreme command of the Luftwaffe and was soon to exchange his general's insignia for the field marshal's baton he had worked so hard to acquire, cherished a very personal conception of how power should be wielded. He felt unique, at least within his own domain, and the feeling was not unfounded.

"I'm expecting a man named Heersdorf," he told one of his aides at Karinhall.

"That's right, General. He's due at nine this morning."

"Well, get this. He's a very shady character, so treat him accordingly. Put him in a room by himself and watch him. I want him softened up. No talking, no smoking, no sneaking off for an unsupervised pee. He can do it down his leg for all I care."

This was one of Göring's virile jests. His underlings took care to register their amusement, if only with a forced smile.

In fact, Göring was merely employing a method that had proved its efficacy in the past: he left his victims to stew in their own juices, be they ministers, generals, or Party bigwigs—or, as in this case, nobodies like Herbert Heersdorf.

Heersdorf turned out to be an athletic-looking and suspiciously handsome man in his early thirties, with an impressive physique which would have endeared him to any SS recruiting officer. He could easily have passed for a ski instructor or a minor film star.

At the present time, however, Heersdorf could fairly claim to be a successful businessman. He had gone into the German-Italian citrus-fruit trade, which was booming. He also claimed to be the legitimate fiancé of a lady who was currently in great demand, one Eva Gruhn. This seemed to have been another promising investment, because it alone could explain his unexpected summons to Karinhall.

He endured his three-hour wait with relative equanimity, but even the hardened businessman in him was thrown by what happened next. He had hardly put his head round the door of Göring's study when a torrent of abuse hit him.

"There you are, you miserable bastard! Stay where you are, damn you—I didn't tell you to come any closer. Breathe on me and I'll cut off your air supply for good!"

Heersdorf felt as if he had suddenly collided with a thick rubber wall. It was an ominous sensation. He stood there dazed, trying to gather himself for a counterattack.

"I honestly don't know what you . . ."

"Don't lie to me, you dirty skunk!" roared Göring. "Nobody does that twice. What are you after? A little talk with the Gestapo? Some friendly persuasion in the cellars at Prinz-Albrecht-Strasse? A rest cure in a concentration camp? I can manage it, if that's what you want. Well, is it?"

Heersdorf grasped that his only course was to look as intimidated as he felt. At the same time, his commercial sense told him some kind of offer might emerge from behind this barrage of threats. What kind? It didn't matter. He'd have to accept in any case.

"Look, General," he said ingratiatingly, "I don't know what I've done wrong, honestly, but you only have to tell me and I'll put it right."

"Aha! That's more like it, Heersdorf. You sound quite human all of a sudden."

"I am, General—human in every way. Maybe that's my trouble. Is it?"

"I can answer that in one sentence, you horny bastard. You've had the gall to get in the way of a German field marshal. As his loyal friend and brother officer, I don't like that at all, understand? What's more, I don't intend to tolerate it."

Heersdorf feigned sudden comprehension. "Excuse me, General, but has this anything to do with Herr von

Blomberg and Fräulein Gruhn?"

"It has," Göring confirmed. "Two's company, three's a crowd. Simple as that."

"I think I see what you mean, General. You want me to back off, is that it?"

"Yes, as far as possible, and I'm prepared to make it worth your while. I was thinking of Argentina. I have some excellent connections there, thanks to my various government agencies. One export-import business is much like another. You'd only have to switch from oranges to meat. Well?"

"It sounds like a paying proposition. Could you put a figure on it?"

"Twice your present income for half the work, formally guaranteed for the next three years—longer, if everything goes smoothly. Are you interested?"

"You bet I am, General, on any terms."

"You're being smart, Heersdorf—I like that. All right, here are my conditions. No more fooling around with the lady in question, and I mean none! No fond farewells, no emotional scenes, no tears, no handholding or promises of undying love, no love letters. You can forget all that crap. As of now, it's over. Is that clear?"

"As daylight, General. As far as I'm concerned, it's so long Fräulein, *buenos días señoritas!*"

Göring's reaction was worthy of the Reich's Huntsman-in-Chief. His eyes narrowed as if he were drawing a bead on a twelve-point stag.

"I smell a rat, Heersdorf. What makes you so goddamned eager to drop the lady?"

"Your generous offer."

"Don't give me that! It isn't a question of what *you're* worth, man, it's what *she's* worth—know what I mean?"

"Yes, General."

Göring delightedly sensed he was on the right track. "Look, if you don't want to diminish my benevolent interest in your future, stop hedging. Is there something not quite kosher about her?"

"That's putting it mildly." Heersdorf could not mistake the menace in Göring's eyes. "It's her past, General," he went on hurriedly. "To be frank, it's not all it might be."

Göring drew a deep breath. Having taken careful note of a similar remark made by Blomberg himself, he was eager to know more.

"So what?" he challenged. "We've all got a past of some kind, and that includes the lady under discussion—after all, she got mixed up with a character like you. There may even have been others, but who cares?" He paused for effect. "Unless there's something else..." He paused again. "Stop playing dumb, man, it won't do you any good. If you know something, let's have it."

"All I know is, the police have taken an occasional interest in her. The Vice Squad, to be exact. They..."

"I didn't hear that," Göring interrupted, "—certainly not from you, understand? You came here to ask for a job, and I viewed your request with favour, but that's all we talked about, get it?"

Heersdorf almost fell over himself with eagerness. "I quite understand, General. If that's what you want, I won't breathe another word."

"You won't have a chance to. You're leaving for Hamburg and South America at your own request— immediately, without contacting anyone. One of my men will make sure of that. As soon as you're safely on board ship, he'll hand you a letter of credit for ten thousand dollars. That's your starting capital. Any objections?"

"None, General. I'm on my way. Heil Hitler!"

General Baron Werner von Fritsch, Commander-in-Chief of the Army, called at the Chancellery on 9 November 1937. The orders and decorations on his tunic jingled as he strode towards the Führer with his cap clamped beneath his arm, moving as mechanically as a man on ceremonial parade. He had come to pay his respects before going on two months' sick leave.

Adolf Hitler saw to it that the general was greeted with full military honours. Colonel Hossbach, his Wehrmacht aide, was stationed at the entrance. A brace of SS sentries belonging to his personal bodyguard presented arms with military precision as the double doors were thrown wide by liveried attendants.

The Führer was standing behind the desk in his official study, which was only slightly smaller than a football field, but he did not remain there. Instead, he almost scurried to meet the general and extended his right hand while still out of range. Fritsch clasped it firmly.

Hitler stood there on the glassy expanse of parquet with several aides in close attendance. War Minister von Blomberg hovered at his elbow. The occasion seemed to demand a cool and calculating show of sympathy.

"So you're deserting us for a month or two, my dear General."

"Not by choice, Herr Chancellor. Needs must, I'm afraid."

"Of course you must go, General. I say that with considerable concern for your health. However, I'm delighted to hear that your condition is far from hopeless. On the contrary, they tell me your rest cure may lead to an almost complete recovery. That would be a cause for mutual congratulation."

"It's a long break, Herr Chancellor. I can't help wondering how my Army will fare in the meantime."

"Come, come, everything's going splendidly,

and fully in accordance with your plans."

Hitler's voice had become even warmer and more vibrant. Nothing in his tone betrayed how much he resented two obvious slights. Fritsch persisted in addressing him as "Herr Chancellor" or sometimes plain "Herr Hitler;" the phrase "my Führer" had never passed his lips. Second, he had dared to speak of "his" army, as though he owned it.

"Don't worry, General," Hitler went on, swallowing his annoyance, "we'll make sure you're left to recuperate in peace." A brief sidelong glance prompted Blomberg to confirm this.

"Your chief of staff will be standing in for you," Blomberg said. "I'm sure you have the utmost faith in General Beck, but I shall also devote special attention to the Army while you're away—in conformity with your ideas, of course. I hope that reassures you."

"I'm much obliged," said Fritsch, looking surly. "However, General Beck should be able to carry on quite adequately with my programme. We'll be in constant touch, but if any problems do come up I'll naturally cut short my leave at once."

"I'm sure that won't be necessary," Blomberg said quickly.

"No," said Hitler, investing the word with solemn finality, "especially as you can rest assured that nothing will be done during your absence to jeopardize your plans for the Army—plans I fully endorse. And that, General, is precisely the message I wanted to convey before you left. I hope it allays your fears."

"Thoroughly, Herr Chancellor." Honest and trusting as ever, Fritsch had heard exactly what he hoped to hear. It filled him with a mixture of relief and gratitude. "In that case, I can leave with an easy mind."

The Führer extended his hand. "We're soldiers to the

marrow," he said as they stood there palm to palm and eye
to eye, "—you, an experienced combat commander, and I,
a veteran of the trenches. Need I say more?"

Only months separated this encounter from the final
confrontations of 27 and 29 January 1938. "We needed that
breathing space," Heydrich said later. "It went like
lightning, but we made the very most of it.

Comments by Counsellor Meller—

Curiously enough, the only person who felt really
sickened by what happened next was my friend Detective
Superintendent Huber.

Huber thought he had plumbed the depths of human
nature. Undaunted by acts of dark violence and unspeak-
able brutality, he had regarded it as his mission to pursue
their perpetrators and render them harmless. But now he
felt he had entered a lunatic age. Germany had become a
free-for-all, its inhabitants a flock of sheep and their
patriotic sentiments the object of criminal exploitation.
The seat of justice, which he had thought it his ultimate
responsibility to serve, was a whorehouse. Justice itself,
for which he had always striven, was in a shambles.

"What have we let ourselves in for?" he asked me in one
of his rare moments of weakness. "It's like a nightmare—
like watching an avalanche bearing down on you and not
being able to move a muscle. I'd never have thought it
possible. What's happening to us?"

"Call it our national destiny," I told him. "If it makes
you feel any better, call it our unwanted and unmerited
national destiny. The phrase has its advantages. At least
we'll be able to use it later on as an excuse for some of the
things that are going on here. If we survive the avalanche,
of course."

5

Stirring
the Cauldron

Weather reports for the last month of 1937 described conditions in Berlin as cold and clear.

The temperature hovered around zero. There was little snow, less rain, and a thin film of ice on the roads until midday. The capital was visited by that steady breeze from the plains of Brandenburg, that cool breeze which seemed to arrive there refreshed after a gentle bath in the many surrounding lakes. The air was good. You could breathe freely—as long as you were prepared to gauge freedom by the state of the barometer.

Berlin was the bustling capital of Greater Germany, a well-groomed reflection of the new National Socialist state. Labourers and artisans worked with a will, commerce and industry flourished. "Cleanliness" assailed the eye at every turn. No beggars in the streets, few prostitutes, and only a dwindling handful of Jews...

The Wehrmacht—the vigilant Army, the dashing Air Force, the staunch and dependable Navy—presented a glorious spectacle. Splendid young men in uniform, proud and confident of their skill at arms, stood ready to defend their Fatherland and the West. Great things seemed to beckon, but it was becoming more and more evident that all this lethal splendour must have cost a fortune—probably several dozen billion marks.

One could hardly fail to be impressed, favourably or otherwise.

Further aspects of the contemporary scene—

In the Soviet Union, Marshal Tukhachevsky and other senior officers were executed at Stalin's bidding. In the United States, John Steinbeck published his novel *Of Mice and Men;* Luise Rainer, an Austrian actress of Jewish extraction, gave an Oscar-winning performance in *The Good Earth;* and Joe Louis, a "black beast" in the racist parlance of Central Europe, became heavyweight boxing champion of the world.

In Germany, Gustav Gründgens accepted an appointment as director-general of the Prussian State Theatre in Berlin. As for Hitler, he seemed intent on resting from his power gathering labours and eager to win acclaim as an architect, patron of the arts, and educator of the young.

But his supporters, especially those in the capital, were into their stride at last. Now that they had been fired with missionary zeal, nothing could prevent them from keeping up the good work. Every street corner, doorway, back yard, bar, and subway station seemed to be haunted by lurking figures, willing instruments of power and loyal auxiliaries of the Party and police—the Secret State Police included. This urge to contribute was not confined to the numerous block and street wardens and their diligent Party cohorts. Many solid citizens from the middle and lower-middle classes rejoiced in their membership of Hitler's "national community" and were equally anxious to pull their weight.

It was the age of the conscientious political eavesdropper, the responsible and public-spirited informant—not inform*er*, heaven forbid! These people were only doing their duty. Having once been alerted to it by the state-controlled press and radio network, they felt satisfied that they were treading the path of conscience.

Together, they busily and effectively ensured that the régime-preservation machine remained in top gear. Nowhere was this activity more noticeable than at the chamber of horrors in Prinz-Albrecht-Strasse. The Central State Security Bureau was busy twenty-four hours a day, and its subterranean cell block permanently filled to overflowing.

"Right, here we go again," Detective Chief Superintendent Meisinger, Heydrich's leading authority on homosexuals, subjected Otto Schmidt to a ferocious grin of encouragement. "Let's see if we can knock our star performer into shape. Ready?"

"Of course, chief," said Otto, feeling flattered. "I'm your man."

"First and foremost, asshole, you're an expert. If I say you are, you are, get it?"

Otto was taken aback, but not for long. His readiness to

cooperate seemed boundless. "An expert? How do you mean?"

"If we're going to build you up into a key witness, we've got to make you convincing. One way would be to present you as a semiofficial expert on homosexual contacts and activities. That's what you're being trained for. I'm going to feed you a mass of information. You'll be an instant expert."

Meisinger sat there hands on thighs, glorying in his role. "The object of the exercise is to expose and convict a big-time fairy. For that we need a watertight case, which is where you come in—an expert known to the department and burning to see justice done, understand?"

"I'm beginning to."

"Fine," Meisinger said briskly. "Then we'll start on your lessons."

With the practised ease of a veteran conjurer, the Gestapo man picked up a sheaf of photographs. He fanned them out and held them under Otto's nose. They were all of General von Fritsch—seated behind his desk, inspecting guards of honour, taking the salute at ceremonial parades. There was something almost invariably stiff and puppetlike about his appearance, but it never lacked dignity.

"You'll be asked if you recognize this man."

"And I'll say I do. I'll say I saw him close up, but not like that—not in uniform. He was in civilian clothes at the time—naturally, considering what he was up to."

"Fine so far. Take a good look at that face and memorize it. If you're asked to confront the man, you'll have to walk straight up to him and point him out without a moment's hesitation. Can I depend on you?" Otto's grin froze at the sight of Meisinger's hard and challenging expression.

"Don't worry, chief. I'm made of cast iron when the heat's on."

"And you'd stick to your story in court, even a military court?"

"Like grim death," Otto assured him. "I don't have any option."

"No, you don't, so let's put you through the rest of your paces. We'll rehearse until you can play the role in your sleep."

Next day, Heydrich called Göring. He sounded very civil. Each man appreciated the other's special status. That made them wary but called for a certain degree of mutual consideration.

"It's just possible," Heydrich said confidentially, "I've turned up something which might interest you."

"Then come and see me, my dear fellow. Make it as soon as you can."

The two met at Karinhall next morning. They greeted each other with exaggerated warmth and retired at once for a private discussion. Its opening phase resembled an intricate card game in which they strove to conceal their weak suits and win as many tricks as possible.

Hermann Göring, who had used the technique with consistent success, regarded a frontal attack as the best method of defence, even against a man like Heydrich.

"You know I couldn't be better disposed towards you if I tried, my dear fellow, but I can't help being irritated by your persistent attempts to meddle with my Research Bureau."

"I naturally respect your sphere of authority, General. My sole aim is to achieve the greatest possible concentration of effort—on the Führer's behalf, of course."

Göring chuckled. "Great minds think alike."

The Research Bureau was Göring's personal creation. Although its name meant little to the outside world, it was a lavishly equipped and funded intelligence agency employing no less than a thousand foreign language experts. This was the unique data-processing and monitoring centre which Heydrich had ordered his men to infiltrate, his object being to get at its vast treasury of secret information. "My dear Heydrich," Göring went on, arrogantly now, with a note of genial menace, "you may be a formidable fencer, but I can't believe you'd be reckless enough to cross swords with a man in my position."

"Quite the reverse, General. That's why I'm here."

"Splendid, but can you prove it?"

"What would you say if I told you of a quick and effective way of removing your opposite number in the Army?"

A glint appeared in Göring's eye. "On what grounds?"

"Active homosexuality."

The Führer's crown prince gave a delighted grunt, but his words failed to echo it. "I'll pretend I didn't hear that. Fritsch a fairy? Good God, Heydrich, you shouldn't go around spreading rumours like that unless you can back them with some really solid evidence."

"We're working on it. Give me another few days—that's if you're interested—and ..."

"No hurry, don't rush things. Do a thorough job. I may come back to you sometime—sooner rather than later."

Heydrich grasped the implication at once. "So I get everything lined up and you say when, right?"

"If you pull this off, Heydrich, you can count on my deep appreciation—even where the Research Bureau's concerned. I'm not saying I'll let you in on everything, but I wouldn't be averse to cooperating on a generous scale."

"That's all I wanted to hear, General," Heydrich said quickly. "We're both on the same side. Fritsch isn't just in your way. He's getting in ours as well, and this seems an ideal opportunity to cancel him out for good."

Göring lolled back in his chair, folded his hands on his paunch, and regarded them lovingly.

"Fine, Heydrich, now that we've reached this understanding perhaps you'd like to do some additional digging for me. I'm sure that versatile organization of yours could cope with another little assignment. Does the name Eva Gruhn mean anything to you?"

"No." Heydrich's negative was a reflex. So was his air of mystification. "Who is she?"

"A daughter of the people." Göring smiled broadly and gave his companion an encouraging wink. "Eva Gruhn, early thirties, resident in Berlin. It would be very nice if, apart from being a daughter of the people, she turned out to have a police record—preferably one that appears in your files. I'd be even more interested in that information, but don't ask me why."

Heydrich, whose predatory instincts were permanently alert, showed every sign of surprise. This came naturally to a power game player of his calibre. No one would have guessed that Göring had just made a monumental blunder.

As premier of Prussia, Göring controlled the Berlin Police Department. Since any records relating to Eva Gruhn would have been kept by the Vice Squad, he could easily have requested them direct. The vice squad obviously had nothing on her, hence this demand for action by the Central State Security Bureau. Göring wanted to hitch the SS to his bandwagon, Heydrich told himself. He planned to leave the dirty work to others and keep his own hands clean. They might be in the same boat, but Göring would let the SS steer it—for the moment.

Heydrich rose and clicked his heels. "Leave it to me, General. As soon as we unearth anything useful, I'll get back to you."

Seventh essay in dramatic reconstruction

...Subject: a dangerous interlude—

Volker Vogelsang, alias Informant No. 134, advanced on Eva Gruhn with his arms outstretched, swaying slightly.

"Eva, darling, you know how I adore you."

Eva dodged him. "Look, Volker," she said imploringly, "you've been a good friend—at least that's what I always thought—but . . ."

"I still am," he assured her drunkenly. "You need me more than ever, now that bastard Heersdorf has walked out on you."

She eluded his embrace. "Now, you know what we agreed the other day, Volker! Our friendship has got to end. I'm starting a new life, Volker—I'm getting married."

"To that man? You honestly think it'll work? You and him—a big wheel and a nobody?" Vogelsang laughed scornfully.

"I've given it a lot of thought. I keep on reminding him about my humble background, but he doesn't care—he's incredibly broadminded. I've finally decided to share my life with him."

"But he's an old man!"

"You don't know the first thing about him, Volker."

"Well, I'm a better bet, and I want to marry you too."

"It's too late for that," Eva said firmly. "You never really understood me, and you aren't capable of understanding him either. He comes from an entirely different world."

"A world *you* don't belong to Eva, that's for sure. Besides, you underestimate me. I've got connections with the Gestapo, and they're starting to take an interest in you. Don't you realize where that could lead?"

"I don't care, my mind's made up. Whatever happens, it won't make any difference. That's what Werner says, and I believe him."

"Don't be too sure," Vogelsang said menacingly. "In your position, you need friends like me. I could be very useful to you."

"Once my mind's made up, that's the end of it—you know me well enough by now. Anyway, I advise you not to interfere."

"What's that, a threat?"

"No, I'm simply asking you not to make trouble."

"*Me* make trouble for you? There are plenty of people better qualified to do that than me. You obviously don't know what a mess you're in. You're beyond helping, but I'll try all the same."

His attempt to be helpful was short-lived. She sidestepped his first lunge. He came after her again, knocked over a lamp and smashed a windowpane, bellowing at the top of his voice.

Startled neighbours called the police, who turned up two minutes later. They burst into Eva Gruhn's apartment and dragged her frustrated admirer away. He was charged with committing a breach of the peace.

Purely as a matter of routine, this incident was cross-indexed in the records under "Gruhn, Eva."

The jigsaw had acquired another piece.

Volker Vogelsang, otherwise know as Informant No. 134, was arrested on Christmas Eve 1937 and consigned to a

concentration camp—on whose orders, no one knows. All
trace of him has been lost.

Meanwhile, spurred on by another injunction from
Heydrich, the scourge of Berlin's homosexuals was
persevering with Otto Schmidt's advanced training course
at Gestapo headquarters in Prinz-Albrecht-Strasse.

"Right," prompted Meisinger, "let's run through the
whole thing again. Have you thought over what I said?"

"You bet I have." Otto did not disguise his growing
self-importance. "You need me badly, from the sound of
it. Okay, chief, I've signed on but what's in it for me?"

Meisinger's eyes became slits. "What!" he hissed. "Who
the hell do you think you are, you miserable little creep.
Try to haggle with me would you?"

"It seemed a good opportunity," Otto replied jauntily.
"After all, chief, nothing in life is free. You said I was an
expert, and experts are expensive."

"I'll show you what you are," roared Meisinger. "You
obviously need an urgent reminder."

His desk was equipped with a red buzzer. He brought
his thumb down on it and kept it there. Ten seconds later,
the office door opened to reveal two men in SS uniform, a
sturdy, genial-looking pair with boyishly inquiring faces.

Meisinger pointed at Otto. "Give him a little workout,"
he said. "Not too energetic—fifteen minutes should be
enough."

"You've got me all wrong!" wailed Otto, panic-stricken.
"I'll say anything you want—anything!"

"Good," said Meisinger, casually. "We'll make sure you
remember that. You'll find our methods most effective."

Otto was dragged out, still begging for mercy.
Meisinger watched him go with a contemptuous smile.
Then, very leisurely, he started to excavate his nails

with a paper knife. They needed it.

Twenty minutes later, Otto was dragged in again and dumped on a chair. He sagged there limply, his face bathed in sweat, his hands trembling. The two SS men withdrew at a nod from Meisinger, their blue eyes shining with honest satisfaction at a job well done. Meisinger bent an amused gaze on his protégé.

"I hope that's straightened you out, you scum. You're at *our* service, not the other way round. Have you got that at last?"

"Yes, sir," moaned Otto. His new found arrogance had evaporated. He had survived, and the realization made him positively grateful.

"So let's get down to business. You're now ready to swear you saw Fritsch performing with Bavarian Joe behind the station, is that right?"

"Yessir, certainly sir," Otto replied in a choking voice. He hugged his stomach, which had been vigorously kicked. His guts felt as if they were on fire.

"And you've thought it over carefully? Is everything clear now—every last little detail, the way we've rehearsed it?"

"Yes, Chief Superintendent, all clear."

"What if I asked a really smart interrogator to cross-examine you?"

"He'd get nowhere, sir. Nothing'll shake me now, I promise you. Not now."

Meisinger rubbed his hands. "Good, we're making progress."

Erich Meller, Heydrich's boyhood friend, was not only an uneasy commuter between two or more worlds. Fate had transformed him into a unique observer of the age he lived in. He now became involved, to some degree unwittingly, in another disastrous chain of events.

One was a meeting which seemed, on the surface, wholly innocuous. Counsellor Meller went to see the woman who cleaned house for him in order to give her some instructions for the coming week.

While in her apartment, he chatted in a friendly way about such general topics as the new spirit of patriotism, the noticeable shortage of food, and the current abundance of plays, concerts, and films in the German capital. He also inquired, sympathetically, whether she was happy living where she did.

"Oh yes, Counsellor, very happy. It may not look like much, but it's a very high-class establishment. These days, that is."

"Really?" Meller's tone was casual. "How do you mean?"

"You'd be surprised," she said proudly. "We've had some really important people calling here lately, and I mean *really* important. One of them's a field marshal! What do you say to that?"

Counsellor Meller said nothing at first. He knew of only one field marshal in Germany, and he was a widower in love. Could this dreary tenement house be the scene of his grand passion?

"He's courting a young lady," the cleaning woman pursued.

"Ah, well," Meller said lightly, "love is everything."

"But an old man like him, chasing a girl like that..."

"That's their business. All I want to know is when you're coming to spring-clean my apartment."

Two days later, Meller paid another call on Reinhard Heydrich. The security chief welcomed him warmly and produced a bottle of Pommery.

"If you hadn't come," he said, "I was going to send for you."

"Officially, you mean?"

"Hardly!" Heydrich was looking unusually cheerful. "Everyone in this department knows you're a friend of mine, and that means hands-off."

"So what's it all about?"

"I wanted to show you a couple of snapshots, Erich. There's an excellent one of you."

Heydrich pushed a black-and-white print across the desk. It showed Meller leaving the tenement where his cleaning woman lived.

"There you are. Taken the day before yesterday."

"Who took it and why?"

"Pure routine, my dear Erich. My men have recently been photographing anyone seen entering or leaving that building—just as a matter of course. I must say I was surprised to find you among the visitors."

"I'll make a deal with you. You tell me why you're watching the house, and I'll tell you why I went there."

"No need to be shy with me, Erich. I'm only human, and it sounds like a pretty lively establishment." Heydrich grinned disarmingly. "I'd still like to know who you went to see. Even if you find it personally embarrassing, you can rely on my discretion. Well?"

"I was calling on a lady," Meller said patiently, "—a Fräulein Maria Winter. She's looked after my apartment for the last few years. There's nothing between us, if that's what you want to know. She cleans my place during office hours, so I hardly ever see her. I only went there to discuss a couple of household matters. Is that good enough for you?"

"Quite good enough." Heydrich refilled their champagne glasses. "Have you been there often?"

"Only two or three times in the past year."

"Know any of the other tenants? What about Eva Gruhn—does that name ring a bell? If so, I'd be interested to hear what you know about her. Just between friends, so to speak."

"Eva Gruhn?" Meller frowned. "Never heard of her. Should I have?"

Heydrich was looking satisfied now, or almost. "No, not necessarily, but if you do, I'd advise you to steer clear of her. That's a friendly word of warning, Erich. In case you didn't know, the road to hell is paved with good intentions."

General Baron Werner von Fritsch, Commander-in-Chief of the Army, was thoroughly enjoying his stay in Cairo. He made several excursions by car from his hotel, the Semiramis, to the Pyramids. The Sphinx aroused his special interest. Though badly mutilated by cannon fire and the elements, it had preserved its air of sovereign indestructibility. Fritsch liked to sit at its feet.

A sober figure formally attired in a dark civilian suit, Fritsch also appreciated his sunset strolls along the banks of the Nile. One evening near the British Embassy, he was politely accosted by an Arab in European dress, a lithe young man with liquid eyes and a face out of the *Arabian Nights*.

"Are you Herr von Fritsch?" he asked in German.

"I am," Fritsch replied with measured courtesy. "What can I do for you?"

But before the young Arab could answer, the general's ADC hurried up. He never walked beside Fritsch during these strolls, because the older man preferred to be alone with his thoughts, but he always remained within hailing distance.

He did not wait for a summons now. Elbowing his way between Fritsch and the Arab youth, he demanded, "Who are you? What do you want?"

"Come, come, my boy," Fritsch said in a faintly resentful tone. "This gentleman obviously wants a word with me."

"I beg your pardon, General, but it's my job..."

The ADC refrained from elaborating on the real nature of his job, which was to protect Fritsch from shady characters. Whoever he was working for, this exquisitely handsome young Arab might be one, just as the proximity of the British Embassy might be more than mere coincidence.

"My name is unimportant," retorted the young man, continuing to fix the general with his beautiful brown eyes. "I have a favour to ask, sir. Will you accompany me to the nearest hospital and visit a patient there—Herr Stander? I'm only acting on his instructions."

"This could be a trap, sir," the ADC said anxiously.

Fritsch ignored him. "Stander is the name of the head receptionist at our hotel—a very pleasant and obliging person. Is that him?"

"Exactly, General. Herr Stander was attacked and beaten up last night, very badly. He thinks it would interest you to know why."

"It could still be a trap, sir," the ADC persisted. "You're here in a private capacity. We don't want any trouble."

"If Herr Stander really wants to see me," said Fritsch, "he shall. Lead the way, young man."

Once at Cairo's Central Hospital, the young Arab threaded his way through various formalities with an ease which betrayed that everything had been arranged in advance. The medical superintendent appeared in person and conducted the party to Room 202.

An injured man lay there, swathed in bandages. He had been severely beaten but was still recognizable—just—as the Herr, Monsieur, or Mr. Stander who normally presided over the reception desk at the Semiramis.

Having been a combat commander in the first war, Fritsch was no stranger to the sight of bandaged figures in hospital beds.

"You wished to see me, Herr Stander? Well, here I am," he said gently. "What was it you wanted to tell me?"

"Something important," Stander replied with an effort. "But only in private, if you don't mind."

Fritsch nodded. The medical superintendent, two nurses, the ADC, and the young Arab withdrew, leaving them alone together.

"I'm listening."

"It's this, General. Thanks to a series of coincidences, I have certain connections—very loose connections—with German Military Intelligence, and Colonel Oster in particular. He asked me to keep an eye on you—I mean, protect you if necessary."

"Very considerate of him," Fritsch said drily, "but rather a waste of time. I'm only here for health reasons."

"But you're being watched."

"Quite possibly, but only as a precaution—by you and my ADC, for example. I suppose I should be grateful."

"No, sir, not just watched—I mean kept under surveillance by Gestapo agents."

This drew a faint smile and a shrug. "A man in my position has to put up with many things, Herr Stander, security measures included."

"I'm not talking about that, General. They're deliberately spying on you—on your private life."

"I don't have one."

"But they broke into your hotel room and searched your baggage—they even examined your bed. I caught them in the act. That's when they did this to me."

"A shocking business, Herr Stander. If what you suspect were true, I should immediately lodge an official complaint in the strongest terms. But couldn't they have been ordinary hotel thieves? It seems pointless to report the matter unless you can positively identify them. Can you?"

"No, sir, I can't." The man in the hospital bed blinked incredulously at his visitor. "So you aren't worried?"

"Worried, my dear sir? Of course not. Without overestimating my personal importance, I know who I am. I also know I have nothing to hide—nothing whatsoever."

Stander sank back on his pillows, stunned by a realization which had dawned on others before him. The general was a man of supreme integrity. He was also supremely ingenuous—and this, in a world teeming with human predators, was an invitation to disaster.

The Egyptian sun might well be the last to smile on him.

At almost the same moment, Field Marshal von Blomberg requested, or rather solicited, another meeting with General Göring. His request was promptly granted.

Their conversation took place over lunch at the Airmen's Building, an exclusive club much favoured by Commander-in-Chief Luftwaffe, for whom a table was permanently reserved in the farthest corner of the farthest dining room. They consumed their plain but ample meal in comparative silence, Göring with gusto, Blomberg less heartily. Little was said until the coffee arrived.

"Well," Blomberg said eagerly, "have you managed to speak to the Führer yet—I mean, about my little problem?"

"But of course, my dear fellow. I took just the line you suggested."

"How did he react?"

"Extremely well. It's all coming along very nicely, thanks to my efforts. The Führer was taken with your idea of marrying a 'daughter of the people.' He thinks it would be a noble and courageous gesture—the act of a social pioneer."

"So he approved?"

"Thoroughly, in principle."

"You mean he has some reservations?"

Göring gave a broad, slightly indulgent smile. "You know the Führer. He's prepared to take my advice, but he'd still like you to consult him in person."

"And then?" Blomberg leant forward avidly. "Will he give his consent?"

"Of course. The Führer would never turn you down—he told me as much. I really vouched for the lady of your choice. Let's hope I never have reason to regret it."

"I can't thank you enough."

"Delighted to be of help. You can always rely on me to support a friend in need. Everything will go like clockwork, believe me—just the way we both want."

At Berlin's police headquarters in Alexanderplatz, Count Helldorf received a visit from his deputy Count von der Schulenburg. He raised his hands in surrender at the sight of him—an established ritual.

"Whatever it is, I don't want to hear. We agreed to operate independently, remember? The less we know about each other's moves, the more room we have for manoeuvre."

"Except," said Schulenburg, "that our security system seems to have broken down. The Gestapo are on the warpath again, and we're right in their line of fire."

"They're always on the warpath, my dear Count. If you're referring to the Fritsch case, so is Military Intelligence."

"Ah, but this time they're after something different. Different but no less important. They want the low-down on a certain Eva Gruhn."

Helldorf looked mystified. "Who's she?"

"A woman whose name has suddenly turned up in our records. Nobody knows how."

The Commissioner's worried frown could have been a sign of personal uneasiness. He was probably thinking of his current affair with a film actress, a harmless relationship based on mutual satisfaction. He emerged from his reverie and shrugged.

"Why are the Gestapo so interested in her?"

"Because she's planning to get married."

"How nice. Who's the lucky man?"

"The lucky man, as you put it, is Field Marshal von Blomberg."

Helldorf burst out laughing. "I thought this farce was funny enough already. Who gets the custard pie this time, a field marshal, some inoffensive girl, or the Gestapo?"

"Take your pick."

"I don't give a damn what we do as long as it doesn't leave us up shit creek without a paddle."

"In that case," said Schulenburg, "I suggest we simply say we don't *have* a file on her. That means it can't be handed over—not to the Gestapo."

Helldorf was frowning again. "Too risky. If there is a

file it must be cross-indexed half a dozen times. Too many people would have worked on it, and some may be Gestapo informers..."

"Files can disappear."

"So can we. If it comes to the crunch—which it will, if the Gestapo decide to step in—are you really prepared to be sacrificed for the sake of an old man's final fling? You may be, I'm not."

"I've run a check on Eva Gruhn. From what I hear, she's an attractive young woman with an engaging personality. All she wants is a chance to live happily ever after."

"With a field marshal?"

"She loves him, and he loves her, that's what matters. They're entitled to a little happiness, wouldn't you say?"

"Touching," Helldorf said with mild sarcasm. "The question is, will the Gestapo share your sentiments?"

"We must try to head them off. I'm sure you'll help, Commissioner, if only for personal reasons."

"Always needling me, aren't you?" Helldorf grinned and shrugged. "All right, I'll try too, but in my own way." He looked suddenly thoughtful, as if he were working out a chess problem. "So the Gestapo insist on having a Gruhn file, do they? Very well, but we'll have to cover ourselves."

"How?"

"By playing the interdepartmental game. It's our duty to cooperate with the Gestapo. Fine, but we'll go through official channels and strangle the bastards with red tape. This department is directly responsible to the Prussian Minister of the Interior, who also happens to be Commander-in-Chief Luftwaffe. We'll simply give the file to him."

"Göring, you mean? You'd really do that?"

"It's the perfect answer. The Gestapo can't touch

Göring, so we'll dig in behind him. That's our insurance policy."

Not for the first time, a fox had been set to keep the geese. The fox in question was a prime specimen with all the predatory instincts of his breed. Who could blame him for doing what came naturally?

Eighth essay in dramatic reconstruction ... Subject: final arrangements—

Their love seemed many-splendoured. They felt alone in the world for hours at a time—lost in an infinity of happiness.

Born of their passion were code words they alone could interpret. One was the date that symbolized the joy of mutual discovery and redemption: Friday the 13th.

It had all begun on a Friday the 13th. That date became their code word for desire. "Ah," Eva would sigh, even in the presence of outsiders, "I feel as if it were Friday the 13th ..."

"It's always Friday the 13th when I'm with you," Blomberg gallantly assured her. "How natural and easy our relationship has grown, Eva—and how very wonderful!"

"You don't see any more problems?"

"None."

"My mother keeps warning me off."

"She mustn't, darling. There's no need. She ought to be glad you're happy. You are, aren't you?"

"Yes," she said. "But that's just what worries her. She says they won't let us be happy together. We've got to be terribly careful, she says, and she should know. She's had a lot of trouble with the authorities in her time."

"She isn't unique," Blomberg said soothingly. "Your mother's a good woman, I'm sure, but I'm here to protect you now. *And* your mother, if she'll let me."

"Thank you, Werner." Eva took his hand. "But wouldn't it be better to leave things the way they are? We love each other, and I'll always be here when you want me. I made a mistake about the baby, so there's no need to marry me because of that."

"A temporary mistake," he said gently. "Next time, the demands of convention will have been safely met, my darling. Our friend Göring has already prepared the ground. He spoke to the Führer, and the Führer intends to give us his blessing."

"Oh, Werner," she said, trembling, "if only it turns out all right..."

He patted her shoulder. "It will, my darling girl, never fear. They're giving General Ludendorff a state funeral in Munich the day after tomorrow, and I'm to be principal speaker. The Führer will be there too. He's agreed to see me after the service and discuss our marriage."

"And then?"

"Then we'll get married—early in January, I think. Let's stop worrying and start looking forward to it."

Counsellor Meller, commenting on his relations with Heydrich.

I never denied the existence of our so-called boyhood friendship—why should I have? It soon became known to insiders and bred a wide variety of attitudes. Some people courted me in the hope that I might be useful to them, others automatically considered me dangerous. I suppose they thought I was a miniature Trojan Horse.

"It's true, though," I told Hans Oster, Admiral Canaris's right-hand man in Military Intelligence, "we really were like blood brothers in the old days."

Oster waved this airily aside. "While we're on the subject, did you know the Führer had a stepbrother? He runs a bar right here in Berlin, but he sees red if anyone mentions Adolf. It's the same with Göring's wife, Emmy. She can't be blamed for everything he does, and his daughter, Edda, isn't responsible for the blood in her veins—quite apart from the fact that Hermann isn't the world's worst husband and father."

"What are you getting at?" I said.

"Well, just because there's some kind of bond or tie between two people it doesn't mean their destinies are inextricably linked forever. There's no reason why boyhood friends should develop into lifelong partners, least of all in this day and age."

I detected a hint of calculation behind his ostentatious broadmindedness, but why not? My own attitude was equally governed by contemporary thought patterns, which was why I had no hesitation in teasing him a little.

"Heydrich has asked me to transfer to his department more than once. Last time we discussed it, he promised I could work there 'in a senior capacity,' as he put it."

"But you naturally turned him down, Erich."

"Naturally, Hans, and for several reasons, one of which I won't disguise from you. I told him I could be more useful to him if I hung on to my job at the Ministry."

"Very shrewd of you." That was Oster's sole comment. It was far from implying that he felt entirely sure of me. In the secret service and at that moment in history, mistrust was part of every man's survival kit.

No mistrust appeared to colour my relations with

Heydrich, though he did once tell me, quite curtly, "I expect and demand nothing of you, Erich—nothing except your friendship in return for mine. But that's saying a lot."

Like Blomberg before him, Count Helldorf had asked to see Göring about a highly confidential matter, and Göring, with his love of the mysterious, had promptly agreed. The meeting took place at Karinhall.

"Well, Count," he said eagerly, "what have you got for me today? No need to beat about the bush—you can safely confide in me. The man who can shock me hasn't been born."

Helldorf was unconscious of what he had let himself in for by embarking on this mission. He came straight to the point.

"It's the Gestapo, General. They've asked us for a file on someone called Eva Gruhn."

Göring shut his eyes in a brilliant display of indifference.

"So the Gestapo have asked you for a file," he said calmly, "and you've stalled them. May I ask why?"

"Because the surrounding circumstances are so exceptional. In the first place, this dossier was compiled very recently—on whose instructions, nobody knows. That makes it our departmental responsibility. Second, it consists of unsubstantiated material, so we aren't bound to release it—certainly not if you don't wish us to."

"And why shouldn't I approve its release, Helldorf?" Göring looked puzzled. "I don't see what's worrying you."

"Allow me to show you the file, General, and you very soon will." Helldorf produced it from his briefcase. "I've marked the salient passages in red."

Göring began to read with a show of reluctance which yielded to mounting interest and consternation. With an expression of anger and disgust, he finally flung the file on the table and smacked it with the flat of his hand.

"It can't be true!" he roared. "I just don't believe it. Honestly, Helldorf, this is too much!"

He shook his head with every appearance of outrage, then drew the file towards him and said grimly, "I can only assume that these documents are based on an unfortunate misunderstanding—a whole series of unfortunate misunderstandings." The next words were uttered solemnly, as though aimed at posterity. "I refuse to be associated with them. Herr von Blomberg is a friend and colleague of mine—kindly note that."

Helldorf caught on at once. Despite his obvious interest, Göring had officially washed his hands of the affair in front of a witness.

"So you'll take charge of the file, General?"

"It will be safe with me," Göring said happily. "I dread to think what might happen if it fell into the wrong hands."

"In that case, may I regard the matter as closed?"

"Far from it, my dear Count. You must dispose of this smear. Check everything thoroughly, or have it checked by a reliable team." Suddenly, Göring had become suspiciously businesslike. "I consider it essential to refute these allegations . . ." He paused. "Or substantiate them, as the case may be. You must dig up more evidence on the lady in question—any kind of evidence, as long as it's conclusive. But be thorough and don't rush things."

"Certainly, General."

Helldorf prepared to depart. Göring rose and shook hands. His face was tinged with pleasurable excitement.

"Thank you for confiding in me, Helldorf. This affair is just between the two of us. We must try to make the best of it, always bearing in mind that the man concerned is a valued friend and colleague of mine. Equally, justice must be done."

The Police Commissioner went his way in a relieved, even hopeful mood. He felt pretty certain his words had found their mark. As soon as he had gone, Göring summoned one of his aides.

"Get hold of Heydrich. I want him here right away. You can hint that I've got something for him."

"A most impressive speech, Field Marshal." This warmly appreciative tribute was addressed to Werner von Blomberg by his Führer and Chancellor. "Your remarks had great creative drive. The nation owes you yet another debt of gratitude."

Hitler's War Minister had indeed proved, yet again, that he combined Prussian military training with a literary turn of phrase. General Ludendorff, the legendary strategist of World War I, had always been a loyal henchman of his field marshal, Paul von Hindenburg. He had then transferred his allegiance to Hitler because, according to the official version, he regarded him as the true redeemer and long-awaited Father of the Fatherland. This story was far from the truth but extremely useful, and Blomberg had taken full advantage of it during his funeral oration.

Today, 22 December 1937, was the day of Ludendorff's state funeral. Munich had witnessed much pomp and circumstance. Fat wreaths were laid, flaring torches filled the air with a stench of oil, and the supreme representatives of the armed forces, Party, and government turned out in force. So did the local inhabitants. The chief mourner was Mathilde, Ludendorff's widow, a heavily veiled, poker-backed figure seated on Hitler's right.

Beside her, displaying manly sorrow in his resplendent uniform, sat Göring. It was a positively Wagnerian occasion.

Immediately after this public spectacle, Hitler had summoned his "nearest and dearest" advisers—his own description—to the Party's Munich headquarters in Königsplatz. There were two of these privileged mortals, Field Marshal von Blomberg and General Göring. They now sat facing him in heavy plush armchairs, looking deferentially man-to-man. Hitler leant towards Blomberg with an encouraging smile.

"You wished to consult me about a personal matter, our friend tells me."

"My Führer," said Blomberg, "I'm thinking of getting married."

"To a daughter of the people, I gather. I was delighted to hear it."

"She's a very charming person," Göring chimed in. "Very attractive too, by all accounts. What if she is twenty or thirty years younger than the field marshal, my Führer? Surely that's no problem?"

Hitler's expression was a mixture of statesmanlike concern and comradely goodwill. He gave Blomberg a sunny smile but quickly qualified it.

"I can't help wondering how our officer corps would react to such a match. We're talking about a body of men who are, by and large, ultraconservative in their ideas and deeply attached to their traditions. I value those sentiments in themselves. However, it's possible that a substantial number of officers are hide-bound by bigoted notions of class. That could provoke some very awkward reactions."

"Oh come, my Führer!" Göring said briskly. "They're soldiers, after all—they'll do as they're told. What does it matter if a senior officer does the unexpected for once? We don't all have to marry generals' daughters, impoverished noblewomen, or busy little members of our secretarial staff—busy on duty and off, eh?" He leered.

Blomberg cleared his throat nervously. "To be honest, my Führer, I've already taken the liberty of dropping a few hints on the subject—to General Beck, among others. Beck isn't the easiest of men, but all he said was, 'That's your affair and no one else's. If the wedding does take place, you and the lady of your choice can expect a telegram conveying my heartiest congratulations.'"

"A very welcome attitude," said Hitler. "Beck is right, of course. The new Germany can't afford to resemble the feudal societies of old. We must do our utmost to develop a true national community. Your marriage, Herr von Blomberg, would be a step in that direction."

"Thank you, my Führer." Blomberg's eyes were moist with gratitude.

Every inch the resolute statesman, Hitler observed, "When one of my country's most senior representatives feels no qualms about marrying a daughter of the people—my people—I can only describe it as an act of faith, courage, and determination."

"Precisely," said Göring, looking delighted. "I think so too, my Führer. Despite that, it wouldn't do any harm to take a few precautions. I suggest, for example, that Herr von Blomberg invite two senior representatives of the armed forces to act as his witnesses at his wedding. If that doesn't silence the conservatives in our ranks, nothing will."

"The same thought occurred to me," Blomberg confided. "I already asked the Commanders-in-Chief of the Army and Navy, and they accepted."

Göring slapped his thigh. "A brilliant idea—it ought to pay off handsomely."

He stopped short sensing that the Führer's gaze was levelled straight at him. Göring felt intimidated. Adolf Hitler could hear the grass grow when he felt like it.

For the moment, however, he seemed determined to prove himself a comrade among comrades, the benevolent Father of the Fatherland and far-seeing custodian of the national interest.

"Permit me to assure you, Field Marshal," he said, "you have my full consent to this union—in fact, my blessing."

"Congratulations!" Göring flung one ham-sized arm round the field marshal's shoulders and gave him a proprietorial hug.

The Führer interrupted this idyll. "Your position is not without its problems, Herr von Blomberg. You must try to make the best of it."

"Don't worry, my Führer," boomed Göring, "he will. I'll see to that."

6

The Perils
of Idealism

From Counsellor Meller's notes—

The events of those weeks can only be described as a malicious plot. Its clearly identifiable target was the Wehrmacht—or, more precisely, the men at its head. Heydrich told me as much over a glass of champagne.

"Well, how do you think our Adolf will react when the full truth hits him?"

He roared with laughter. It may be of historical interest to note that his laughter sounded thoroughly genuine, with none of the malice or contempt that might have been expected. Reinhard Heydrich was then in his prime. Whatever he turned his hand to gave him unalloyed pleasure. He seemed to have the Midas touch in those days, and his unbroken string of successes would have been enough to make any man feel invincible.

"I know Göring pretty well," he went on, "—which doesn't take much doing. He's far too frightened of Hitler to stab him in the back. In a situation like this, you can always take for granted that he's acting on the Führer's instructions, if only indirectly."

"So Hitler stays in the background," I said. "He doesn't want to know what's happening, not officially and not at the moment. Meanwhile, you and Göring go on with the spadework."

"That's what we're here for," Heydrich said tersely. "They had a saying in the Middle Ages: 'Even the executioner belongs to the king's train'—or words to that effect."

He dropped the subject. I hurriedly advertised my lack of interest in it, which seemed to please him. The rest of the time, we amused ourselves by brushing up our Russian. Heydrich went into raptures over Stalin.

"As far as I can judge," he said, "he's got a lot of personal qualities in common with the Führer. For instance, they're both equally ruthless when their spheres of interest are at stake. I think we're going to see some fascinating historical developments before we're through."

It was also at this period that I requested an interview with Field Marshal von Blomberg, ostensibly because I wanted to present him with a copy of a book by my uncle, "Blood-and-Guts" Meller. It was dedicated to Blomberg and resoundingly entitled *Verdun: The Moment of Truth*. The field marshal greeted me warmly and gave a dinner in my honour at Kempinski's. His future wife, Fräulein Gruhn, played hostess.

I was curious to see her at close quarters and was privileged to do so for nearly three hours. They made an odd couple, though touching might be a better description of the way they leant towards each other and exchanged glances, he with infinite tenderness, she with a mixture of joy and gratitude.

The evening made a deep impression on me. I simply couldn't bring myself to warn Blomberg. Apart from anything else, I felt I had no moral right to interfere—a rare attack of scruples which I very soon regretted. After all, we were up against a man like Hitler.

Ninth essay in dramatic reconstruction... Subject: Werner stands firm—

"Everything must be as simple and dignified as possible," Blomberg told Eva, meaning their wedding ceremony. "I owe it to my position."

Even at this late stage, Eva seemed hesitant to take the final step. Not that she was deliberately playing hard to get, her reluctance only endeared her to him more.

"You don't have to shackle yourself to me," she implored him. "I'll always be here when you want me—I've told you that a thousand times. You can't just ignore my background."

"Remember Counsellor Meller?" he said. "The man we dined with the other night? Well, he knows all about you, thanks to his connections and his official position—that's partly why I invited him. I could see he was taken with you, with us both—with our relationship. I must say, it warmed my heart."

"But there were times when I caught him watching us with a strange expression, Werner. Almost pitying."

"Not pitying, Eva—sad. Counsellor Meller lost his wife and child in a very unfortunate accident. He's lived alone for years."

"I'm so sorry. He certainly seemed a likeable man, but rather on the deep side. At least, that's the impression I got."

"You're an excellent judge of character, my darling. Meeting him was important to us—you must have sensed that."

They were sitting over tea in her living room. Blomberg had brought a genuine English fruitcake with him. Eva took his hands in hers.

"If you're really set on a wedding, Werner, the answer's yes. Just as long as there's no fuss."

"I don't want any fuss either, sweetheart. We won't be able to avoid it altogether in view of my job, but I think it'll all go off as discreetly as we both want. A private ceremony—apart from the registrar, only the witnesses and one personal friend. My family won't be represented, but I think your mother should come."

Eva looked startled. "Please don't insist, Werner. I love my mother, really I do, but she's a simple soul. I wouldn't want to burden you with her. Not that on top of everything else, I beg of you!"

"But darling, she's the mother of the bride. I'm sure her pressure would make an excellent impression."

"If you insist," Eva said resignedly, "I'll try and arrange it."

"Anyway," Blomberg went on, "it's very probable the Führer will want to congratulate us in person. Göring too, of course. All the newspapers will carry an announcement and publish the names of the witnesses. I've already invited them, by the way—two very distinguished colleagues of mine."

"Goodness," sighed Eva, half impressed and half aghast, "all this because of you and me! And Mother there too? She'll feel like a fish out of water."

"Your dear devoted mother will be immensely proud of you, I'm sure. After all, her daughter's marrying a field marshal—the only one in the country. Doesn't she care?"

"Of course, that's why she's always begging me not to get involved in this 'escapade,' as she calls it. She's very impressed by the way you've behaved, Werner, but all the same, my mother at the wedding..."

Blomberg drew on his store of erudition. "Frederick the Great had a cavalry commander named Hans von Ziethen. After one of the general's victories, he invited him to dinner. Ziethen brought his mother along too—a humble farmer's wife. The king was so enchanted that he congratulated him. His exact words were 'Your filial devotion does you credit, General.'"

"But Hitler's no Frederick the Great," said Eva. "I mean," she tactfully amended, "times have changed since then."

"Some values are timeless, Eva. The Führer has restored this country's awareness of its moral foundations—the Germanic, Prussian virtues of loyalty, integrity, and family feeling. All these principles have regained their proper place in our new national community."

"Are you absolutely positive, Werner?"

"Not positive, perhaps, but confident."

The head of the Central State Security Bureau had a keenly observant eye. It told Heydrich his visit to Göring's luxurious country seat was regarded as something of a state occasion, albeit a confidential one. One ADC was

awaiting him at the front gate, another at the entrance, and
a footman at the double doors of Göring's inner sanctum.

The general pranced towards his visitor like an elephant
on tiptoe. He half-embraced Heydrich and drew him into
the study with a parting injunction to his senior aids.

"No interruptions, please." A superfluous thought
struck him. "Unless, of course, the Führer phones."

After a polite inquiry as to whether his honoured guest
desired some form of refreshment, which he didn't,
Göring got down to business.

"Well, Gruppenführer, what about Eva Gruhn? Can we
make anything out of her?"

"Possibly, General. I've compiled some information on
the lady, as you suggested, but it hasn't been easy.
Someone at Police Headquarters seems to be sitting on her
file. Still, we're making progress."

"In what direction?"

Heydrich smiled enigmatically and opened his briefcase. "It doesn't amount to much in itself, but it's a start.
Fräulein Gruhn appears to have a PSH rating." In police
jargon, whose refinements were not entirely unknown to
Göring, this signified "promiscuous sexual habits."

Göring's agitated intake of breath was an admirable
piece of theatre. He accompanied it with a look of
childlike amazement. "Can you prove that? I hesitate to
think of the implications if you're right."

"You underestimate my experts' abilities, General. Of
course we can prove it. Why, doesn't it suit you?"

"You know very well what I mean," said Göring,
regaining his composure with an effort. "Put yourself in
my place, Gruppenführer. If the Gestapo presented me
with a file on this woman, I might feel compelled to submit
it to the Führer. I wouldn't find it easy, of course. That's
why I'd have to be convinced the evidence was absolutely

conclusive. Everything must be checked and double-checked. I want some really solid proof, understand?"

Heydrich understood perfectly. "I take it you intend Blomberg to go ahead. As soon as he's safely married, you'll gun him down with ammunition supplied by us."

Göring smiled coldly. "Any objections?"

"Of course not, General, but I'm sure you won't mind if I cover myself too. I'll hardly be able to avoid informing Himmler, though with all due discretion. If I know him, his first reaction will be to ask what's in it for the SS."

"And what answer would he like to hear?"

"I can hazard a guess. In return for Blomberg's replacement by yourself as Commander-in-Chief Wehrmacht, the SS would appreciate the removal of General von Fritsch as well. Fritsch is a constant source of trouble to us, and to Himmler in particular. Fritsch says we're militarily incompetent, dismisses the SS as second-rate, and does his best to exclude us. He's our sworn enemy. That means he'll have to go—with your help, General, or at least with your connivance. May we count on you?"

"Indeed you may." Göring frowned deeply. "There's only one thing that bothers me. Do you really have enough on that obstinate old man to shoot him down? You'd have to produce some pretty damning evidence."

"We've got it—now."

"You don't say!" Göring wavered between skepticism and rapture. "Can you really make it stick?"

"As long as it's presented with sufficient force."

"By me, you mean?"

"This is a most delicate matter, General. If anyone can broach it to the Führer and persuade him to take the appropriate action, it's you. He listens to you."

"I'd only do it if I absolutely had to, and then with extreme reluctance. However, I don't propose to shirk my responsibilities. As long as your case is watertight, you can depend on me."

General Baron Werner von Fritsch was still recuperating in Cairo. His spacious room on the fifth floor of the Hotel Semiramis was solidly furnished in the Swiss style and had a balcony from which he could see the sluggish waters of the Nile and, beyond the Zoological Gardens, the Pyramids of Gizeh.

Fritsch's ADC had been given a room on the second floor. His job was to shield the general from any unwelcome outsiders who might penetrate his tourist's disguise. He accompanied him on walks, dealt with his mail, and kept in touch with Berlin by phone. He also kept him company at two meals a day, lunch and dinner.

The table permanently reserved for "Herr Fritsch from Germany" was in the far right corner of the spacious dining room and could be reached via a side door. The general, who always wore a plain dark suit, had banned the use of his rank and title. Official matters were also taboo. He usually conversed, if conversation seemed unavoidable, about literature.

This evening—just before Christmas 1937—he appeared in the hotel restaurant with his customary book. Fritsch was currently studying the libretti of Wagner's operas. He was also reading Hölderlin's poems, which he found too daring for his taste. Personally, he preferred the historical plays of Shakespeare.

The general sat down, not forgetting to give his constant companion a friendly but dignified nod. As he did so, he noticed that a third place had been laid. He looked inquiringly at the ADC, who had also turned out in a dark suit but cut a slightly more stylish figure.

"I beg your pardon, General," the ADC said quickly. "You have a last-minute visitor, a nephew of our ambassador here. Colonel Oster of Military Intelligence warned me to expect him. He only arrived this afternoon, and he's flying on to Athens tomorrow morning. His instructions are to brief you on developments in Berlin."

Fritsch nodded, clearly resenting the intrusion. He did not think much of these confidential briefings on events at home, because they so often degenerated into rumour-mongering. It was characteristic of him to set store by concise language, hard facts, and accurate figures.

The budding German diplomat got an appropriately cool reception. He proved a remarkably self-assured young man who made frequent references to "my uncle the ambassador." He was also loquacious—so loquacious that he blithely launched into a stream of Berlin gossip, undeterred by the general's increasingly icy expression.

Clearly relishing his inside knowledge of the capital's goings-on, he reported that "Jupp," alias Propaganda Minister Goebbels, had taken a new mistress. Another film star, of course, but this time he had caused something of a flutter by picking a young Czech beauty. Meanwhile, "Jupp's Magda," alias Frau Goebbels, was making time with her husband's ministerial deputy...

Oh yes, and "the dashing Count," meaning Police Commissioner Helldorf, had also become emotionally entangled with a goddess of the silver screen—a beautiful blonde who was doing her best to hook him. Rumour had it he was infatuated with her.

Best of all, though, "the other Werner"—meaning Werner von Blomberg, as distinct from Werner von Fritsch—was courting hard. His prospective bride was said to be a woman with a past, and several cuts below him socially.

No one could have told whether Fritsch was listening to this survey of the Berlin social scene with even half an ear. He said nothing and seemed wholly preoccupied with his excellent Turkish coffee. The ADC strove to conceal his growing impatience and embarrassment. As for the visiting diplomat, he talked on and on.

He showed no sign of coming to the point until a final brandy appeared on the table. The dining room was almost deserted, the waiters having beaten a deferential retreat. Still in a cheerfully conversational tone, the visitor broached the actual purpose of his mission.

"There's dirty work afoot in Berlin, General. That's what Colonel Oster and Admiral Canaris told me to tell you. The SS authorities are becoming more and more active, and their activities are unmistakably directed against the Army and yourself. I was asked to make that absolutely clear."

Fritsch preserved a dogged silence but looked fractionally more interested. His ADC felt called on to fill the breach.

"That's nothing new. Everyone knows the SS are planning to expand their own military formations. The Army's firmly opposed. So is the general. The only body entitled to bear arms in Germany is the Wehrmacht, Hitler says so himself. We have his solemn pledge."

The visitor raised his eyebrows. "My dear fellow, surely you don't believe everything Adolf says? Besides, even if he meant it the SS would wriggle out from under. Those gentlemen are only interested in manoeuvring their opponents up against a wall, and that includes you. They're trying to produce a *fait accompli* so Hitler can give it his blessing after the event. Why? Because the Army's a thorn in his flesh—too independent, not revolutionary enough from the Nazi point of view. It certainly isn't noted for its doglike devotion to the Führer."

"Permit me," said Fritsch, with unruffled dignity, "to draw your attention to the following. Without actively seeking my present position, I have become one of our country's most senior soldiers. As such, I owe absolute loyalty and obedience to my head of state, be his name Paul von Hindenburg or Adolf Hitler."

The visitor gave a snort of impatience. "But that's just what they're all counting on, General, and by all I mean Heydrich, Himmler, and Göring. Hitler too. They're gambling on your integrity—on their ability to predict your gentlemanly reactions. What's more, they're prepared to stoop to methods you and your friends would consider unthinkable."

"Just a moment," said the ADC, perturbed by his general's obvious indignation. "You're talking about the legally constituted government of Germany, not a gang of crooks."

"Are you sure?" the young man retorted firmly. "You've fallen for a gigantic confidence trick, can't you see?"

The ADC rose, modelling his mask of disapproval on the general's. "If that's all you came to say, thank you and good night."

Fritsch, who looked pained and hurt, said nothing. His aide hurriedly escorted the visitor out. When he returned, Fritsch was still staring into space.

"I'm sorry about that, General. I should have headed him off."

"And I," Fritsch said after a long pause, "should never have left my post."

"In your state of health, General? You had no choice."

"Compared to the issues at stake, my health is unimportant."

"He was all hot air, sir. Don't let it worry you."

Fritsch thought for a moment, then issued their marching orders in a crisp and businesslike tone. "Our time in Cairo is up. We leave tomorrow, initially for Rome, where we shall spend a few days. We shall then return to Berlin. I intend to resume my duties there by 2 January at latest."

Very early in the new year, 1938, Counsellor Meller paid another call on his boyhood friend. Heydrich, who had issued the invitation, gave him a warm welcome.

"Good to see you again, Erich. A human being at last, after all these fools and asslickers! Let's start by splitting a bottle. After that you're invited to dine at my expense."

"What are we celebrating?" Meller noted Heydrich's mysterious grin. "You're a glutton for surprises, Reinhard. What is it this time?"

"They've just opened a Russian-style restaurant in Friedrichstrasse. The Troika—a hilarious name. I'll tell you why in due course, but first let's have a glass of champagne."

"You seem happy enough."

"I am. Everything's going fine." Heydrich beamed. "The so-called military élite of this country are due for the axe. Another few days and we'll have the lot of them— medals, monocles, and all."

"Anyone in particular?" Meller asked casually.

"Wouldn't you like to know!"

"Of course I would," Meller said, even more casually. "I always prefer to get my information first-hand."

Heydrich could not contain his high spirits that evening, switching erratically from subject to subject. He waxed eloquent about the fortunes of war and the pleasures of the chase; a mediocre but enthusiastic fiddle player, he even discussed the relative merits of several violin concertos.

Erich Meller took care to be a patient, attentive listener. Knowing Heydrich as well as he did, which was better than anyone, he realized that the wisest policy during these rare spells of exuberance was to let him talk. Heydrich was suspicious by nature and profession. One ill-timed question could transform him at lightning speed into a predator scenting enemies on every side. No such transformation occurred this time.

Instead, they breezed into the Troika and commandeered an alcove near the door. Here they consumed quantities of caviar and sank vodka by the tumbler. Reverting to a favourite theme, Heydrich recalled the practical jokes they had played as boys. One involved sabotage at a country wedding.

"Do you remember, Erich?"

Meller certainly did. They had stolen the parson's sermon for use as lavatory paper and filched the cutlery, compelling several dozen hungry wedding guests to attack the ample feast with their bare hands. They had switched off the lights, stolen the fuses, and got the band drunk on beer spiked with schnapps...

"Ah yes," said Meller, "those were the days. They won't come back again."

"Everything comes back one way or another." Heydrich draped an arm round Meller's shoulders. "History does repeat itself, Erich, even if it does so in a different form. Know why that wedding's so fresh in my mind? Because I'm going to wreck another one in the near future—a big one this time. Blomberg's."

"Blomberg marrying again—at his age? Has he invited you, Reinhard?"

"Of course not. I wouldn't have accepted anyway. I ask

you, can *I* afford to compromise myself by kissing the
hand of a registered prostitute and risk being photographed in the act? No, but I'll be taking a close
behind-the-scenes interest."

"This wedding—is it all arranged or just on the cards?"

"Not only arranged but announced, old boy!" Heydrich
was almost beside himself with glee. "It's set for the
twelfth, or three days from now, and it's going to be a real
sensation. But that isn't all."

Meller raised his eyebrows.

"Hang on, Erich, I've left the best till last." Heydrich
slapped him on the back and glanced at the door, where
one of his most reliable security men had been posted.
Smiling, he clinked glasses with Meller.

"Remember me telling you earlier how uproariously
funny I found the name of this restaurant? Like me to tell
you why?"

"You will if it suits you, Reinhard."

"I will indeed, just between friends. A troika's a
three-horse team right? Whip up the horses, point them in
the right direction, and away they go, hell for leather. This
is much the same."

Meller played a waiting game. He made no immediate
response—he even contrived to look faintly bored and
indifferent.

"Well?" he said at last.

"The troika I'm talking about consists of Blomberg, the
bridegroom of a part-time prostitute, plus two witnesses.
By the time I'm through, they'll all be up to their necks in
mire."

"You really think Blomberg's that dumb?"

The Gruppenführer ordered some Crimean champagne. A bottle had been chilled in readiness. The waiter
quickly opened it and poured. Heydrich tried it.

"Third-rate!" was his verdict, but he seemed to enjoy it just the same. He leant towards his table companion.

"You wouldn't *believe* how dumb some people can be. The witnesses have already committed themselves. Guess who they are? The Commanders-in-Chief of the Army and Navy!"

Meller tried to conceal the full extent of his shock and surprise. He deliberately drained his glass. "Fritsch and Raeder? Are you sure there's no mistake, Reinhard?"

"I've seen my troika listed in writing—only a copy, of course, but still. The race'll be run in three days' time, Erich, and then I'll have them. Let's drink to that!"

Interlude No. 1—

Counsellor Meller promptly tried to contact General von Fritsch, with no immediate success. The general's outer office was guarded by the aide who had escorted him to Cairo.

"I'm sorry, Counsellor," he said. "I realize that the general knows you personally, but he can't be disturbed right now. Just between you and me, he's engaged on some new and extremely important projects. He and his strategic planning staff have been working on them for days."

"I'm sorry too," said Meller, "but I'll have to insist on seeing him. It's absolutely vital. Colonel Oster of Military Intelligence agrees. If you don't believe me, ask him yourself."

This proved unnecessary. Fifteen minutes later the Commander-in-Chief emerged, looking as urbane and composed as ever. He granted Meller's request for a word in private but did not demur when his ADC urged the visitor to be as brief as possible.

"General," Meller said when they were alone together, "I'll come straight to the point. You've been invited to act as a witness at Herr von Blomberg's wedding. I strongly advise you to withdraw. I don't have access to the full picture, but the Gestapo appear to have compiled a dossier proving that the future Frau von Blomberg has an unsavoury past—you know what they're capable of. They'll be launching a smear campaign immediately after the wedding."

The general did not seem unduly surprised. "I'd already heard similar rumours but dismissed them as malicious gossip. Why come to me, Counsellor? Why not inform the field marshal direct?"

"I've tried that, but it's no use. He flatly refuses to discuss his fiancée's past with a third party. According to him, she doesn't have one."

"There you are, then. Blomberg should know."

"But think of the repercussions on you and the officer corps as a whole, General. If the Gestapo produce this file, many officers may believe its libellous allegations. They'll regard them as an infringement of their code of honour."

"A code of honour which also stipulates that a promise, once given, must be kept. The field marshal asked me to act as his witness, and I accepted."

"Don't think me presumptuous, General, but the least you should do is get in touch with the other person concerned. I advise you to contact Admiral Raeder at once."

Interlude No. 2—
Commander-in-Chief Army called at the Navy Directorate and asked to see his opposite number without delay. He was ushered into Raeder's office.

"If you hadn't come to see me," Raeder confided as he offered Fritsch a chair, "I'd have come to see you. For the same deplorable reason, I suspect. It's Blomberg's marriage, isn't it?"

"Precisely. I just received a visit from Counsellor Meller, whom you doubtless know. A reliable man, so I'm told, even if he does have some rather shady connections."

"Connections reputed to range from Heydrich to Canaris. That's not a black mark, of course—not in this day and age."

"My immediate impulse was to tell him to mind his own business. However, a couple of things have occurred to me. One of my corps commanders telephoned me yesterday. They didn't put him through because I was in conference, but he left a message with my ADC. It read: 'Tell the general that Field Marshal von Blomberg is about to marry a prostitute.'"

"Do you believe it?" asked Raeder.

"No, I don't. I think it's a malicious fabrication on the part of the Gestapo, the SS, or some other interested party, but I don't think that alters our problem. You know how thorough these people can be. Think what will happen if this spurious evidence *does* exist—think how long it may take to *prove* it's a fabrication. Meanwhile..."

"Meanwhile, as far as the public, the armed forces, and the officer corps are concerned, the War Minister will have married a prostitute with a police record..."

"And we, the senior representatives of two armed services steeped in tradition, will have given our seal of approval."

Raeder stroked his jaw. "I'm beginning to see the object of the exercise. We must put a stop to it."

"But we've already given our word. Besides, the marriage has been vigorously sponsored by Göring and expressly approved by the Chancellor."

"Well said, General! You've hit the nail on the head, don't you see? *That's* our chance to escape in the nick of time and leave someone else holding the baby—someone who may even have fathered the damn thing."

"I don't follow you," said Fritsch.

"It's quite simple. We each call Blomberg—independently—and thank him again for doing us the honour of inviting us to be his witnesses. On mature consideration, however, we feel bound to decline. Why? Because this great and exceptional privilege does not, unfortunately, belong to us. It should only be conferred on the sponsors and patrons of Blomberg's marriage, namely Adolf Hitler and Hermann Göring. We respectfully step down and persuade him to give them first refusal. And that, General, gets us off the hook!"

Interlude No. 3—

The War Minister and Commander-in-Chief of the Wehrmacht, Field Marshal Werner von Blomberg, paid another call on Hermann Göring, who received him with exaggerated warmth.

"Problems, my dear fellow?"

"Only one, but it's rather pressing. As I already informed you and the Führer, I'd earmarked Fritsch and Raeder as my witnesses. They accepted, too, but now ..."

"What! Don't tell me they're backing out!"

"Not exactly. They say—and I must confess I see the force of their argument—that the honour shouldn't go to them. They say the only people entitled to witness such a union are the Führer and yourself. This situation has been dumped in my lap, Herr Göring. Reluctant as I am to bring it up, I'd much appreciate your views on the matter."

Göring took his time. He thought hard, breathing heavily. Then he smiled with catlike complacency.

"I don't see why it shouldn't be arranged, my dear fellow."

"So I can depend on you as before?"

"Of course, in every conceivable way. What's one little problem more or less? It'll be a pleasure."

Interlude No. 4—

Hermann Göring arrived at the Chancellory for a heart-to-heart talk in Hitler's study. He came straight to the point.

"It's those stiff-jointed, stiff-necked old war-horses of yours, my Führer. They'd shy at their own shadow."

Hitler reacted with his usual acumen. "What is it, Blomberg's marriage? Are some of the generals acting up?"

"Incorrigible," fumed Göring, "that's what they are. No revolutionary vigor—no conception of what it means to live in a dynamic new society like ours. Inbred, that's their trouble. It doesn't matter if a woman's fat, scrawny, or swaybacked, with a face like a Gorgon and buttocks like a brood mare, they'll marry her as long as her pedigree's right. They wouldn't know a daughter of the people if they saw one."

"Come to the point, Göring. What's the matter?"

"Fritsch and Raeder don't want to act as witnesses at Blomberg's wedding."

"Really? Why not?" Hitler showed little curiosity. "Are they critical of his choice?"

"Not outwardly—they wouldn't have the nerve. It's just that the social angle has become too much for them. They're trying to slip out of the picture. They aren't worthy of such honour, they say. The War Minister has their warmest good wishes but they don't deserve to act as witnesses."

"And who does? You and I, Göring—is that it?"

Adolf Hitler regarded his henchman with the pensive, almost indulgent expression he always assumed after effortlessly reading Göring's devious mind. Göring saw his Führer smile and nodded vigorously.

"In that case," Hitler said, "I suppose we shall have to support our worthy field marshal in his hour of need, as true friends should. We must only hope our confidence isn't misplaced."

Interlude No. 5—

Field Marshal Werner von Blomberg married Fräulein Eva Gruhn, a government employee, at noon on 12 January 1938. The simple but dignified ceremony was held at the War Ministry. Only a civil wedding had been planned. There were no religious rites and few outsiders present.

Blomberg's grown-up children stayed away. So did his daughter's father-in-law, General Keitel, whose career owed much to Blomberg's help. The field marshal's family had privately and unanimously agreed to ignore the occasion.

Those who did turn up included one of Blomberg's very few personal friends, his ex-naval aide Lieutenant Commander von Friedeburg, who came without a second thought. Attired in uniform and wearing his full complement of orders and decorations, Friedeburg was almost alone in betraying a hint of subdued emotion. It did not surprise him to note that his friend's obvious happiness was alloyed with apprehension—even with a trace of gloom. His words of congratulation were restrained but came straight from the heart.

The registrar stood humbly in his corner beside the farthest window, watching what was probably the most extraordinary spectacle he had ever witnessed. The field marshal stood conversing in low tones with his friend. The bride, who could fairly be described as lovely to look at but showing faint signs of strain, stood a little to one side with her mother. Frau Gruhn smiled soothingly at her daughter, twitched her dark-brown suit into place, and plucked stray hairs from the padded shoulders. Near the door lurked one of Blomberg's aides, tensely awaiting the climax of this state occasion.

It came at noon precisely. Punctual to the minute, the Führer strode in as stiff-legged and stern-faced as if he were about to inspect a guard of honour. Göring trotted at his heels. He was the only person present who radiated unclouded cheerfulness, and his voice, which matched his expression, pierced the solemn hush like a clarion.

The registrar commented on this later, still under the spell of his recent experience. "I might have been forgiven," he said, "for thinking that Göring was the bridegroom. He certainly gave an impression of profound pleasure and close personal involvement."

Blomberg hurried towards Hitler, welcomed him, thanked him devoutly for coming, and assured him how much he appreciated the honour his presence conferred. Hitler declared that the pleasure was his and that he, in his turn, considered it an honour to be present. He was then introduced to such members of the party as he did not already know.

"Delighted to make your acquaintance," he told Eva Gruhn, sounding admirably rehearsed. "It is always a pleasure to meet those close to those who are close to oneself."

Then he turned to the mother of the bride. "Your

daughter, Madam, is about to become the wife of one of our country's most distinguished figures. Her new life will make very special demands on her. I hope you will lend her your fullest support."

Finally, he addressed the registrar in a commandingly statesmanlike tone.

"And now, sir, do your duty."

The ceremony took only a few minutes. The registrar recited his standard text. Blomberg said "Yes." So did Eva. Then they signed the register. Their witnesses—Hitler, Adolf, and Göring, Hermann—followed suit. The formalities were quickly completed. Nobody in the room could wait to get them over, that much was obvious.

Immediately afterwards, champagne was served by a mess waiter. Although he was only a chance witness of the proceedings and seemed a faceless and anonymous figure in such company, he too had a name. It was Ewald Liedtke.

Information supplied, several decades later, by Ewald Liedtke—

I was doing my two years' military service at the time. Trust the Army to stick a square peg in a round hole! They put me through months of latrine cleaning before they remembered I was a trainee waiter and posted me to an officers' mess instead. Not just any old officers' mess, mind you. I was assigned to the War Ministry and hired out for special occasions. That was how I came to be on duty at the field marshal's wedding. Three bottles of champagne, nine glasses. Eight for the guests and one on the side for yours truly.

Jesus, what a party! More like a wake than a wedding.

Nobody spoke above a whisper except Göring, who kept roaring with laughter. The rest might have been a collection of wax-works. That was because of Hitler, I suppose. He stood there gazing into space, all solemn and dignified, while the others gaped at him.

The field marshal was very attentive. He put his arm round the bride's shoulders, and she clung to him like ivy. Her mother couldn't take her eyes off them. Göring was all over the mother, by the way. "Well, my dear lady," he thundered, "you're the mother-in-law of Germany's top soldier. How does it feel?"

Frau Gruhn bridled. "Eva always did aim high, even as a girl."

"And higher you can't get!" Göring gave a delighted chuckle. "A remarkable young woman, your daughter, but how could she fail to be with a mother like you! We must get together sometime for a chat—I'd enjoy that."

Before Frau Gruhn could accept this invitation, which she doubtless found flattering, the Führer barked out his intention of leaving. He discarded his untouched glass of champagne, conferred a limp handshake on everyone present, and nodded mechanically in all directions.

"Well," he said, turning to the bridegroom, "what happens now?"

"Are you referring to our personal plans, my Führer?"

"Yes, I imagine you'll be taking the usual honeymoon. Where have you chosen?"

"Where else but our beloved Germany, my Führer! I'm planning to take Eva—my wife, I mean—to my native Saxony. Most of our time will be spent in Leipzig, but I shall naturally remain in constant touch with the Ministry."

"In that case, have a good trip." Hitler turned on his heel and strode briskly out. Göring followed him.

Each of them thought he had scored a decisive victory. In one case—though not in Hitler's—this proved a horrendous mistake.

Next day, an official announcement appeared in Nazi Germany's leading daily, the *Völkischer Beobachter*, which carried the following inconspicuous report on page one:

> Berlin, 12 January—The Reich War Minister, Field Marshal von Blomberg, has married Fräulein Eva Gruhn. The Führer and Reich Chancellor and General Göring were witnesses.
>
> Field Marshal von Blomberg may rest assured that he and his wife enjoy the heartfelt good wishes of the entire German people.

That was all, but it was enough—quite enough for all hell to break loose.

Storm clouds were looming over the SS nerve centre in Prinz-Albrecht-Strasse. Gruppenführer Reinhard Heydrich was furious. Everything seemed to be going wrong, so he summoned his heads of section.

"What's the matter with you?" he demanded. "You're half asleep. Are you getting fat and complacent? Are you tired—tired of living, maybe? I was bang on target, and what happens? Fritsch and Raeder gallop out of range at the last minute."

One of his devoted yes-men hazarded a suggestion. "There could be a leak, Gruppenführer—here at headquarters, I mean."

"Just what I was thinking." Heydrich's eyes narrowed.

"It looks as if somebody in our outfit can't keep his mouth shut—either that or he's deliberately selling us out. He could even be a plant. Whoever the bastard is, find him. I'll deal with him personally."

There was a murmured chorus of assent.

"From now on," Heydrich said in a voice like a knife, "double-check your security procedures. I want everyone in this organization rescreened. That order takes priority over everything else. Turn the department inside out. Be absolutely ruthless. We've got to find that leak."

The heads of section departed, suitably chastened. Next, Heydrich directed a special blast at Meisinger.

"What the devil are you thinking of? How dare you submit this trash? Only a complete fool would have done what you did. You gave the man a look at that file, and he's made a monkey out of you."

Meisinger, pale and shaking, strove to explain. "I only did it as a precaution, Gruppenführer. I wanted to make absolutely sure..."

"Then you're a damn sight stupider than I thought you were," snarled Heydrich. He tapped the report in front of him with an accusing forefinger. "What do you call that, an insurance policy? I wouldn't use it to wipe my ass! Results, that's all I want—results we can use."

Meisinger was almost wringing his hands. "I'm sorry, Gruppenführer, but I was so anxious to leave nothing to chance I thought a second opinion would..."

"Second opinion be damned! You've screwed it up completely. Thanks to your stupidity, another of these blasted generals may slip through our fingers. Can't you read, Meisinger?"

The document in front of Heydrich was a species of "check report" drafted by a Berlin CID officer who had been seconded to State Security on the strength of a personal recommendation. His name was Huber.

Heydrich shook his head and groaned. "The man's an obvious outsider—a foreign body. Who the hell palmed him off on you?"

From the Meller report—

It was a tricky situation. So tricky that, when things became really hot, I felt compelled to send for Huber.

"Well," I said with a mixture of regret and encouragement, "the time has come."

"The time for what, Counsellor?"

"I've found it urgently necessary to sing your praises, Huber. The Police Department has seconded you to State Security on my recommendation—they value my advice at Prinz-Albrecht-Strasse, as you know. You'll be welcomed with open arms."

"As what?"

"As a first-class detective, which you are."

"I know, and I plan to stay one." -

"I was counting on that. Anyway, you're now on loan to the Gestapo. Meisinger needs you in his section."

"That lousy bastard?" Huber's reaction was grimly sincere. "You really think it's essential? All right, I'll go if you say so, but Meisinger's in for a big surprise."

Meisinger was indeed. Eager to cover himself from every conceivable angle, he had hit on the bright but risky idea of subjecting his star witness, Otto Schmidt, to cross-examination by the vice squad's leading interrogator, George Huber. Huber's assignment was to put Schmidt through his paces once again and try to trip him up. The results were alarming.

Huber took only a few days to persuade Meisinger and his men that certain aspects of the case against Fritsch were extremely shaky. In particular, discrepancies existed between various recorded statements and the important details they contained.

"Then we'll have to iron them out," was Meisinger's casual comment. "Pure routine, old man. I'll get my men to run through Schmidt's statements again. He's ready to repeat the whole story under oath, surely that's the main thing?"

"Ah," Huber said amiably, "but what if the defence digs up some witnesses of its own? What if evidence comes to light which proves that Schmidt has perjured himself—or that his statements have been doctored?"

Meisinger grunted impatiently. "You're just shadow-boxing."

"That's what I'm paid for," Huber persisted. "There's another thing. This story about Schmidt being a regular police informant—I doubt if you can make it stick. As far as I recall, he was an active member of the Berlin homosexual community before graduating to blackmail. Other people might remember that too, with a little pressure or financial encouragement from the defence side. Anyway, I've drafted you a report on the subject."

And that was the report that went to Heydrich.

"Good God, Meisinger, what's this rubbish supposed to prove. You must be crazy!" Heydrich's tone did not match his words. It was almost affable. "Don't you see what it could mean?"

Even a man of Meisinger's limited imagination could see that. He looked imploring, humbly requested fresh instructions, and promised to comply with them faithfully. He ended on an almost reverential note.

"I always try to be worthy of your trust, Gruppen-führer."

"Then get cracking. The whole thing's really quite simple. I do as the Führer wants, you do as I want, and your subordinates do as you want. That way, everything's fine."

"Yessir!"

"So why let yourself be sidetracked by this man—what's his name again?"

"Huber."

"Who is he?"

"A detective superintendent on loan from the vice squad, Gruppenführer—an expert in his own field. CID assigned him to us on the personal recommendation of Counsellor Meller."

"You idiot, Meisinger, why didn't you say so before?" Heydrich sounded relieved. "Don't you know who Meller is? We're old friends—he's one hundred per cent reliable. If the Counsellor sends us an expert, he must be all right. You'll have to do the best you can with him."

"I will, sir." Meisinger seemed finally to have grasped what was expected of him. "I'm only using the man as a final check on our case. Any holes he picks will be personally plugged by me. He won't get a chance to interfere direct, I've already seen to that."

Meisinger was positively smirking with relief. Heydrich's expression had softened a little.

"It's your show, Meisinger. Get it rolling properly—stage it to my complete satisfaction and turn in a really convincing performance—and you won't regret it. Otherwise..."

Tenth essay in dramatic reconstruction... Subject: an attempted honeymoon—

"Werner," said Eva von Blomberg, née Gruhn,

nestling close to her husband, "are you happy?"

"Very happy, darling," he assured her tenderly.

"But... You don't look it, somehow."

"I'm not a debonair young man any more."

"Don't say that," she reprimanded him, laughing gaily. "I can think of lots of times when you act like a *very* young man!"

"If I do, it's all because of you." He beamed at her. "You're wonderful in bed."

"I'd do anything for you, Werner."

It was only a few days since their wedding. They were now in Leipzig, where they had visited the zoo. A light drizzle was falling. Eva had put up a big black umbrella and was holding it over them. She wore a dark brown floppy felt hat and kept gazing up at her husband, who was a full head taller.

Without knowing it, they were photographed in front of the monkey cage. The picture was later printed in the *Berliner Illustrierte*. Whether or not it appeared in the connivance of the Propaganda Ministry, this outwardly touching and innocuous photograph caused a stir.

Although Blomberg could not have foreseen it, it was soon brought home to him by a flood of hurtful asides. One came from his daughter's father-in-law, General Keitel, who was heard to say, "Did he have to do that *too*!" Colonel Hossbach, the Führer's Wehrmacht aide, put it another way. "Our field marshal," he complained, "seems determined to spare us nothing, but I suppose we'll have to grin and bear it." As for one unnamed general, his terse comment was, "Brothel outing!"

To crown everything, Hitler was reported as having made a remark "in the strictest confidence" to Göring, which was one way of ensuring it received maximum publicity. "As soon as I saw the bride's mother at that wedding," he declared, "I knew what she was and where she came from. Her past was written all over her."

Meanwhile, Eva and her husband had returned to their hotel after a stroll through Leipzig.

"It depresses me to see you brooding," she told him. "I only hope it's nothing to do with me."

"My dearest girl," he admonished her gallantly, "I could never regret my decision to marry you, so please put the idea out of your head. For the first time in sixty years, I feel truly alive, and I'm not afraid to admit it."

"Thank you." She put her arms round him. "But there must be something wrong, I can see it in your face."

"Every successful man has enemies," he sighed, "and I'm no exception. There are one or two generals who begrudge me my rank and appointment. They're only waiting for me to put a foot wrong."

"That's terrible!" Eva's face clouded. "But does it really have nothing to do with me? Be absolutely honest."

"No, my beautiful, gentle darling. You're a pure and unadulterated source of joy. Nothing else matters to me but you."

"If you mean that, Werner, it makes me very happy."

"I mean every word!" he said, hugging her fiercely. "Don't worry, I'll deal with those vipers. As soon as we get back from our honeymoon, I'm going to clean out the whole nest."

Further aspects of the contemporary scene, early 1938—

The Nansen International Office for Refugees was awarded the Nobel Peace Prize. The Nobel Prize for Literature went to Pearl S. Buck of the USA. The black contralto Marian Anderson, born 1902, received an honorary doctorate from Harvard University.

Italy mourned Gabriele d'Annunzio, nationalist bard
and novelist, intimate friend of Duse, devoted admirer of
the Duce. The dead of those days also included Ernst
Barlach, probably the most spirited and spontaneous of all
the Expressionists. He was buried without ceremony. Not
one German newspaper published a word about him.

Georges Bernanos, the most pugnacious of France's
Catholic writers, castigated supporters of Franco in *A
Diary of My Times*. Oskar Kokoschka applied for British
citizenship. Ernst Ludwig Kirchner, German Expression-
ist and creator of glowing abstractions on canvas, chose
suicide.

Bartok composed another piano concerto. Like him,
the painter and sculptor Hans Arp strove to make a living
in Switzerland. Both succeeded, thanks to financial
support provided by the citizens of Basle.

At the same time, that unique novelist Joseph Roth was
trying to drown the sorrows of his Parisian exile in drink,
which finally killed him. The brothers Mann, Heinrich and
Thomas, seemed to have abandoned all hope of their
country's redemption. They promptly converted their
lamentations into accusations.

Meanwhile, Hitler paid a brief visit to Rome. Sundry
British politicians declared that developments inside the
Third Reich should be viewed as objectively as possible, in
other words, without emotional bias. Paris was preparing
for another world exhibition. The colossal German
pavilion, a ponderous and imposing edifice, had already
been designed by Albert Speer, the Führer's faithful court
architect.

Corporal Schmiedinger, General von Fritsch's batman,
was a cheerful and uninhibited character who sometimes

treated his Commander-in-Chief with a lack of ceremony which visibly shocked him but did not cause offence. The general made it a rule to encourage absolute candour in his subordinates.

And candour was what he got now, after Schmiedinger had imparted a dazzling shine to his boots and shoes and produced his uniforms for inspection, neatly pressed and stain-free.

"Excuse me, General, but may I make a personal remark?"

"Why ask, Schmiedinger? There's no need to request my permission before you inform me—or, to use your own vernacular, tip me off—about something."

"Do you remember Corporal Freiberg, sir?"

Fritsch gave a faint smile. "Another pointless question, Schmiedinger. I never forget anyone who has served with me."

Corporal Freiberg was one of Schmiedinger's predecessors, a respectable and agreeably self-effacing man—efficient too. Fritsch had lost track of him but surmised that he must be holding down a responsible job in an officers' mess somewhere.

"A decent type," said Schmiedinger. "Very dependable, sir, wouldn't you say?"

"Absolutely," the general agreed. "I'm glad you share my opinion of him."

"The thing is, we meet now and then—to swap experiences, in a manner of speaking. Well, yesterday we had a few drinks together, and this time I didn't like the look of him at all. Shall I tell you why, sir?"

"If you insist."

"All right, General, I'll give it to you straight. Our old pal Freiberg has fallen foul of the Gestapo. They've really been putting the screws on him, poor bastard. That's nothing out of the ordinary, not these days, but there's something else. You'll be wondering what it's all about, so here it is. You, General—*that's* who they're after!"

Fritsch, who was seated at his desk, leant back and slowly shook his head. "I can't believe it."

"Maybe not, sir, but it's the gospel truth." Schmiedinger was well away now. "And guess what those Gestapo bastards have been trying to squeeze out of him? Whether he was ever subjected to improper advances while he worked for you, and if so, what sort. I hope you realize what they're driving at, sir."

Fritsch had risen stiffly to his feet, a stern and disapproving figure. "What an appalling story, Schmiedinger! Knowing me as well as you do, you should never have inflicted it on me."

"Don't take it that way, General." The corporal stared anxiously at his Commander-in-Chief. "It's the Gestapo— they're trying to frame you, can't you see?"

"What business is it of yours or mine, Schmiedinger? Those people can do as they think fit. I've no intention of descending to their level."

"But that won't stop them, sir. They don't give a damn about anyone."

"I refuse even to acknowledge such a thing—everything inside me rebels at the thought."

"I understand, sir." Corporal Schmiedinger was impressed by this lofty attitude but not unduly deterred by it. He was now convinced, and rightly so, that the general had a blind spot. However conceivable Fritsch had thought it that the Gestapo were planning to oust Field Marshal von Blomberg with the aid of fabricated evidence, he greeted his own exposure to such underhanded methods with suicidal incomprehension. His innocence may have been commendable, but it was just that innocence which made the fast approaching tidal wave of filth so perilous.

Fritsch's days as Commander-in-Chief were numbered. Sensing this, Schmiedinger tried to exorcize his sorrow with a stream of curses uttered in the privacy of his room. But it was no use. His only way of emerging unscathed, it seemed, was to request a transfer.

Eleventh essay in dramatic reconstruction ... Subject: death of a mother—

"You're just in time to watch the sunset." Blomberg turned to greet his bride with a radiant smile. He always tried to show how blissfully happy he was to see her. "The world seems to light up whenever you walk in."

Eva hurriedly closed the door of their Leipzig hotel room and leant against it.

"I've got some bad news for you, Werner."

"Nothing that affects the two of us, I hope?"

"Not in that way."

"Then it can't be so bad." He sensed her mounting concern and uneasiness. "Aren't you feeling well, darling? What's the matter?"

"This came for you," she said flatly, holding out a sheet of paper, but he only had eyes for her. Her pale face was tinged with evening sunlight. "A telegram from your family—it's signed by one of your sons."

"If they're wiring their congratulations, they've left it too late."

"Your mother's dead."

Blomberg drew himself up, breathing heavily. He swayed a little and turned to hide his tears. Even at this moment, it was as if he were commanding himself to demonstrate that German field marshals never cry—never! He disappeared into the bathroom.

When he emerged, many minutes later, his air of soldierly calm and composure was fully restored. He nodded gravely at Eva.

"There's nothing more inevitable in life than death. My dear and deeply respected mother said so more than once, with her own inimitable brand of humour. I've never told you much about her, have I? I ought to have done so long ago, just as I ought to have introduced you to her. She'd have seen for herself how happy you've made me. That would have made her happy too, quite apart from making things a good deal easier for us. All we can do now is drink to her memory."

His mother, he went on, putting his arm round Eva's shoulders, had recently developed a taste for French wines, notably Château Lafite-Rothschild. He had even managed to procure a case of the 1933, an outstanding year, for her last birthday.

He called the reception desk. Yes, he was informed a few minutes later, the hotel cellars could produce some Château Lafite-Rothschild 1933, but only two bottles. He sent for them both.

Blomberg filled Eva's glass, then his own. He held the dark red wine to the light, and it glowed like liquid fire. They drank sitting side by side on the double bed. Eva covertly watched her husband as he drained his glass with silent ceremony.

Then he began to speak, quietly. Although his body rested against hers, he might have been talking to himself—addressing something inside him.

"My God, what a mother she was! I always felt safe with her. She could detect every stirring of emotion I ever had. There was nothing I couldn't confide in her, as far back as I can remember. When I was still a boy, and going through the torments of adolescence, she'd put her arms around me and all would be well. Later on, when I joined the Army and became an officer, she only had to take my hand when she sensed that I was depressed or unsure of myself, and all my misgivings vanished. One look from her and perfect harmony reigned between us.

"I shall never forget visiting her as a brand-new field marshal—immediately after calling on the Führer. I turned up in uniform with all my orders and decorations and saluted her with my baton. And what did she do?

"She just smiled at me with a tenderness nobody else could convey—I hadn't met you then, darling Eva. And what did she say? 'Werner, my boy, that uniform looks awfully tight. Never mind, though, you've risen high enough in the world not to be vain about trifles. At last you can be yourself.' That's the way she was.

"She was in bed the last time I saw her, with a bad case of flu. She was bathed in perspiration and fighting for breath, but she still managed a smile. 'I'm worried about you, Mother,' I told her. 'The Führer's expecting me, but I'll stay if you like.'

"What I really meant was, 'Mother, nobody means more to me than you.' She realized that, but it didn't make any difference. 'Werner, my boy,' she said—she still called me 'her boy,' even after nearly sixty years—'Werner, my boy, I don't want you to make any special allowances for me. As long as you're content with life, so am I.'"

The bridal pair sat side by side for hours that night. They reverently finished both bottles of wine. Eva was very silent. She wanted to say, "If your mother was such a wonderful person, she might even have accepted me." But it was too late for that now.

"I shall naturally attend my mother's funeral," Blomberg said, "—with you. Now she's gone, you're all I have left."

The general who had requested an interview with his Commander-in-Chief was a divisional commander from the Königsberg-East Prussia area, a military man whose self-assurance was exceeded only by his devotion to the Prussian officer's code.

Fritsch gave him a cool reception, partly because he resented the visitor's brusque and peremptory manner. He did not invite him to sit down but stood facing him stiffly across the desk.

"Well," he said, "what brings you here?"

The general's reply was militarily concise and delivered without the slightest hesitation. "It's the field marshal, sir. His marriage is quite unacceptable."

"I see," Fritsch said, still comparatively civil. "And what gives you the right to pronounce on his private life?"

"A German field marshal isn't a private individual, he's a symbol."

"He may also be a married man. In that capacity he can surely do as he pleases."

"Yes, sir, but only within certain well-defined limits. Our code of honour is absolutely clear on that point. None of our number can be permitted to involve himself with a person of doubtful repute—not to put too fine a point on it, with a whore."

"That's a monstrous charge, General. I hope you realize what you're saying. Have you given the matter careful thought?"

"Very careful thought, and I felt fully entitled to raise it, not as an individual but as the spokesman of numerous brother officers and fellow generals. Their demands are as follows: Herr von Blomberg must resign and you, sir, must compel him to. The honour of our nation is at stake."

"By which you doubtless mean something other than I do, General." Fritsch's smile was characteristically bleak.

"What counts is Herr von Blomberg's long and meritorious career, not his private life."

"But, sir, can't you see the inescapable implications of this latest development? By recklessly embarking on marriage, the field marshal has signed his professional death warrant. He's finished, so a successor will have to be found. In the opinion of a large section of the officer corps, on whose behalf I speak, there's only one possible choice—yourself."

"I didn't hear that," Fritsch said simply. "What's more, I flatly forbid my officers to engage in idle speculation. I'm a soldier, not a politician."

The funeral of Werner von Blomberg's mother took place in Berlin towards the end of January 1938. It was a dignified but simple ceremony. The officiating clergyman, who had been instructed to confine himself to the barest essentials, conjured up an atmosphere of Lutheran austerity in keeping with the character of the field marshal's late and greatly revered parent.

The weather was seasonable: temperature just above zero, sky overcast, no snow or rain. The rich brown soil which was to receive the plain oak coffin was heavy with moisture.

Those present—in addition to the pastor, the pallbearers and a protective screen of cemetery attendants—included almost every member of the Blomberg clan: the sons and their wives, the daughters and their husbands. Also present was General Keitel, who stared at the ground in an attitude of the deepest sorrow, but only so as to avoid looking his son's father-in-law in the eye if he dared to turn up. Although Blomberg was his patron and senior officer, their connection by marriage inspired a sense of reflected ignominy.

He gave a slight start when the field marshal arrived. Blomberg made a last-minute appearance but tactfully refrained from elbowing his way into the foreground. He was accompanied by a heavily veiled woman, presumably his wife.

Greeting and greeted by no one, the late arrivals stood frozen-faced and silent at the edge of the grave. They lingered there even when the coffin was lowered and earth began to patter on its lid.

"Ashes to ashes, dust to dust..."

Blomberg and Eva were the first to leave the cemetery, pursued by observant eyes. Arm in arm they hurried off—or "fled," as one witness put it.

On reaching the cemetery gate, however, they were accosted by one of Hitler's aides. He saluted smartly and delivered a message.

"I have the honour, sir, to convey our Führer's personal and heartfelt condolences on the occasion of your sad bereavement."

"Thank you," said Blomberg, not unmoved by the apparent sincerity of this gesture. "Kindly convey my deep appreciation of his sympathy."

"Certainly, sir. I have also been instructed to inform you that the Führer requests your continued presence in Berlin for the next few days. It may become necessary to consult you on matters of the utmost importance."

"Of course. I'm always at the Führer's service—please tell him that."

Blomberg half-raised his right hand to an imaginary cap or helmet. Then, remembering that he was not in uniform, he draped his arm protectively round Eva's shoulders. She was shivering.

7

Treachery
at the Top

From Counsellor Meller's notes—

The history of power politics is no real guide to what happened next. But, as so often, even this orgy of destruction had its humorous side.

There is firm evidence that Hitler had known of the "Fritsch file" for several months. We may also assume he knew of the Gruhn file. If he agreed to join Göring as a witness at Blomberg's wedding despite this, it can only have been because he thought it a peculiarly brilliant move. Hitler ruled men's destinies like a theatrical producer. That was why he could now afford to stage his

Twilight of the Generals on a truly Wagnerian scale:
superman versus dwarfs!

Three days before 26 January 1938, a date which was later
acknowledged to be historically crucial, the Führer and
Chancellor rearranged his list of appointments in Göring's
favour.

Göring was transparently delighted, even though he
made every effort to assume the grave and grief-stricken
demeanour of a man compelled to attend the obsequies of
someone whose death moved him deeply.

Hitler, who seemed to enjoy this spectacle did not omit
to glance at Colonel Hossbach with a twinkle in his eye. He
had summoned his Wehrmacht aide to be present—"a
highly confidential matter, so Göring assures me"—with
the evident intention of making him a witness. At this
point, he probably considered it essential to record who
had conveyed the fateful information and who had
received it. Apart from that, Hossbach's personal reaction
would be interesting in its own right.

Göring began by declaring how much he regretted
having to be the bearer of evil tidings. But alas, the facts
were incontrovertible. Although he found it hard to
broach them, he had always been noted for his candour.

"Yes, yes," said Hitler, who could hardly conceal his
glee and impatience. Another glance at Hossbach revealed
the colonel's mounting uneasiness, so he promptly
switched to a more businesslike tone. "Colonel Hossbach
and I aren't easily shocked, Göring. Let your facts speak
for themselves."

Göring fumbled in his briefcase and produced a slim
sheaf of papers, which he placed on the Führer's desk.

Hitler made no move to take them. He waited, partly for Hossbach's benefit, until Göring had summarized their contents.

"Item one, my Führer, contains various particulars concerning Herr von Blomberg's recent and regrettable marriage to a woman who has violated the public decency sections of the penal code on more than one occasion. Item two details aberrations of a homosexual nature. The person concerned is General von Fritsch."

Adolf Hitler drew in his breath with a sharp hiss. He seemed overwhelmed, cut to the quick, an impression he managed to sustain for some time. It conveyed that even he, the mightiest and most eloquent orator of his age, was temporarily at a loss for words. He turned an almost imploring gaze on his Wehrmacht adjutant, who was looking predictably dismayed and bewildered.

"This," Hitler blurted out at length, "—this is monstrous. I simply can't believe it." Colonel Hossbach bowed his head in what Hitler took to be a sign of mournful resignation. "Am I to be spared *nothing*!" he lamented.

Adolf Hitler was a gifted actor commanding a wide range of histrionic effects. He used them readily and, for the most part, convincingly. This was apparent even to Alfred Rosenberg, his devoted and assiduous cultural henchman. "The Führer," Rosenberg declared in one of his more perceptive moments, "is his own Shakespeare."

Göring, an actor whose more modest talents were to some extent enhanced by vocal power and sheer enthusiasm, joined Hitler in a thoroughly professional duologue. The Führer's first line was an unwitting echo of his latest victim's response to the news that he had been earmarked for a Gestapo frame-up.

"Everything inside me rebels at the thought of

accepting such a possibility, but I suppose I must. I assume, Göring, that this information of yours is one hundred per cent accurate?"

"It is, my Führer, and we'll have to make the best of it."

The Führer seemed ready to do just that, but not without a rider intended for his Wehrmacht aide. "This is a tragedy," he declared. "My heart bleeds." He turned to Hossbach as though urgently seeking his advice. "What do you say, Colonel?"

"The colonel is flabbergasted," said Göring, sounding grimly jocose, "—aren't you, Hossbach?"

Colonel Hossbach, a naturally truthful man, looked almost numb with shock. His face wore an expression of sorrow and solicitude. "Well—yes, I'm bound to admit I didn't think the field marshal's choice a particularly happy one. However, the most charitable course would be to treat his marriage as an entirely personal matter. Since you ask me, my Führer, I suggest we drop the subject."

"Precisely my own view, Hossbach!" Hitler's reaction sounded spontaneous. "On the other hand, are we justified in accepting such a situation? Can we expect the officer corps and the public to accept it? Is it historically defensible?"

Göring jumped in quickly. "What about the Fritsch case, Hossbach? What's your opinion on that?"

"Even simpler, General. Those charges against the Commander-in-Chief are absurd, not to say utter nonsense."

"You're forgetting the evidence in that file. It contains several statements."

"There may be something else involved," Hossbach said stoutly. "General von Fritsch is no friend of the Gestapo, everyone knows that. They might be only too happy to pin something on him. The first priority is to go to him and clear the air. I'd willingly approach him myself."

"What do you mean, Colonel?" Göring scowled menacingly. "Are you proposing to warn the general and give him a chance to cover his tracks? That would be asking for trouble. It would create innumerable problems—problems affecting national security. Is that what you want?"

"Knowing Colonel Hossbach as I do," Hitler interposed smoothly, radiating confidence, "I can assure you his constant concern in any dispute is to arrive at a fair and reasonable compromise. I'm sure that's so in this case, Hossbach, isn't it?"

"Absolutely, my Führer. That's why I beg you to let me confront General von Fritsch with these monstrous allegations. I feel sure the whole thing can be cleared up in minutes."

Hitler preserved a thoughtful silence. His gaze travelled from Hossbach to Göring, who sprang to life again.

"How can you be so naïve, Colonel? Homosexuals are notoriously corrupt. They're born liars and potential criminals. You can't expect a man of that type to admit his disgusting practices."

Hossbach clung to his dignity. "May I take it, General, that your remarks are of a purely abstract nature and do not presuppose the Commander-in-Chief's guilt?"

"Of course," Hitler put in quickly, aware Hossbach was anything but a yes-man. "But you must try to understand General Göring's justifiable concern."

"Yes, my Führer, but the more I try, the more essential it seems to ask General von Fritsch for his immediate comments."

"I don't think you'll do that." Hitler's tone was startlingly brusque. "Not if I expressly forbid you to."

"I'm sure Colonel Hossbach won't make any unauthorized moves," said Göring. "This matter has been discussed in absolute confidence. He wouldn't be here now if we didn't have the utmost faith in his discretion."

But Hossbach was unmoved. "I consider these charges premature, suspect, and unproven. They require urgent clarification. I request permission to investigate them at once."

"No," Hitler insisted, "not now—not yet. That's to say, not before they've been thoroughly investigated by me. Do I make myself clear, Colonel Hossbach?"

"Yes." Hossbach lingered over the word. "Your suggestion has been noted, my Führer."

"Let's hope you act on it," Göring threatened with an encouraging smile. "We value your cooperation, Colonel. You could go far—to the very top, with luck. I'm sure you wouldn't want to compromise your career. We need you, so be sensible."

Colonel Hossbach withdrew, leaving the Führer and his lieutenant alone. They brooded in silence for a minute or two. When he finally spoke, Göring sounded very apprehensive.

"If Fritsch gets to hear of this too soon he may go berserk."

"No," Hitler said firmly, "not Fritsch."

"What about his colleagues, though? I could name two or three corps commanders who are itching to launch a palace revolution."

"You don't know them, my friend—not as well as I do." Hitler was unperturbed.

Knowing what his master expected of him in perilous and precarious situations, Göring promptly showed his belligerent side. "Never mind, we'll straighten them out."

"We shall have to." Hitler thoughtfully stroked his chin. "Hossbach's reaction was quite unmistakable, but no matter. We've already identified our target and pulled the trigger. Nothing can stop the bullet from finding its mark." He paused. "As long as I can rely on you and your ammunition..."

"You can, my Führer. Anyone who isn't for us is against us, that's my motto, and I'm afraid it applies to Hossbach. He'll have to be replaced. There are plenty of eager candidates for his job—"

Colonel Hossbach didn't hesitate for an instant after leaving the Chancellery. He drove straight to the Tirpitzufer, where Commander-in-Chief Army presided over a warren of shabby offices linked by labyrinthine red-tiled corridors.

Here behind his uncluttered desk, as aloof and imperturbable as ever, sat General von Fritsch. There was, however, a hint of paternal affection in the way he greeted his visitor. Being a man of his own stamp and a member of his own set, Hossbach was always welcome.

"What brings you here, my dear Hossbach?"

"A matter of extreme delicacy, General."

"Come now, I'm proof against anything these days."

"I know I can be absolutely frank with you, General, but this time—well, I don't know where to begin. It's all most embarrassing."

"Embarrassing? For whom?" Fritsch had lost none of his composure.

Hossbach's confusion made him dodge the issue yet again. "It appears, General, that someone has had the audacity to charge you with a certain type of offence. The Central State Security Bureau is said to possess some sworn statements compiled in the course of a police investigation."

"Statements about what? Can't you be more specific?"

"Well, a form of sexual perversion—homosexual, to be precise. Please forgive me for imposing on you like this, General, but someone had to."

"You'll notice I'm not unduly surprised or shocked, Hossbach. Rumours of this type have been reaching me for some considerable time."

"That makes my task a lot easier, General. I'd have hated to be the first to broach the matter. Would you care to comment?"

"No, Hossbach, I wouldn't." Fritsch dismissed the question with dignity. "Suspicions of this kind are completely alien to me. Quite apart from that, I have no wish to see you involved in them. They are no business of yours."

Hossbach looked dismayed. "How am I to take that, General? Don't you trust me?"

"Of course I do, my dear Hossbach, but you aren't my father-confessor. You're more in the nature of a son—a favourite son, I admit, but fathers expect their offspring to have faith in them. To borrow your own question, don't you trust me?"

"That goes without saying, General, but please think carefully. These allegations are meant to destroy you. You *must* defend yourself against them before it's too late."

"If it ever came to that," Fritsch replied gravely, "one word would be enough—my word of honour. I should give the Führer my personal undertaking, and that would clinch the matter."

"You honestly think so?" Hossbach looked more dismayed than ever. "Haven't you seen through him yet? There's no one he wouldn't trample on if he had to, you included."

Fritsch smiled at him indulgently. "Ah, Hossbach, my boy, I was something of a rebel myself at your age. Since then I've learned a few things, one being that nothing and no one is perfect—no emperor, no political system, no national leader."

"So you're giving up?"

"No, Hossbach, I'm simply trying to make the best of a bad job."

"And you extend that principle to a man like Hitler?"

"The Chancellor is a fact of life. We have to live with him, but that doesn't mean we have to abandon all hope of doing so in a decent and responsible manner."

"And if we fail? What then?"

"I don't think we should be too quick to judge someone so obviously ordained by providence to lead his native land. In my experience, historic figures often rise to the tasks that confront them—rise and surpass themselves. Besides, no one would deny that Hitler is a man of many qualities."

"Precisely. The only question is, what sort?"

From the Meller report—

The next phase began at 10 A.M. on 25 January 1938. It inaugurated a firework display which was destined to last for several days, almost without a break, and included a series of set pieces unprecedented even in the colourful history of the Third Reich.

The event I refer to was an "extended staff meeting" at the Chancellery, "extended" implying that there would be no definite theme and no fixed agenda, just a general *tour d'horizon*. Topics for discussion were arbitrarily tabled or shelved by Hitler at the best of times, but on this occasion everything seemed even more nebulous than usual.

The attendance list itself presented certain puzzling

features and created an atmosphere of tense expectancy.
Hitler's personal advisers, several junior ministers, and the
Minister of Justice himself had been summoned, but the
occasion was further graced by Göring and Heydrich,
who turned up together with masklike faces. The cast list,
extras included, was virtually complete.

Hitler was the last to enter. He walked to his place
looking careworn, shoulders slightly drooping, arm limply
raised in the quasi-benedictory gesture that was his version
of the Nazi salute.

As Heydrich confided to me some hours later in his
most affable mood, "Half of them were scared shitless,
Erich. The Führer's expression spelt trouble. You could
almost see the tears in his eyes."

Hitler proceeded to inform those present of his
"profound disquiet" and "abiding concern." Why? Because of certain occurrences which might already have
come to their ears. "I keep asking myself how best to clear
the air without damaging the prestige of our country and
our armed forces."

He made no accusations, merely deplored what had
happened and expressed genuine anxiety. The cruder and
more blatant aspects of this well-planned assault he
delegated to his trusted lieutenant, Göring, who promptly
referred to "obscene behavior," "betrayal of our Führer's
faith" and, finally, to a "pigsty" which was "long overdue
for a cleanup."

Hitler kept well in character by taking exception to this
last remark. Nevertheless: "I must and shall do all in my
power to preserve my people from harm in the certain
knowledge that you, my colleagues and companions, will
lend me your fullest sympathy and support."

Heydrich's comment on this résumé: "That floored
them. Nobody said a word, naturally. There were no

objections—not even a whisper of dissent. He had them all neatly hog-tied."

"So he's got the audience he needs?"

"Exactly, Erich. The Führer's in the middle of the arena now. He can't leave until he's killed his bulls—three of them."

That same afternoon, the afternoon of 25 January 1938, Göring requested a brief meeting with Field Marshal von Blomberg. Its purpose, he hinted, was "highly confidential and extremely personal." The field marshal readily agreed.

Göring thanked him briskly. "In that case, may I invite you to call at my office? I wouldn't ask, but I've certain documents to show you, and I'd sooner they didn't leave the premises."

Blomberg, wearing civilian clothes, drove at once to the Air Ministry, a slablike fortress of concrete and glass. Göring received him in a vast office not unlike the one inhabited by his Führer.

"As I intimated on the phone, Herr von Blomberg, I don't intend to take up much of your time." Göring had, in fact, allowed only fifteen minutes for this interview. "I propose to brief you in confidence about a matter which will inevitably be raised at your next meeting with the Führer, probably tomorrow. May I proceed?"

"By all means." Still completely unsuspecting, Blomberg sat down. He gave his host a trusting smile, but Göring's very next words alarmed him. They were uttered with a melancholy expression and an undertone of sorrow.

"Herr von Blomberg," he said. He had recently taken to addressing him as "My dear fellow" but did not use the phrase on this occasion. "Herr von Blomberg, permit me to begin by reminding you of a certain fact. You saw fit to induce not only me but the Führer himself to attend your wedding in a formal capacity."

"Not induced, Herr Göring. I wouldn't have ventured to ask, even, but I was greatly honoured by your readiness to act as my witnesses. I shall always be grateful to you both."

"And very glad we were to attend, Herr von Blomberg. We did so in good faith—out of a natural sense of comradeship, so to speak. But now, I'm afraid—and I find it painful to have to say this—it transpires that we were the victims of a deplorable deception, if not a deliberate abuse of trust affecting the Führer's person. I don't care about myself, Herr von Blomberg, but you should never have subjected the Führer to such treatment."

Blomberg struggled for composure. "I don't know what you're talking about!" he said angrily.

"I'm talking about your marriage to that—that creature!"

"I take the strongest exception to your choice of words, General. You're referring to someone I love—to my wife."

"I beg your pardon," Göring trumpeted, "but you can hardly blame me for being disturbed by your wife's past."

"Her past? I took the precaution of emphasizing her humble origins when I asked you to approach the Führer on my behalf—our behalf. You did so, and I'm grateful to you. I fully conceded that our marriage couldn't be represented as 'suitable' in the conventional sense. It conflicted with the traditions of the officer corps, I know, but we both agreed that the time had come to adopt a more down-to-earth approach."

"Quite so, Herr von Blomberg, but there are limits."

"I still don't follow you."

"The Vice Squad has a file on your wife. Would you call that 'down-to-earth'?"

"Impossible!" Blomberg wavered between horror and indignation. "If any such records do exist, they must be based on false information. They may even be deliberate forgeries."

"They're official records nonetheless. I have them here, ready for your inspection."

"I decline to acknowledge their existence."

"But you should. I strongly advise you to brief yourself before seeing the Führer tomorrow morning."

"I trust the Führer implicitly. What's more, he trusts me."

Göring gave a pitying shrug. He had finally recognized Blomberg for what he was, a born loser.

Hitler would be able to deliver the coup de grâce with ease.

General Baron Werner von Fritsch was often regarded as an extremely complex, inscrutable, and idiosyncratic figure, though some people thought him childishly ingenuous. His response to the greatest crisis in his career was to bury himself in his work. The product of this strategic withdrawal was a tense and oppressive atmosphere in his immediate entourage.

The general put in eleven or twelve hours' work a day. One aide recalls that he seemed obsessed with the idea of completing his last major plans for Army reorganization. Another describes him as virtually unapproachable and totally uncommunicative at this period, but General Beck, the Army Chief of Staff, put it more simply: "He was the same as ever."

Other testimony comes from Fritsch's housekeeper, the baroness who looked after his domestic needs. "There was nothing to be done with him," she reported. "He'd never eaten much of a breakfast, but now he hardly bothered with lunch either, even at the mess—I checked. As for supper, it didn't matter what I gave him—even his mother's favourite dishes, which I had the recipes for—he barely touched a thing."

Corporal Schmiedinger may have been the only person who caught a glimpse of what was going on inside his general. He made persistent efforts to do so, partly because of an alarming report from his friend Sergeant Meier to the effect that Fritsch seldom went riding now. In other words, he was neglecting his horse—a sure sign of extreme agitation.

Schmiedinger commented on this in later years. "After all, what was I in those days? Just another member of the herd. As long as I grazed where they told me, there was a fair chance I wouldn't be sent for slaughter. Okay, so I felt like a dumb ox, but do you know what the general reminded me of? A statue of himself in marble—the kind you see on top of a tomb."

Hitler greeted Blomberg with a marked courtesy which did not conceal his obvious show of concern. Göring hovered in the background at first, a benign smirk on his face.

The Führer invited Blomberg to sit close beside him. For a few brief moments, all seemed unchanged.

"Of all the people I've met," Hitler said gently, "people who form part of my world, people to whom I owe much and feel deeply attached, none means more to me than you, my dear Herr von Blomberg."

The field marshal looked devoutly gratified. "Thank you, my Führer. Your sentiments are reciprocated in full."

"However," said Göring, in response to a quick glance from Hitler, "there's no escaping the gravity of the information that's come to light. I'm sorry, but there it is."

Blomberg shook his head. "It must be based on a misunderstanding."

Hitler stared pensively at his field marshal. "Perhaps," he began, "we should view it in the following light. Once upon a time, there was a young, attractive, and vivacious girl who grew up in the slough of the Weimar Republic before Berlin had been purged of its iniquities. She was merely a chance victim of the moral decay and unbridled promiscuity fostered by unscrupulous Jews."

"Thank you, my Führer!" Blomberg inclined his head. Hitler's remarks seemed to imply that he meant to play down the contents of the file on his desk.

"I'm sorry," Göring interposed, miming regret, "but I'm afraid it wasn't like that." Swiftly, he went on the attack. "The record shows that sums of money were paid for the said lady's favours—in other words, she was for hire. What's more, there are a number of compromising photographs on file, some of them flagrantly pornographic."

"But that's inconceivable!" Blomberg greeted his assertion with genuine horror. He gazed imploringly at the Führer, who sprang to his aid.

"You must be mistaken, Göring—surely!"

"No," Göring said harshly. "The evidence is perfectly official and absolutely conclusive. Would you like me to particularize?"

The Führer rose like a startled pheasant and began pacing to and fro near his desk. Blomberg watched him, ashen-faced but—even at this late stage—not entirely without hope. Göring deemed it wiser to keep silent.

"It goes against the grain even to acknowledge the possibility of such a thing!" Hitler said at last, in a tremulous voice. He stood rooted to the spot, fixing his field marshal with a magnetic gaze. "You certainly didn't deserve this, my dear Herr von Blomberg. Neither did I, for that matter. I've always considered you a man of honour, and I still do, but there's no point in disputing the official nature of those revolting allegations. If they prove well founded, they pose an inescapable question. What can be done to shield you from the consequences?'"

With Blomberg temporarily dumbstruck, Göring redoubled his activity. "A quick divorce might salvage something from the wreck. For instance, Herr von Blomberg might secure a decree of nullity on the grounds of gross deception and deliberate concealment of material information relating to the lady's antecedents. He need only make a formal break and . . ."

"I'll do nothing of the kind!" snapped Blomberg. Göring's suggestion had brought his willpower flooding back. He refused to be branded a man with no sense of honour or obligation. "She's my—my wife. Nothing can alter that."

"You've got a point there," Göring said. "Even if you did divorce her, she could still use your name for the rest of her life, and where would that leave us?"

"A depressing thought," mused Hitler. He gazed at Blomberg as though tormented by the possibility. "Nevertheless, we shall stop at nothing in our efforts to resolve this matter sensibly. That much I owe you."

Blomberg was immensely touched to note the extent of his Führer's personal concern. Boundless gratitude welled inside him. Hitler knew the meaning of true comradeship. He underlined this a moment later by turning to his lieutenant.

"Göring, you may leave us. Whatever happens next—
and something must be done without delay—will be
decided in private by the field marshal and myself."

It was not Corporal Schmiedinger who brought General
von Fritsch his usual glass of warm, sleep-inducing
milk—not tonight. For the first time in many years, his
housekeeper ventured into his bedroom.

Fritsch stared at her aghast. "My dear lady, the rules of
this house are simple and straightforward. I beg you to
observe them at all times, if only for your reputation's
sake."

"Rules can be broken, General."

Rumour had it that the baroness who ran Fritsch's
bachelor establishment was as old as Methuselah. This was
a myth. Widowed at an early age, she was the daughter of
a brother officer who had been killed in the first war.
Fritsch had semiadopted her. Now just over forty, she was
far from unattractive and might have been described as a
mature beauty of faintly Slav appearance. She had a small
but full-lipped mouth and a tip-tilted nose whose nostrils
tended to quiver slightly. Many men thought she emitted
an aura of languid but unmistakable sensuality. Fritsch
was not among them.

There was something strange about her tonight,
though—even he noticed that. Her tone was insistent
rather than deferential.

"Like it or not, General, I'm part of your life. Gratitude
isn't all I feel for you. I feel affection and admiration as
well. You ought to take advantage of that if ever the need
arises. Now, for instance."

"My dear lady!" Fritsch repeated, horror-struck. He sat
up in bed, taking care not to expose any part of his
anatomy. This presented little difficulty, because he

always wore closely woven ankle-length nightshirts—snow-white, of course. He regained his composure.

"Your presence is an unfailing source of pleasure to me, Baroness—but not here in my bedroom. You mean a great deal to me as a person. However, I'm not as unsophisticated as you might suppose. Such energy as I still possess is reserved for my official duties. It still suffices, but only for them. I hope you understand."

The baroness smiled. "I didn't expect you to say or do anything else, General. A form of personal insurance was all I had in mind—a safety measure, nothing more. A woman friend of mine has achieved some excellent results with it in Munich recently. If you like, we can take a leaf out of her book."

"I don't quite follow," said Fritsch, who followed very little these days.

"It's an unconventional but highly effective idea. She and her girlfriends got together on behalf of some male acquaintances—I use the term loosely—who were in danger of prosecution for certain offences. They systematically fabricated exonerating evidence in the shape of love letters referring to their passionate relationship with the suspects, reminiscing about the blissful times they'd spent together and longing for a repeat performance—and so on. In other words, they built up a defence not even the Gestapo could crack."

"But what are you trying to say?" Fritsch asked. "Precisely what do you take me for?"

"A man in danger, General. Grave charges are going to be brought against you, that's clear. They're groundless, of course, but you *must* take precautions. That's why I want to help you in the only way I can. Will you let me?"

Fritsch stiffened. "No, Baroness, certainly not! I wouldn't wish that on anyone, least of all you. And kindly note the following: I'm not a homosexual, so I can never be justly suspected of any such tendencies. I'm grateful for your offer of assistance but must naturally decline. I don't feel threatened in any way, I assure you. Whatever lies in store for me, I shall deal with it. Alone."

Göring disappeared through the doors of Hitler's study, which closed behind him. The Führer, who seemed profoundly uneasy, was left alone with Blomberg. They exchanged a long but not wholly despairing look. Finally, after some hesitation, Blomberg broke the silence.

"May I say something in complete confidence, my Führer? I don't understand Herr Göring's attitude. I'd always thought he was a friend of mine—or at least a loyal colleague."

"Which he is," said Hitler, "in his own peculiar way. However, Göring considers himself a political animal with a highly developed instinct for the potentialities of power. You must never forget that when dealing with him."

Blomberg's bewilderment persisted. "But I don't see what he's after. Does he hope to inherit my job?"

Hitler dismissed this supposition with a sweeping gesture. "Don't overrate him, Blomberg—and don't underestimate me. Why should I be willing to entrust him, of all people, with the Wehrmacht—our country's most valuable source of power? Göring lacks patience and industry, perseverance and creative insight. He may lend himself to employment as a figurehead—an impressive figurehead, sometimes—and he occasionally serves as a useful battering ram, but that's as far as it goes."

Blomberg, who felt that Göring had duped him, was not displeased to hear these confidences, especially as they offered a glimmer of hope. "Even so," he objected, "you did appoint him your *de facto* deputy."

"Yes, quite deliberately, because it marked him out as a number two—a second-rater, if you like. My most important associates, led by you as Commander-in-Chief of the Wehrmacht, must be absolutely first-rate. And that you always were, at least until this distressing affair."

"A misunderstanding, my Führer, not an affair."

"Whatever you choose to call it, my dear Blomberg, we must nip it in the bud."

"But how?"

"Well, one way would be to announce your intention of leaving this woman—but that you firmly decline to do. However much your attitude does you credit as a man, I, as head of state, am bound to deplore it. I can't simply destroy this file, so that leaves me no choice. I shall have to take steps to cover us both. Nobody could be sorrier than I am, Blomberg, but there it is."

The field marshal took several seconds to grasp the nature of the sentence that had just been meted out. While accepting the possibility, he would never have believed the axe could fall so swiftly. There was nothing to do but submit with soldierly good grace.

"I see," he said dully. "So you want my resignation."

"Let's phrase it a little differently," the Führer amended in sympathetic tones. "Like this, for example. You temporarily vacate your post and return it to my safekeeping, whereupon I grant you indefinite leave of absence. That will give you and your charming wife an opportunity to take an extended trip abroad which I—and please permit me to do this—shall personally finance. You will, of course, retain your field marshal's rank plus full pay and allowances. The pack will be baying at your heels, Blomberg. All that matters is to get you out of range as soon as possible. The rest you can safely leave to me."

"Thank you, my Führer. I appreciate your kindness and generosity more than I can say."

"Don't mention it. After all, I can't afford to dispense with a man of your talents. I shall continue to need you as an adviser, friend, and comrade-in-arms—especially if war comes, which seems inevitable."

"If it does, may I look forward to receiving an active command?"

"Of course. I shall insist on your reemployment in a major sphere of operations—one of vital strategic importance."

Blomberg gazed at the Führer with relief and gratitude. What a man, and how worthy of his trust! He was going to fix everything—salvage his reputation, preserve his name untarnished and his marriage intact. "Thank you," he said fervently.

"And now," said Hitler, "please lend me your continued assistance." Realizing that this intricate and not unhazardous part of his scheme had succeeded, he followed it up promptly. "The next point to consider is this. I shall have to appoint someone to deputize for you in your various capacities, but only on your recommendation. Do you have any ideas?"

Blomberg obediently knit his brow. The Führer needed him—he valued his advice! "Someone to deputize for me until the situation finally resolves itself..." he mused. "From the point of view of seniority, my Führer, Commander-in-Chief Army is the only possible candidate. It has to be General von Fritsch."

"A splendid man," Hitler said quickly. "Present company excepted, he's by far the best of my senior military commanders. I'd accept your recommendation on the spot—if I could afford to."

"What's to stop you, my Führer?"

"Something I'd never have thought possible. Fritsch has become the object of some very grave allegations. According to them, the general has persistently violated the penal code—to be more specific, those sections concerned with public decency."

"I'd heard something similar myself, off the record, but I never imagined there could be any truth to it. I'd be terribly sorry if there were. In either case, everything possible should be done to spare the general embarrassment."

"I quite agree. The matter will be thoroughly investigated, though I fear we must be prepared for the worst. That still presents us with the problem of finding you a suitable deputy." Hitler deliberately eschewed the word "successor." "It can't be Göring, and Fritsch is temporarily out of the running, so who does that leave?"

The harassed field marshal had a sudden flash of inspiration. It proved a direct hit. "Why not take over the post yourself, my Führer? Think of it! Führer, Chancellor, and Commander-in-Chief of the Wehrmacht—all the reins of power concentrated in one strong pair of hands. It would be an impressive combination."

"But a depressing prospect for me personally." Hitler rose and turned away with every sign of trepidation. He did not want Blomberg to look into his eyes, or they might have betrayed his triumph. He stopped pacing and came to a halt in front of him.

"I should be profoundly reluctant to shoulder any additional burden, but if that's your advice I must give it serious consideration." A thought seemed to strike him. "Especially as it would, in a sense, neutralize the post until you resume when the dust has settled—as I shall ensure that it does."

Still unwitting, Blomberg drove the last nail into his

own coffin. "Until then, my Führer, I'm sure there couldn't be a better solution."

Late on the afternoon of 26 January 1938, a number of people assembled in the Chancellery at Hitler's behest.

One of them was General Baron Werner von Fritsch, Commander-in-Chief of the Army. He had been summoned by Colonel Hossbach, who greeted him at the main entrance, respectfully but with deep anxiety. "Be careful, sir," he whispered, "—very careful!"

Someone else was simultaneously sneaked in through a side entrance, namely Otto Schmidt, appearing in his well-rehearsed role as witness for the prosecution. He was escorted by two wooden-faced Gestapo officers. Meisinger would normally have been in charge of the party but was absent on leave, so the party was led by one Detective Superintendent Huber.

Hitler received Fritsch in the Chancellery library with Göring at his elbow. He greeted the general with a carefully gauged nod. Fritsch responded with a smart salute and was promptly accosted by the Führer's lieutenant.

"Frightful business, this, eh!" Göring ventured in friendly tones.

"Indeed," said Fritsch.

Despite his air of infinite dejection, Hitler roused himself sufficiently to address the general with a faint note of menace. "I deeply regret having to submit you to this confrontation, my dear General. All that consoles me is the certainty that it will prove absolutely unproductive from the Gestapo's point of view. That would dispose of this whole obnoxious affair. Is my confidence justified?"

"I give you my word of honour," Fritsch said calmly. "I

have nothing to fear from such allegations—nothing whatever."

"I accept that without question. However, the decision no longer rests with me. These charges are a matter of record. They will have to be dealt with."

"Then let's get it over with!" cried Göring, beaming with malicious glee. "It'll only take a minute or two. Are you ready, General?"

"Yes," said Fritsch. "If you really consider it necessary—yes."

Göring bustled on ahead and flung open the door to the stairs. Hitler courteously invited Fritsch to precede him.

The landing was brilliantly lit. Every detail stood out with preternatural clarity—gleaming marble, crimson stair carpet, gilt and crystal chandeliers. Four men were standing at the foot of the stairs: Huber, the two Gestapo officers, and, flanked by his escorts, Otto Schmidt.

The quartet gave two Hitler salutes in quick succession, one when they caught sight of Göring and another when the Führer himself appeared. They gazed reverently upwards. Otto felt overcome. He had known his great moment was at hand but never imagined it would be as awe-inspiring as this. His bowels churned with excitement.

Yet it was all quite simple, he told himself. He had only to behave as Meisinger had instructed him a score of times with the aid of numerous photographs. Besides, he had already caught two glimpses of his prospective victim in the flesh—distant glimpses but quite close enough for identification. A pair of Gestapo officers had pointed him out while riding in the Tiergarten.

The crucial question was put to Huber by the Führer himself. "That man you've brought along—ask him if he's met anyone present, and if so where."

Huber just said, "Well, Schmidt?"

"Yes, yes—I know that gentleman!" Excitement had reduced Otto's voice to a hoarse croak. "That's him—I'd know him anywhere!" He took a step forward and pointed straight at Fritsch. "That's him all right. I saw him at Wannsee Station..."

The Führer addressed Huber once more. His tone was brusque, businesslike, and imperious. "Ask your witness if he's absolutely certain."

"Well, Schmidt?"

"No, there's no mistake. I'd swear to it in court if I had to."

Göring leant against the wall, breathing stertorously. Hitler looked thunderstruck. Fritsch confined himself to a disdainful shrug. "Quite absurd," he murmured.

"See that?" cried Otto, ad-libbing. "I'd know him just by the way he shrugs his shoulders—it's a sort of habit he's got!" The two Gestapo watchdogs gave him an approving glance. Huber stared at the floor. "It was him all right," Otto repeated, "I'd stake my life on it."

Göring's indignation seemed to get the better of him. "That," he said with every sign of horror and disgust, "will be quite enough."

It looked as if he was right.

From the Meller report—

A lot of people thought this "confrontation" a gamble from the Gestapo's point of view. It was, in fact, little more than the product of a thorough advance evaluation of the general's behaviour patterns. Given his disastrous naïveté, Fritsch's reactions could be predicted with consummate ease, especially by a shrewd judge of character like Hitler.

It was conceivable that another man subjected to this

terrible ordeal—which did not remain a lone example—
might have vented his wrath, if not on the Führer, at least
on Göring. A veteran general of the hardier type would
certainly have tried to bully this suspect "witness" in the
approved parade-ground manner.

Equally, one can visualize the reaction of a solidly
self-assured general like Beck, the Army Chief of Staff. He
would probably have been outraged and stalked off,
contemptuously turning his back on the Führer and
Göring alike. Fritsch did nothing of the kind.

Huber gave me a first-hand description of the picture
he presented: "At first, he just stood there like a statue. He
didn't flinch—he stood firm. Against what? Well, against
Fate, you might say. He obviously believed justice would
prevail. It hadn't dawned on him that the dice were loaded
against him."

Georg Huber, a well-trained and thoroughly objective
observer, had obviously been in the right place at the right
time. "So it's a criminal conspiracy," I said. "Even you
accept that now."

"Oh, sure," said Huber, "but knowing something and
proving it are two different things. State Security have
probably withheld various pieces of evidence. I might be
able to do something if I could get at them, but I haven't
managed to yet. Maybe you can help a little there,
Counsellor. Through your friend Heydrich, I mean."

I promised to try, but with no real hope of success. If
this back-stage drama were really as suspect as it looked, it
couldn't be spun out indefinitely. And a smart operator
like Heydrich might well be alive to the fact.

Fritsch could be expected to hit back as soon as the case
reached court. He would then be armed with a defence
counsel—preferably one of our own men—who could
speak out on his behalf and present all the arguments

Fritsch himself was either unwilling to advance or inhibited by his very character from bringing into the open.

Göring, who believed that one of his finest hours had struck, flung himself into a bravura display of histrionics.

Immediately after Otto's cry of "That's him!" and his own cry of "That's enough!" the Führer's deputy made an elephantine dash from the landing to the library. Here, breathless and sweat-beaded, he made an announcement to all who cared to listen—aides, advisers, domestic staff, and Colonel Hossbach.

"It was him! It was him!"

He then hurled himself onto the nearest sofa, which miraculously withstood his weight. Next, according to the unanimous testimony of several eyewitnesses, he proceeded to "howl" as if in "extreme agony of mind." Close to tears, and with his hands clasped to his face, he uttered a third despairing cry.

"It was him!"

Numerous observers watched Göring's solo performance, some with compassion. The more devoted members of Hitler's Chancellery staff looked quite emotional themselves. Not so Colonel Hossbach, who made yet another disagreeable exhibition of himself by boldly questioning the cause of Göring's grief.

"Who would you rather believe, a small-time criminal or a general?"

Göring sat up like a sleeper jolted awake. He lowered his hands, still looking agonized, but his grim determination was all too plain. "The Führer has the highest regard for General von Fritsch. So do I. Kindly remember that, Colonel."

"With pleasure, General, but what form does your regard take?"

Göring heaved his colossal bulk erect. He already weighed well over three hundred pounds and had a tendency to consume vast quantities of food in times of crisis. Not a larder at Karinhall was safe from his depredations, even in the small hours.

"There's nothing I wouldn't do for the Führer, the Reich, or the Wehrmacht," he groaned piteously, "and the same goes for your friend—our friend—the general. I'm going to dig him out of this mess if it's the last thing I do, Colonel, take my word for it."

Meanwhile, Hitler had retired to his study with the Army Commander-in-Chief. Once there, he slumped into a leather armchair near the window, looking exhausted, and limply waved Fritsch into the chair beside his own.

"What an appalling situation!" Hitler's eyes stared vacantly into an imaginary fog bank. "How are we going to extricate ourselves, that's what I want to know?"

"This affair is more than an unparalleled piece of effrontery, Chancellor. It goes against the grain to say so, but it may be a malicious conspiracy—an indirect attack on the Army through me."

Hitler stared at him. "You don't seem unduly perturbed by these accusations—in fact, you seem to be taking them calmly. May I ask why?"

"For two reasons, Chancellor. First, the charges against me are absolutely unfounded, and second, I trust you."

"As well you may."

Hitler could afford to give this assurance with an easy mind. Sooner or later, even men of granite like Fritsch crumbled, collapsed, and fell to dust. He knew from experience that this process could be accelerated.

He appeared to receive prompt confirmation of this when Göring bustled in.

"Everyone's horrified!" he proclaimed funereally. "Of course, I've done my best to calm them down. I hinted that the Führer would sort things out. Was I right?"

"Absolutely," said Hitler, still looking at Fritsch. "Please don't think I'd ever believe you capable of such conduct, General. Far from it, but we must try and deal with this embarrassing situation somehow. The question I ask myself—and you—is, how?"

"No problem there," Göring said gleefully, right on cue. "Herr von Fritsch retires—he resigns his post at once. That will spare him any further embarrassment and guarantee him immunity from prosecution. Wouldn't that be the best answer, my Führer?"

Hitler expressed his prompt but qualified assent. "Perhaps, but my own suggestion would be as follows. We let it be known that the general has been granted indefinite leave of absence for medical grounds. It's already been rumoured that you're gravely ill, General, so a statement along those lines would simplify matters considerably. No fuss! None of us could afford that at this stage."

"Quite right," said Göring, following up fast. "We'll let the dust settle, then we can see what to do next. The main thing to remember is this, General. The Führer is determined to retain your services."

"Indeed I am," Hitler agreed with some solemnity. "I have two courses in mind, General. One, if we succeed in clearing the air as quickly and thoroughly as I believe we shall, you can resume your duties at once. Two, I would then invite you to become Herr von Blomberg's successor."

"Not through any wish of mine, Chancellor."

"Perhaps not, but we must allow for every contingency. Anyone who has served me as loyally as you, General, deserves to be suitable rewarded."

"In what way?"

"My dear Herr von Fritsch, please note the following points. If, after this problem has been resolved, you wish to resume your duties as Commander-in-Chief Army, do so, by all means. If you were further prepared to accede to my wish and take command of the armed forces as a whole, I should be delighted. There is, however, a third possibility."

"Which is?"

Hitler gave Fritsch an amiable, statesmanly, beguiling smile. "I should invite you to go to Moscow as our ambassador. I need hardly tell you what a mark of trust this would be. Soviet Russia is the ultimate threat to our nation and the Western world. I need an absolutely dependable man there—someone capable of thinking in military terms. Someone of your calibre, General."

"Congratulations!" cried Göring. "The Führer is making things easy for you. What more do you want?"

"Only one thing," Fritsch said with utter simplicity. "My name has been sullied. I want it cleared."

"But how?" Göring bellowed. "How, without harming the country?"

"Our country's true worth can be only gauged by the proven integrity of its leading citizens." Fritsch was still convinced of this, even now. "No stigma must attach to a man in my position. I therefore request the appointment of a court of honour and will gladly appear before it in due course."

From his point of view, there was no more to be said. He stood there stiffly, his monocle glinting like a beacon. Then he saluted and withdrew, dragging his feet a little.

A clear and frosty winter's night greeted him when he left the Chancellery, silently escorted by Hossbach. Fritsch removed his cap and took several deep breaths. He seemed to be smiling faintly, perhaps at himself. Whatever the reason, he was smiling just the same.

Extract from the Meller report—
The lines of battle had been drawn at last. As any insider could have predicted, Fritsch had refused to take the easy way out. No one could horse-trade with a man like him.

He confided some of his impressions to me and Colonel Oster immediately after this interview. He had, he said, been struck by the number of stock phrases used, like "in the event of," "to the extent that," "should the situation arise," "use our best endeavours," "make every effort to"—in other words, the sort of language that doesn't figure in my lawyer's vocabulary because of its imprecision. It all sounded ambiguous.

"Very perceptive of you, General," Oster told him. "Those two"—he meant Hitler and Göring—"are a pair of devious, double-dealing liars. You must do the logical thing. Confront them head-on, and a lot of people will back you to the hilt."

I wholeheartedly and enthusiastically endorsed this— even I had my reckless moments!—but the general merely fixed us with a stern gaze.

"I'm a soldier, gentlemen, not a revolutionary. I've already taken the only course I care to contemplate by insisting my name be cleared. As I see it, any slur on me is a slur on the Army."

8

General
Retreat

By 4 P.M. on 26 January 1938, the Chancellory had
received another visitor. The man who answered Hitler's
summons was soon to prove one of his most faithful
henchmen and remained so to the bitter end. His name
was Wilhelm Keitel.

Keitel headed the Wehrmachtamt, or Armed Forces
Department, which made him a close associate and
immediate subordinate of Field Marshal von Blomberg.
He had presided over the department since 1935, not least
because of his personal connection with the field marshal.

Hitler was naturally aware of this. He had studied the
relevant papers and, with a swiftness of perception all his

own, picked out the essential point. Apart from being a
fine figure of a man, Keitel fitted the popular conception
of an adaptable subordinate and was generally regarded
by his peers as "pleasant to work with." The Führer's
manner towards him was correspondingly civil.

"My dear Herr Keitel," he said, feeling his way with
unerring skill, "these latest developments have come as a
great personal shock. I have always cherished the highest
regard for Blomberg. That he should have become
embroiled in such a deplorable situation grieves me
deeply, as I'm sure it does you, being a friend *and* relative.
You both served with the same regiment in the last war,
didn't you?"

"We commanded infantry units in adjacent sectors of
the front line, my Führer. A splendid soldier, the field
marshal—a man of supreme refinement but remarkably
warm and human as well. And now this!"

Hitler looked solemn. "We mustn't be too quick to
condemn him. On the other hand, distressing as the facts
appear to be, we must take them into account. How do
you see matters, Herr Keitel?"

"It's a difficult business, my Führer, I know that all too
well. I tried to reason with the field marshal. I even went so
far as to describe his present wife as a potentially
undesirable character and his marriage as an utterly
unsuitable liaison which ought to be terminated without
delay."

"Your advice was wasted, of course," Hitler said
confidently. "It says a lot for him as an individual, but I
happen to be our country's Führer and Chancellor. Can
you see what conclusions *I* am forced to draw?"

"Of course, my Führer. There's no room for compromise in a situation of this sort. Our officer corps has a
long-established code of honour. To flout it would be a

disgrace, if not a threat to national security. I've impressed that on Werner—I mean, the field marshal—over and over again, and I haven't minced my words. I told him as much only last night."

"And how did he react?"

"He flatly rejected what he called my 'presumption' and assured me that his marriage was a love match—in fact, he even said he'd sooner blow his brains out than give the woman up. He actually had tears in his eyes!"

"How tragic!" said Hitler, looking deeply moved. "And how regrettable for us all! We shan't be able to count on him for an indefinite period, I fear, but our work must go on. Nobody's indispensable, so the saying goes. It doesn't apply to my good friend Blomberg, but we shall have to try and cope without him. Can you suggest a possible successor, General?"

"Ordinarily I'd have said General von Fritsch, but he's ruled out too now—for the time being."

"More's the pity." Hitler bowed his head.

"There's always General Göring, but I hear you don't intend to give him the job."

"True," said Hitler.

"That narrows the field to one. As Führer and Chancellor, you must fill the post yourself."

"I take it you're aware the field marshal made a similar suggestion? He was most insistent that I should assume personal command of the armed forces."

"It would certainly be the best solution," Keitel said promptly.

"I view the whole prospect with reluctance, but I suppose there's no alternative." Hitler paused. "If I follow your advice, I shall need a man at my side I can trust and depend on to the hilt—you, General! I'm sure the field marshal will approve of my choice. Would you be

prepared to continue as head of the Wehrmachtamt but
with considerably wider responsibilities, increased powers, and greater seniority—financially speaking too, of
course? You would also work closely with me. What do
you say?"

General Keitel was overwhelmed. "My Führer," he said
humbly, "I accept."

"Thank you. Devote some constructive thought to the
subject and let me have your ideas as soon as possible—by
one P.M. tomorrow, let's say. I'm putting a good deal of
faith in you."

General Baron Werner von Fritsch, Commander-in-Chief
of the Army, was plagued with insomnia in the nights that
followed. He laced his glass of milk with brandy or drank a
bottle of wine to numb his aching brain, but even then he
remained awake for hours, haunted by dark and
amorphous phantoms.

Lying stiffly on his back with his arms clamped to his
sides, he stared at the ceiling. Often, when it was long past
midnight and the chill winter darkness closed in on him, he
seemed to see, flickering wanly like a silent movie, the
various stages in his career.

Himself as a child, grave-faced even then. Beside him,
his mother, gazing down kindly but just as unsmiling. He
longed to nestle against her warm body but dared not.
Then as a soldier in the Great War. Still a boy but already
an officer and, as such, a youthful father to the men from
whom he never asked more than he demanded of himself.
He refused all preferential treatment, shared his meals
with them, slept in the same trenches, and led them into
battle. Finally, as a general toiling day and night for the
reconstruction, as he saw it, of his country, intent on

nothing save the restoration of Germany's military prestige and her national resurgence—a man who was known as Prussia incarnate.

He had no private life as even soldiers understood the term. No boisterous mess parties for him, no gastronomic orgies, no gossip among friends. No women either. He was a man who lived by a self-imposed code. Service was his lifelong watchword and the sole criterion of his increasingly Spartan existence.

What hurt him personally, defied his comprehension, and caused him to brood for hour after sleepless hour, was the Chancellor's attitude to him. And so, at this stage in his honest confusion, he hit on the idea of writing Adolf Hitler a letter.

In it, he thanked the Führer in moving terms for the trust bestowed on him—"save in this case"—and expressed the confident hope that his head of state would continue to extend him the goodwill and understanding he had always enjoyed in the past. Hitler's role in the plot still escaped him, just as he failed, even now, to detect the complicity of Hermann Göring and several fellow generals.

"God Almighty," said Corporal Schmiedinger, "the general's at the end of his rope. How could they do such a thing to a fine man like him?"

The general's friend and physician, Professor Dr. Karl Nissen, gave it as his sober professional opinion that Fritsch was on the verge of collapse, deeply depressed, and suffering from acute nervous exhaustion. "One cannot," he said, "rule out the possibility of suicide."

The members of his immediate circle, notably his aides, made no secret of their sympathetic concern but were powerless to help. Why? Because their Commander-in-Chief, that retiring and ultrasensitive soul whom some had

lately described as dangerously "introverted," seemed to
be in an almost pathological state of submission to—of all
people—Hitler, whom he evidently regarded as his
"destiny."

Fritsch was still in this disastrous condition when he
received a visit from his predecessor as Commander-in-
Chief Army, General von Hammerstein, a tough, resolute
character who felt "sickened" by Hitler and blithely said
so to anyone prepared to listen. He marched in and looked
Fritsch up and down with grim solicitude.

"Good God, man, surely you're not going to let these
people walk all over you?"

"My dear Hammerstein," Fritsch replied gloomily,
"however much it may look as if they're trying to destroy
my reputation, I refuse to demean myself by stooping to
their level."

"Very noble of you, I'm sure!" Hammerstein gave a
snort of derision. "My dear General, we're up against a
bunch of swine whose sole ambition is to gorge themselves
and wallow in filth—that's all they're fit for. Haven't you
ever taken a close look at that man Göring?"

This was distasteful language to someone of the
Commander-in-Chief's refinement. He knew Hammerstein as a fire-eater who doggedly pursued a patriotic line
of his own. His frequent references to "that charlatan"
Hitler were assuming the dimensions of a public scandal.
A confirmed disciplinarian like Fritsch belonged to an
entirely different world—one governed solely by a
soldier's oath of allegiance. He reacted with due dismay
and disapproval, especially when Hammerstein grew
even more outspoken. "General, you're Commander-in-
Chief Army. You only have to say the word—we're all
waiting."

Fritsch uneasily brushed the implication aside. "I prefer not to understand you, Herr von Hammerstein."

But Hammerstein was undeterred. "General, I came here to deliver a message on my own behalf and that of several colleagues. We're ready. One word from you and we'll march wherever you point us."

"I still don't understand," said Fritsch, rising abruptly. "In fact, I didn't even hear what you said."

"But you'll think about it," his visitor retorted without rancour. "Don't take too long, though. Time's running out."

Within minutes of this clash, the Commander-in-Chief received a visit from his Chief of Staff, Ludwig Beck, someone of very different mettle from the rugged warrior who had just left. Beck was universally regarded as a shrewd intellectual and natural aristocrat who needed no "von" to advertise his nobility. He might have been predestined to figure prominently in a book entitled *Great Germans*—which he eventually did.

It would not be long before Ludwig Beck's opposition of the Führer's more and more patently warlike plans became so unmistakable that he was banished to the wilderness. Hitler adopted the course he found effective in such cases by retiring him honourably on full pay. He was not snuffed out until the night of 20–21 July 1944, when the attempt on Hitler's life had failed.

At this stage, however, he seemed quite as unable to fathom the course of developments as his friend and comrade, Fritsch. His attitude was puzzled but dignified. "I simply can't believe," he said, "that anyone would act with such an unparalleled lack of scruple. I can't believe it even of a man like Hitler."

"Nor can I," said Fritsch. "But the whole affair will soon

be settled. The Chancellor has strongly advised me to sort
it out with the department in possession of this spurious
evidence."

Beck's eyebrows shot up. "The Gestapo? Surely you
aren't going to get involved with that crowd?"

"I'd rather sup with the devil than let things drag on. If
the Chancellor himself recommends it, why should I
hesitate?"

The Army Chief of Staff looked highly perturbed.
"Allow me to remind you of something. Jurisdiction over
the Army and Wehrmacht is vested in our own military
courts. No other authority in the country has any legal right
to intervene, least of all a branch of the SS. You've always
insisted on upholding that rule."

"For my subordinates, yes, never for myself. I have
nothing to hide. Why shouldn't I consent to such an
interview?"

"You know how ruthless they are. This interview of
yours could degenerate into an interrogation with all the
usual trimmings. What would you do then?"

Fritsch looked steadfastly optimistic. "My conscience is
absolutely clear."

On 27 February 1938, only twenty-four hours after their
first meeting, General Keitel was given every opportunity
to gladden his Führer's heart. The conference began at 1
P.M. It lasted nearly three hours and got off to a promising
start. Hitler's manner was as cordial as before.

"Your friend and comrade-in-arms, Herr von Blomberg, is our country's senior soldier and will remain so. For
the moment, however, he must be granted a long leave. I
suggest twelve months, preferably spent abroad."

Keitel swiftly grasped that he was expected to convey

some form of approval. "An excellent decision, my Führer. Most appropriate!"

"I propose to place at least fifty thousand marks at his disposal, drawn from my private funds. I shall instruct the Reichsbank to pay this sum in any foreign currency required, at a favourable rate of exchange. Would you consider that appropriate too, Herr Keitel?"

"More than that, my Führer. It's extremely generous of you."

"I try to be generous—to borrow your own expression—whenever I think circumstances warrant it. I'm particularly generous to my friends, but I also have opponents—enemies, even. A man in my position has to allow for that, which makes it doubly important for me to have aides and advisers I can trust implicitly. I should be delighted to include you among them from now on."

"You may, my Führer. Your wish is my command."

A momentous pact had been sealed. At long last, Hitler had found the general he needed—a uniquely dependable recipient and transmitter of orders. As soon as he realized this, he got down to business.

"Herr von Blomberg's marriage has caused the Wehrmacht extreme embarrassment. We shall now make a concerted effort to dispel that. I see every prospect of success, especially as the field marshal himself, to his credit, is doing all he can to avoid harming the national interest. However, that still leaves the Fritsch case."

"You think he's guilty?"

"Certainly not! I've always thought most highly of the man—that's why I put him in charge of the Army. General von Fritsch has fulfilled all my expectations, and you can say so to anyone who expresses interest. I stand by that statement, but I must also bow to reality."

Keitel was an attentive listener. He had a marked

capacity for reading other people's thoughts, notably Hitler's, and retained it almost intact for seven long years. "You came to an arrangement with Blomberg," he said cautiously. "Couldn't we do the same with Fritsch?"

"That's just what I've already tried to do, my dear Keitel—several times. His health is poor, as you know. I offered him a long spell of sick leave on the most favourable terms, but he won't hear of it. He's being dangerously obstructive. He insists on a complete rebuttal of the charges against him."

"You mean he actually *wants* some form of legal hearing, my Führer?" Even now, Keitel was displaying an admirable knack of echoing his master's ideas. "That could be risky from his point of view."

Hitler nodded, then handed him a document. It turned out to be a written opinion supplied by the then Minister of Justice, Franz Gürtner, and was all the Führer could have wished for from such a dependable source. The nub of Gürtner's comments on the "Fritsch case" read as follows:

"As the record stands, it could furnish the Director of Public Prosecutions with grounds for an indictment."

In other words, the country's senior judicial officer had declared that it would be legitimate to proceed against Fritsch. With that matter provisionally settled by himself and his new-found confidant, Hitler swiftly passed to another point.

"Tell me, Keitel, what do you think of Hossbach?"

The general realized at once that this question required an unequivocal answer. "Hossbach is a man of integrity, I'm sure, but he can hardly be described as an officer imbued with the true National Socialist spirit. I seem to recall Blomberg telling me, in the strictest confidence, that he found him very trying."

"Precisely my own opinion, Keitel, and his recent

behaviour has only confirmed it. Hossbach warned Fritsch prematurely of the charges pending against him. What's more—and you'll hardly credit this—he did so in defiance of my express order to refrain from any such action. What do you say to that!"

"Outrageously irresponsible conduct, my Führer, and utterly unworthy of a German officer!" Keitel shared his master's indignation. "Fortunately, General von Fritsch is a levelheaded and self-disciplined individual. I shudder to think what someone more impetuous might have done in his place." He paused. "So Hossbach has disqualified himself from further employment as your aide."

"Precisely." Hitler gave several nods of approval. "So one of your first jobs will be to find a suitable replacement as quickly and unobtrusively as you can."

"Of course, my Führer. From what I gather, Colonel Hossbach has often expressed a wish to return to field duties. We mustn't disappoint him. I think the best answer would be a regimental command as far from Berlin as possible, perhaps in East Prussia."

"Excellent, Keitel, excellent! Draft some suitable recommendations—likewise on the appointment of a new Commander-in-Chief Army. I need someone absolutely trustworthy in that post. Will you give your mind to the problem?"

"Certainly, my Führer."

Each man felt he had found the ideal teammate. Their partnership was, in fact, destined to produce some cataclysmic decisions—decisions which shattered a country and destroyed a nation, not to mention scores of millions of lives.

"So we're agreed, General." Hitler's voice took on a portentous note. "I shall swallow my reluctance and assume personal command of the Wehrmacht—

unofficially, for the time being, though we shan't be able
to postpone an announcement for long. You have now
become one of my principal confidants and advisers. As of
now, you will have access to me at any time and place
without prior notification. I hereby appoint you head of
the Wehrmacht High Command."

It dawned on Keitel that he had become virtually
indispensable to his country's supreme leader.

Deeply moved, he gave a pledge which he kept for the
seven or eight years of life that remained to him.

"My Führer, I shall always strive to justify the faith you
have placed in me."

From early the same morning onwards, turmoil reigned at
No. 8 Prinz-Albrecht-Strasse, otherwise known as the
Central State Security Bureau.

Gruppenführer Heydrich prowled the offices like a
wolf, snapping and snarling in a way which betrayed
pent-up excitement. Discounting his own office, the grey
stone box of a building looked shabby and neglected as a
result of the activities that went on there day and night.
The torture chambers in the basement were almost always
occupied.

But even in this building there was one room that
looked comparatively civilized, though its sumptuous
décor contrasted almost grotesquely with the rest of the
interior. Gestapo cognoscenti referred to it, usually with a
faint smirk, as the "front parlour," but its official title was
Interrogation Room No. 1. It was reserved for very special
visitors, one of whom was expected at any moment.

Two men were lurking in this plush-and-mahogany lair.
One was the Gestapo's senior legal adviser, Dr. Werner
Best, whose professional expertise still commanded some

respect outside Prinz-Albrecht-Strasse. Beside him sat a detective superintendent named Huber, who owed his presence to Counsellor Meller's recommendation. A crimson folder lay in front of each.

Heydrich stalked into the room and treated its occupants to a cold stare—his "official look," as the department called it. "Think he'll turn up?" he asked, meaning Fritsch.

"Why should he?" drawled Huber, lolling back in his chair. "The Gestapo doesn't have any jurisdiction over the armed forces. I expect he knows that. If not, some of his friends will have pointed it out."

Heydrich shrugged. "But he accepted the Führer's advice."

"Yesterday or the day before, perhaps." Huber's tone was discreetly provocative. "There are any number of reasons why he may have changed his mind since then. Anyway, I know what I'd do in his place..."

Heydrich nodded at the superintendent with a hint of approval. He liked the look of him. Huber evidently wasn't a yes-man. So Erich Meller had sent him a hound, not a lapdog... Well, a man of his own superior calibre could use assistants like that.

He turned an inquiring gaze on Dr. Best, the Gestapo's trusty legal expert. Best felt obliged to endorse the policeman's view but amplified it in accordance with his own.

"Well, yes—he's under no compulsion to come, naturally. All the same, Fritsch is a man with a strong sense of duty, at least, so I'm led to believe. My guess is, he'll keep his promise." He glanced at his watch. "Another three minutes to go. I'm banking on the general's punctuality—it's one of his foibles."

Best was right. Punctual to the minute, General Baron

Werner von Fritsch marched into Gestapo headquarters
wearing a dark-grey civilian suit. It was 10 A.M. precisely.

A young SS officer had been detailed to meet him at the
entrance. He gave the general a snappy salute and
respectfully conducted him through the shabby but
spacious hall. Some anonymous figures cringed back
against the walls to let him pass—two dozen of them, all
male, all watching him. They were a motley collection,
some unkempt and seedy, with worn faces and dull eyes,
others almost feminine in their good looks and daintily
affected movements, others barrel-chested and bulging
with muscle like professional wrestlers, but all subjected
Fritsch to the same glassily indifferent stare of appraisal.
They were homosexuals interspersed with Gestapo
gorillas, and they had gathered for a look at Heydrich's
latest exhibit.

This process was known in Prinz-Albrecht-Strasse
parlance as a "mannequin parade." It differed from an
identity parade in that a single suspect was displayed
before a number of potential witnesses. Most of these
witnesses were professional informers, and all were
guaranteed "bonuses" or other concessions in the event of
a positive ID.

Fritsch strode haughtily through this sordid array of
would-be prosecution witnesses. He ignored their existence—especially as the reason for their presence
completely escaped him—and marched straight on with
his usual brisk, unswerving tread.

The SS officer ushered him politely into Interrogation
Room No. 1. Heydrich had just slipped out through
another door after receiving the news of Fritsch's arrival
by telephone, but not before he had exhorted Best and
Huber to "do their damndest." Best got off to a good start

by hurrying over to Fritsch and extending a courteous welcome.

"Thank you for coming, General. I should like to begin by assuring you that my instructions, which come from the highest possible source, are to treat you with the utmost consideration and do everything in my power to clear your name."

"Delighted to hear it," said the unsuspecting Fritsch. "After all, why shouldn't I put myself in your hands? In the first place, you're a public servant. In the second, I've done nothing to be ashamed of. My dearest wish is to dispose of these unfounded allegations once and for all."

"And I," said Best, "shall be only too glad to assist you. The Führer wants to see you cleared. So do Göring and Himmler—they told me so themselves. They're all on your side. So, of course, am I."

Best's assurance did not remain unqualified for long. "However," he went on, "the only way of bringing this affair to a satisfactory conclusion—the conclusion we all desire—is to investigate it thoroughly. I may have to raise some embarrassing, even distressing details, General, but please bear with me. You've landed yourself in a mess—innocently, I'm sure—and we shall simply have to wade through it together. May I count on your sympathetic understanding?"

"Whatever the Chancellor considers necessary will be done."

Huber pushed his chair away from the conference table and against the wall, avoiding Fritsch's eye. To a first-class detective and connoisseur of interrogation methods, the general's docility seemed positively alarming.

He bent an almost hypnotic gaze on the crudely concealed microphone built into the conference table, trying to steer Fritsch's eyes in the same direction. Its leads ran to a loudspeaker in a nearby room, where a fat stenographer sat impassively, his right hand scurrying across the pad. Not that Fritsch knew it, every word uttered in the "front parlour" was being recorded.

"And now, General," Best said amiably, "permit me to confront you once more with the principal witness, Otto Schmidt. I know it's asking a great deal, believe me. Between ourselves, I find the man quite as loathsome as you must, but I'm afraid we can't ignore his existence—not any longer."

"Bring him in!" The general's grim alacrity suggested that he was still very sure of his ground.

Otto materialized like a jack-in-the-box. He remained near the door, smooth-faced and shifty-eyed. His hoarse voice sounded overloud and overincisive, as if sheer volume would alchemize lies into truth.

"Schmidt," Best said with a mixture of menace and encouragement, "think carefully before you speak. Anything you say must be absolutely unimpeachable, otherwise you'll find yourself in the dock for slander, defamation, perjury, and half a dozen other offenses."

"Yessir," croaked Otto.

"General," the lawyer went on, turning to Fritsch, "please listen to what this man says. However much his story tries your patience, take it in your stride. I advise you to dissect his statements and give him a chance to amend them in your favour. Do you agree?"

Huber, who had been fidgeting in his chair, looked faintly appalled and shook his head, but the general didn't notice. He said yes.

Now it was Otto's turn. Well rehearsed and serenely self-assured, he declared that he had no reason to depart from his previous statements. "It was Fritsch," he repeated. "I can swear it was him and Bavarian Joe who..."

"Are you *quite* sure, Schmidt?" Best put the question in an undertone of horror and disbelief. "Think again—think carefully. Couldn't there be some mistake?"

"Impossible, sir. There's no mistake."

"A resemblance, maybe. Perhaps you've simply..."

"There's no maybe about it, sir. It was this gentleman—I'd know him anywhere."

While Best shook his head and looked pained, Otto produced further details. After seeing Fritsch commit an act of gross indecency, he had accosted him in his capacity as a police informant of long standing and been offered a sum of hush money—a bribe, in fact...

"Five hundred marks to begin with. Later he offered me another two thousand."

"So he offered you money, Schmidt. Did you take it?" Best homed in on this point though he already knew the answer. "Did you accept this alleged bribe?"

"Only for show, sir." Otto went on to state that he had pocketed the cash in front of witnesses in a railway café but promptly reported the matter to a police officer with whom he enjoyed a close and confidential working relationship.

"And he followed it up?"

"Not officially, sir, but he took down the details—time, date, particulars, personal description, method of payment, and so on. There must be a record of them somewhere in your files."

"That's enough, Schmidt—quite enough." The Gestapo's legal expert turned to Fritsch with an air of grave concern. "General, may I ask you to comment on these allegations?"

To everyone's surprise, Detective Superintendent

Huber made his first contribution. "The general needn't say a thing unless he wants to. He has the right to remain silent."

"Of course, of course." Best strove to conceal his astonishment at this unwelcome piece of advise. He eyed Huber with ill-disguised annoyance, but the policeman continued to stand there with his back against the wall.

"The right to which my colleague alludes," Best went on, weighing his words, "is fully consonant with legal procedure. It may be exercised by an accused person if he feels that further testimony would tend to incriminate him. But that's hardly so in your case, General—or is it?"

"Of course not. I want everything brought out into the open."

"Then I repeat my question. What have you to say to Schmidt's allegations? Please make your comments as detailed as possible."

Huber loudly cleared his throat. It was an unmistakable warning, but Fritsch ignored it. He had now been forced on to the defensive—put on a par with his criminal opponent and inveigled into producing counterarguments. These fell into three main categories.

One: "You must be mistaken, Herr Schmidt. I don't know you—I'd never seen you before we met at the Chancellery. Whoever you saw that night, it certainly wasn't me."

Two: "Even if I *had* managed to raise five hundred marks in cash, as you claim, I certainly wouldn't have been carrying such a sum around. My monthly pay is allocated with some care—I've kept an accurate and detailed record of my expenses for years. My accounts are at your disposal, Dr. Best. *They'll* prove whether or not I paid this man two thousand marks."

"You could have borrowed the money," Otto scoffed.

"One of your pals could have lent it to you."

Best turned on him with ostentatious severity. "Kindly confine yourself to statements as required, Schmidt. If there's any theorizing to be done, you can safely leave it to us. Please go on, General."

Three: "I find it difficult to say this, but I suppose I must. I've now reached an age at which certain—er, escapades can be virtually ruled out. I've always led a very simple, Spartan life, especially where my physical needs are concerned. I'm sure you know what I mean. Ask anyone who's ever been close to me, and they'll tell you so themselves."

Otto Schmidt looked scornful and actually laughed aloud. He was feeling thoroughly pleased with himself. Everything had gone according to plan. Fritsch was hooked.

"You can go!" snapped Best.

Otto went, but not before he had bowed deeply in Fritsch's direction—a gesture the general greeted with mute astonishment.

"A revolting type," said Best, wrinkling his nose. "However, General, we're in trouble. It's your word against his. Oh yes, I know what you're going to say—the word of a police informer against that of a prominent national figure."

"Would you ignore that?"

"Of course not—speaking as an individual. Unhappily, this is a legal proceeding based on a police investigation. I'm sure Herr Huber will confirm that there are no discrepancies between Schmidt's statements and the information so far gathered by the police."

"No," Huber said tersely, "none, on the face of it."

"What do you mean, on the face of it? Does anything strike you as dubious?"

"There's such a thing as credibility, that's all I mean."

The general gave an approving nod. He adjusted his monocle and examined the policeman with a trace of benevolence. Then he stiffened again, smiling faintly as if consoled by the knowledge that, even here in Prinz-Albrecht-Strasse, someone understood him.

"Credibility matters to me too," said Best. "I attach crucial importance to it, General, which is why I'm so unreservedly on your side. However, I also owe a duty to current legal criteria and the law as it stands. I'm their slave, if you like."

"These current legal criteria of yours," said Fritsch, "—how do they apply in my case?"

"I must regretfully state, General, that a witness is a witness. His profession and social standing are immaterial. If this man sticks to his story, as I'm very much afraid he may, an extremely difficult situation will arise. What I want to know is, how are we going to dispose of it?" Best fell silent for a moment. "For your own good, General, I suggest we have a word in private."

Further Interlude No. 1—

Time: two minutes later. Place: Interrogation Room No. 1, Central State Security Bureau, Prinz-Albrecht-Strasse. Dramatis personae: General Baron Werner von Fritsch and legal expert Dr. Werner Best.

Although they have agreed to talk in private, the microphone remains live and the stenographer in the neighbouring room continues to scribble away. Every word of this "confidential" discussion is being taken down—a dirty trick but thoroughly consistent with the times.

Best: Well, we can now exchange ideas in complete privacy—off the record, so to speak.

Fritsch: "I don't see the absolute necessity."

Best: "Perhaps not, but you don't know the pitfalls of the legal system—any legal system. Please let me help you. I should be only too glad, especially as the Führer himself has urged me to clear you at all costs and by all available means. I'm sure you grasp the implication."

Fritsch: "No."

Best: "The Führer wants to save you—for his own sake as well as the Army's. That's why, if we're to get you out of this mess, we shall have to be absolutely frank with each other. I beg your pardon in advance for being outspoken, but it's essential."

Fritsch: "Haven't you been outspoken enough as it is?"

Best: "Let's face the facts as calmly as we can, General. Permit me to ask you this. Is there any possibility, however remote, that your private life has at some time involved activities of a so-called homosexual nature?"

Fritsch: "None whatever."

Best: "Please bear the following points in mind. Incidents of this kind may sometimes be forced on one. They can happen on the spur of the moment—they may even be the product of misunderstanding or chance. These things can happen to anyone. They don't matter much. What does matter is to safeguard oneself against graver allegations by being frank about them. Well?"

Fritsch: "No, there's nothing to tell."

Best: "Very well. I suggest we approach the problem from another angle. The witness stubbornly asserts that you're homosexually inclined—that you've actively engaged in homosexual practices. Can you think of any effective way of refuting his charges, for instance, by bringing definite evidence to show that you're sexually normal!"

Fritsch: "I don't understand. What on earth do you mean?"

Best: "What I mean is this. Would it be possible to demonstrate the past or present existence in your life of female persons—persons with whom you've been on intimate terms? Could you produce firm and convincing evidence to that effect? Would you be prepared to supply particulars?"

Fritsch: "Certainly not! What do you take me for? That would be an indiscreet and dishonourable course of action. I flatly refuse even to consider it."

Further Interlude No. 2—

Place: the monitoring room at Prinz-Albrecht-Strasse, equipped with all the latest US listening devices. In the background, looking bored stiff, stands an SS officer. The stenographer, a grey, tortoiselike individual with a furrowed brow, is hard at work, pencil still racing across his pad. Two equally stolid observers of the scene are lounging around. Behind them, listening to the "confidential" chat in Interrogation Room No. 1, stands Detective Superintendent Huber. He soon gives vent to some unbridled remarks.

Huber: "This is too much! What's Fritsch doing, falling for such an obvious act? Is he naïve, dumb, or just an honest-to-God soldier? His kind of innocence can be a public menace!"

Stenographer: "Please keep it down a bit, Herr Huber, otherwise I won't catch it all."

Huber: "Why doesn't he say, 'The hell with you and your insinuations!'? Why doesn't he slam his sword down on the table, metaphorically speaking, and tell everyone to get stuffed—or words to that effect? He's in charge of the Army, so why doesn't he call out his men? I'd raise hell if I were in his place—anything rather than sit there and let some lawyer rummage around in my sex life."

Stenographer: "Do you mind! I missed a couple of words that time."

Huber: "It doesn't matter a damn what he says, the result'll be the same. It's like taking candy from a baby."

SS officer: "Why get so worked up, Huber?"

Huber: "Pushovers always annoy me. I like my opposition tough."

SS officer: "So who's talking about fun? These types are our bread and butter. If they aren't genuine fairies, we frame 'em. They all crack sooner or later—usually sooner."

Huber: "Is that a fact?"

SS officer: "You can walk all over them. The Gestapo gets everybody to confess in the end—it doesn't matter whether he's a general or a lavatory attendant. This is routine stuff, Huber. The sooner you get used to it, the better."

Stenographer: "Pipe down, can't you! Now I've missed something else. How can I be expected to do a decent job in all this racket?"

Further Interlude No. 3—

Situation report drafted by Dr. Werner Best immediately after General von Fritsch's interview with the Gestapo. Promptly passed by Best to Heydrich and by Heydrich to Göring via Himmler. Text, as transmitted by Göring to the Führer:

"Schmidt, Otto, is proving virtually unshakeable. He has stuck to his incriminating testimony, even after a second confrontation with the accused. The attitude of this chief prosecution witness may be termed reliable.

"Although the accused persists in denying any connection with the affair, he has failed to present any cogent arguments in his own defence. He cannot, therefore, be said to have cleared himself beyond reasonable doubt.

"On the contrary, his inertia seems genuinely suspicious. In view of his failure to produce an effective answer to the charges, one is forced to conclude that he is guilty."

Hitler's comment: "How terrible! The effrontery of the man! I don't care how it's done, but we've got to make him see the light."

Further Interlude No. 4—

The same evening (to quote from Counsellor Meller's notes) I received a visit from Detective Superintendent Huber. At my suggestion, Colonel Oster turned up too. We met at 24 Uhlandstrasse. It was the safest rendezvous I could think of, being the home of an absent friend who not only shared our political beliefs but kept his establishment well stocked with liquor. I held keys to the front door and the wine cellar.

Colonel Oster, who turned up shortly after I did, asked for a dry sherry. He seemed as tense as I was. Huber didn't keep us waiting long. He was looking truculent—in fact I'd never seen him in such a nasty mood. He barely said hello, just glared at his surroundings.

"Classy, I must say," he growled. "I wonder what you have to be or do to afford a place like this. The world's a rotten apple whichever way you look at it. I guess it always was, but it's never been so obvious before."

He sounded quite hostile; Oster quickly put his finger on the trouble. "You're feeling down, Huber. Has something gone wrong?"

"You can say that again!" Huber tossed his threadbare overcoat and crumpled hat on to an armchair. He demanded some brandy "in a tumbler, please," but he was off and running before I handed him the glass.

"You can't railroad someone so obviously," he said angrily. "It's too much to expect of Fritsch—or me, for that matter."

Enlightenment dawned. The Gestapo had obviously got the general in their clutches, though that couldn't alone account for Huber's almost malign truculence. He accepted his brandy but didn't drink. Instead, he stared at us accusingly.

"How could you let it happen? I thought you were experienced tacticians, but you let the man put his head in the noose. Didn't you warn him what to expect—didn't you coach him at all? My God, he was a lamb to the slaughter!"

"Was it really as bad as that?" asked Oster, looking genuinely concerned.

"But Huber," I said, "that's why we infiltrated you into Prinz-Albrecht-Strasse in the first place. You're a resourceful type—we hoped you'd fix things."

"You're talking crap, Meller!" he thundered, even more resentfully. His outrage was pretty convincing. Oster seemed to think so too.

"Look," Huber went on, "let's be realistic. The Gestapo had their loose ends just about tied up by the time I appeared on the scene. They handed me a cut-and-dried case, and I had to take it as it stood. If I hadn't, they'd soon have spotted there was something wrong with me—or Heydrich would. And that would have raised two awkward questions. One, what's Huber's game, and two, who dumped him on us?"

"And you'd have got it in the neck, Meller," said Oster. "At best, our Gestapo friends would have put you on their suspect list, and that might have landed all three of us in trouble." Oster was obviously waiting for me to put up a fight, but all I could produce was a stopgap.

"It certainly sounds like a very tricky situation," I said.

Huber stared at me with a mixture of scorn and inquiry. Oster was looking critical too—very. I racked my brains for a way out and found one.

"Well," I said, "the best thing you can do, Oster, is to get the general a first-rate defence counsel and fast—someone he's willing and able to accept. All right?"

"Leave it to me. Anything else?"

"That's all for the moment—for you. Personally, I'm going to pay an immediate call on my old friend Heydrich. I plan to be very discreet but extremely insistent. The Gestapo's case against Fritsch won't hold water, I shall tell him. I shall also hint that this opinion is shared by the High Command, Military Intelligence, and numerous Army officers including sundry generals—not to mention several police experts."

Oster looked please. "It might work, at that. Heydrich's no fool. He won't lend his name to a bunch of false insinuations if he's afraid they'll blow up in his face."

"That's exactly why I'm going to try to convey how much wiser he'd be to quit the line of fire. However, to put the point over properly, I'd have to be in a position to offer him some really solid facts."

"With my assistance?" asked Huber, who had been listening intently. "All right, I'll try—on your responsibility, Meller. I hope you know what you're getting yourself into."

I said I did, though at that stage I couldn't have foreseen the consequences.

Further Interlude No. 5—

Time: later the same night. Place: a suite of offices in the Central State Security Bureau. Overladen desks and overflowing shelves but few staff in sight because even death's central office worked regular hours. Most of the nocturnal operations conducted by specialist teams took place in the cellars beneath the reception hall.

The upstairs offices allotted to Meisinger's "Control of Homosexuality" section were dark and deserted until Huber appeared. He switched on the main lights and began a systematic search.

Huber knew exactly what to look for and where. He was a practical detective of the first order, cool, unflinchingly determined, and exceptionally well informed. Being all these things, he had instantly realized that the file on which Fritsch's "interview" had been based was an elaborate concoction prepared by Gestapo officers acting on orders from Meisinger.

Meisinger was abroad, soaking up the sun on a "Strength through Joy" cruise liner, but the suppressed information must be somewhere in his department. Huber went to work.

Swiftly and unerringly, he searched the desks occupied by Meisinger's underlings, and there in the bottom left-hand drawer of one desk he unearthed a file about twice as thick as the official "Fritsch dossier." It proved to be a supplementary volume containing information gathered by the Gestapo but not used—not used, quite obviously, because it confounded their case.

Huber leafed through this welcome but disconcerting find, taking his time, and made a number of detailed notes. He couldn't help shaking his head in rueful amazement as he did so—a reaction which had lately gained such a hold on him that it was developing into a nervous tic.

"That's that," he muttered at last, and replaced the file where he had found it—accurately to the nearest millimetre. He might never have touched it, nor did anyone ever suspect he had. Ten seconds later, the office was dark and deserted once more.

Further Interlude No. 6—

Time: an hour past midnight. Place: the office of Deputy Commissioner Count Fritz-Dietlof von der Schulenburg, Police Headquarters, Berlin. A surprisingly untidy room. The tables, chairs, and windowsills are littered with newspapers and books. More books are stacked on the floor. Huber had just walked in.

Schulenburg: "Well, well, if it isn't our star performer—the Gestapo's latest acquisition. If I know you, Huber, you aren't here for old time's sake."

Huber: "No, Count, it's slightly more awkward than that."

Schulenburg: "Don't say you've come to arrest me?."

Huber: "Somebody'll do that sooner or later, but it won't be me."

Schulenburg: "If you want to rejoin the department, I'll do my best to fix it."

Huber: "It isn't that, Count. I can't set the clock back now. I only came to give you some information and ask a favour."

Schulenburg: "Right, but make it quick. I'm just tidying up, as you see. I'm off to the mountains with my family tomorrow morning—skiing, tobogganing, long walks. I need a change of air. You aren't going to stop me, I hope?"

Huber: "Far from it. I'd do the same if I could, but I can't afford the time. They've put me on the Fritsch case."

Schulenburg: "I've heard of it. I thought it was a departmental joke at first—not a particularly funny one, but still ... Why come to me about it?"

Huber: "Because I've dug up some fresh evidence, most of which wouldn't stand up in court. The bulk of it consists of extracts from police records—copies, I mean. The originals are what I need, Count, and they ought to be here on the premises."

Schulenburg: "What are you getting at? You want the run of our records department, is that it?"

Huber: "More or less. What I really want are the Vice Squad records—all of them. They'd have to be taken out of circulation for the next couple of weeks so the Gestapo couldn't get their hands on them. I'd use that time to sift the material and extract anything I considered important. Will you give me a free hand?"

Schulenburg: "Yes, if you insist, but it's the last thing I'm going to do before I take a break from this sweatshop. I shall be away for just about as long as you say you need. I'll have the stuff desposited where nobody can get at it, not even the Gestapo—only you. Will that do?"

Huber: "Thank you, Count. I ought to be able to manage something in that time."

Schulenburg: "So I'm free to absent myself from our National Socialist paradise?"

Huber: "Yes, and bon voyage."

Schulenburg: "Perhaps you could pay me a visit in the mountains—officially, to brief or interrogate me at public expense. You'd be welcome either way."

Huber: "That's nice to know. I may be taking some leave myself in the near future—a long spell, probably, but I plan to earn it. Then I can really enjoy it."

Further Interlude No. 7—

By next morning, Gruppenführer Heydrich was facing Detective Superintendent Huber across his desk in the Central State Security Bureau. Huber hadn't requested the meeting; he had been sent for.

"Last night," Heydrich confided amiably, "I had an interesting chat with my old and valued friend Counsellor Meller. Some awkward misunderstandings have cropped up. He says you may be able to dispel them before it's too late."

Huber hesitated a moment. "I have reason to believe, Gruppenführer, that the charges against General von Fritsch cannot be fully substantiated."

Heydrich frowned. "You mean there's some conflicting evidence somewhere?"

"I'm convinced of it, Gruppenführer. My instructions were to act as observer on behalf of your department. According to some inquiries I conducted for that purpose, the man seen and subsequently blackmailed by Otto Schmidt was not General von Fritsch but someone with a similar-sounding name."

Heydrich's frown deepened. "Are you absolutely certain? All right, Huber, I'll take your word for it. You're an expert in your field. Quite apart from that, you were highly recommended by Counsellor Meller, whose opinion means a lot to me. Where is this evidence?"

"It obviously exists in duplicate. Our own department holds one batch, though only in the form of copies and extracts. Those are here on the premises in Section II-H. I assume the originals are held by the records department at Police Headquarters."

Heydrich reacted with characteristic agility. "Herr Huber," he said in a tone of command, "I appreciate your efforts. I'm relying on your official pledge of secrecy—but I'm sure I don't have to stress that, in view of the delicacy of the situation. Thank you. You'll be hearing from me in the very near future."

As soon as Huber had gone, the Gruppenführer's first step was to telephone Göring.

"General, it's the Fritsch case. I think we've hit a snag."

Göring was predictably irate. "Then deal with it, man!" he barked. "Snags are *your* business, not mine. You've handled things well up to now—I appreciate that. Fritsch is hooked. Don't let him get away, whatever you do. Pile on the pressure until he admits everything—everything! I hope you aren't going to disappoint me."

"Of course not."

"I wouldn't advise you to. The boat's already sailed, Heydrich—the Führer says so himself, and that means it can't be stopped by you or anyone, understand? All right, so make sure it has a smooth voyage. Is that clear?"

It was. Heydrich promptly summoned two of his most trusted lieutenants, who trotted into the office like well-trained gun-dogs.

"I want to see Commissioner Helldorf at once," he told them. "You know Huber, that CID man who joined us recently? He's overworked—needs a long leave of absence. While he's gone, get him quietly transferred to an outstation—somewhere as far from Berlin as possible. And send Meisinger in here. I want him immediately."

"He's away on a cruise, Gruppenführer."

"So what? Tell him to fly back at once. If I know Göring, he'll send a plane to pick him up. I want cast-iron results, and I don't care how I get them."

Twelfth essay in dramatic reconstruction
... Subject: an Italian journey—

To Werner von Blomberg, the days he was privileged to spend in Italy with his beloved bride seemed altogether tranquil at first. Capri was stepped in a pellucid winter sunlight which accentuated the picturesque outlines of the rugged cliffs overlooking the silver strand, the pines that never lost their greenery, the brilliant white houses and the many-coloured fishing boats in the distance.

Here in Capri the couple were treated with extreme courtesy, at least by the hotel staff. Blomberg had asked them to refrain from using his rank. "Please address me as Herr von Blomberg. My wife and I are on holiday, and we want to enjoy ourselves with the maximum of privacy."

But he was still addressed as "Field Marshal"—for instance, when the manager bustled up and obsequiously announced that he was wanted on the phone.

"It's Berlin, Field Marshal—the War Ministry."

So they still need me, thought Blomberg. Keitel, doubtless at the Führer's prompting, was civility personified. He respectfully requested information, invited suggestions, and solicited advice. Werner von Blomberg was only too happy to oblige.

"Well, my dear Keitel, how are things at your end? . . . So it's all going just as the Führer planned—in consultation with me . . . I'm delighted."

Blomberg also received letters from a few brother officers, some exaggeratedly cordial and others distressingly curt. He realized from their stilted tone that the writers had no wish to arouse the vigilance of the German censorship authorities, who might have withheld such communications or passed them to the police and Gestapo. But even these letters were addressed with a pleasing lack of ambiguity to "Field Marshal von Blomberg, Grand Hotel, Capri, Italy."

And there in the wardrobe, alongside several Savile Row suits ranging in shade from pearl grey to midnight blue, hung his best uniform. It glinted alluringly at him whenever he opened the door, with its embroidered oak leaves, brilliant scarlet collar, and impressive array of orders and decorations; and beneath it in a velvet case, forever within reach, lay his marshal's baton. He was gratified to discover that his beloved insisted on looking after all this martial splendour herself.

"What a lovely uniform," she sighed as he fondly watched her plying a clothesbrush. "I only hope you'll soon have another chance to wear it."

"I'm bound to sooner or later, darling." He sounded positive. "The Führer needs me—he told me so himself, more than once. That filth was fabricated by a handful of ambitious rivals. I'll be back in harness as soon as the dust settles."

"But will I still be your wife?"

"What a question, sweetheart. Promise you'll put such dismal thoughts out of your head." She nestled against him and he put his arms around her. "My life wouldn't be complete without you."

Eva felt infinitely grateful and proved it over and over again by giving herself to him with tender and whole-hearted affection. In her company, the sixty-year-old soldier felt like a man in the prime of life.

They spent their days together in a mood of carefree enjoyment, blissful relaxation and idleness. They lingered over their excellent meals and drank the choice white wines of Frascati and Orvieto.

"What a wonderful country," Eva kept saying, "and what a glorious time we're having!"

"This is only the beginning," he assured her.

They did not talk much during their morning walks. Hand in hand or arms entwined, they strolled like young lovers through the little streets, across the rocks, and into the pinewoods.

They usually watched the radiant sunsets from their balcony, mute and content—almost spellbound. Their love had reached the stage at which silence becomes a language of its own. Side by side, they gazed out across the velvet blue expanse of softly gleaming sea. They had never felt so close, just as Germany had never seemed so infinitely far away.

"I could shout for joy!" she said.

"Yes," he replied, "we've found happiness at last. Nothing else matters."

But one of these halcyon days brought a visitor, a stern-faced man wearing a formal suit and carrying a bulky briefcase he never relinquished for an instant, presumably to demonstrate that he had come on official business.

The visitor was a colonel on the staff of the Wehrmacht High Command. Blomberg had personally selected and promoted him, given him important work to do, and even earned his gratitude by introducing him to his private circle. One of the field marshal's last official acts had been to recommend his promotion to major-general.

But now, as he stood facing the Blombergs, his manner was formal, aloof, and wholly governed by military conventions.

He bowed, first to Blomberg with the deepest respect. "Field Marshal!" Then came another bow, but only a ghost of one, in his wife's direction. "Frau Blomberg," he murmured.

The field marshal shook his hand warmly. "It's a pleasure to see you, Colonel. What brings you here?"

"I've been instructed to hand you some papers from the War Ministry, Field Marshal. I don't know what they are—I'm only acting as courier. You're invited to look through them and give your comments in writing. General Keitel has sent them on the Führer's instructions—they both asked me to convey their regards, by the way. I gather he's listed the salient points on a separate sheet."

"I'll get down to it at once," said Blomberg, transparently delighted that his views were still sought. If the documents had been brought him by a special courier of such senior rank, they could relate only to policy decisions of the utmost importance. Gratefully, he put out his hand for the briefcase. "I'll take this next door—I can work in peace there. Meanwhile, Eva my dear, please look after our guest."

The colonel seemed unaware of her touching efforts to play the hostess, presumably because he chose to ignore them. He responded to her invitation to sit down by taking a chair some distance away and pushing it back still farther.

Eva did her best to be hospitable. Would he care for an espresso? He declined. Wine, mineral water, Campari? "I can strongly recommend a Campari, Colonel—it goes with the landscape, somehow. Or would you prefer some champagne?"

"Neither, thank you." The colonel stared boldly at her as though confronted by a carnival freak. He had seen sundry photographs of the field marshal's bride in a file which had made the rounds at headquarters.

And yet he had to admit the woman was far less unappealing than he had imagined. On the contrary, she was a splendidly feminine creature. But as for marrying her! Never! She wouldn't make a colonel's wife, far less a field marshal's.

Eva made strenuous efforts to penetrate the visitor's wary reserve. She found it hard going, especially as she couldn't help noticing that he addressed her—when he spoke at all—as "Frau Blomberg" and pointedly omitted the "von" she was entitled to by marriage.

That rattled her—badly. She tried to drown the obvious insult in stride, but the more voluble she became the more her insecurity showed. "I hope," she said coaxingly, "that when Werner and I are back in Berlin you'll come and visit us. I know my husband thinks a lot of you, Colonel. We could have some good times together."

"Good times, eh?" drawled the colonel, aloof as ever. "That sounds intriguing..."

"All done," said Blomberg, appearing from next door. "The Führer should be satisfied—Keitel too. Will you be dining with us tonight, Colonel?"

"I'm afraid not, sir. General Keitel intimated that my mission was urgent as well as important. I must return to Berlin at once." He bowed as he had on arrival—"Field Marshal, Frau Blomberg!"—and beat a hasty retreat. Blomberg turned to Eva.

"Well, my love, did you charm the gallant colonel?"

"I tried," she said, looking distracted, "but I don't think I succeeded. Not properly."

"Never mind, darling. You aren't used to your new environment yet, but you won't find it hard—you're a wonderfully adaptable person. There's a power-game going on, that's the trouble. The colonel isn't a bad man at heart. It's just that he doesn't know which way to turn—which side to come down on."

But the first thing the colonel did on reaching Berlin was to broadcast the following announcement: "You should have heard the woman. She tried to proposition me!"

How Hitler got himself a new C-in-C Army—
1. Paving the way

Hitler had summoned the two new repositories of his trust: General Keitel, soon to be officially appointed "Chief of the Armed Forces Department," and Major Rudolf Schmundt, who has already succeeded Colonel Hossbach as the Führer's Wehrmacht aide. Like Keitel, Schmundt was a lucky find. He too had a phenomenal knack of divining his master's intentions.

"Gentlemen," the Führer began, "I'm afraid we're going to lose General von Fritsch, whatever happens. Like it or not, we shall have to find a replacement for him."

In response to his request for constructive suggestions, Hitler's new advisers submitted a list of candidates. It was not particularly long, and they accompanied it with a brief summary of the essential points.

The first and most obvious choice was Ludwig Beck, the Army Chief of Staff. Beck was fully acquainted with Fritsch's important reorganization plans. He was also an administrator and theorist of high standing. Against this, his independent approach to military policy might prove awkward, if not downright dangerous.

Next, General von Rundstedt, an outstanding field commander and first-rate soldier but five or ten years too old for such an onerous job. Next, General von Witzleben, a gifted strategist who enjoyed the respect of all ranks but was insufficiently orthodox in his politics. The same objection applied to General von Stülpnagel, who had been known to utter remarks so questionable as to cast doubt on his loyalty to the regime.

"So who does that leave?"

"Well, my Führer, what about General von Reichenau?"

2. Weighing the odds

"Reichenau..." Adolph Hitler nodded at his advisers with an air of interest. He had been waiting for them to mention that name—that and that one other. "An excellent suggestion, but it needs careful thought. Let me have your pros and cons, and please be absolutely frank."

To many of the hidebound veterans who still dominated the German armed forces, General Walther von Reichenau was an abomination who made them see red—or, rather, Brownshirt-brown. This athletic, football-playing general was widely regarded as a devout Nazi—sometimes, even, as the Führer's pet. It was he who had devised the controversial oath of loyalty to Hitler's person after Hindenburg's death.

To quite a number of people, however, and eventually to Hitler himself, Reichenau seemed a glamorous enigma. Like Blomberg, he was something of a cosmopolitan. He had once accompanied his father on a successful sales trip to Latin America, selling guns, ammunition, and spare parts for Krupp. He had travelled in the United States, the Middle East, and Central Europe. He also spoke several languages, and his English was reputed to be excellent.

English was the language in which he had nonchalantly addressed the following remark to his wife at an important official function: "I detest these swastika men!" These words were promptly relayed to Hitler, who just as promptly dismissed them as malicious slander—a fact many found suspect.

"Reichenau, then. How do you rate him, Keitel?"

"Very highly, my Führer, though I do have certain reservations. I think I can claim to know him pretty well. He worked closely with Blomberg at the War Ministry for a considerable time, but then—well, they had some major disagreements."

"What sort of disagreements?"

"Reichenau persistently tried to revolutionize our military conventions—addressing superior officers in the third person, for instance. He made a premature attempt to abolish the practice—in fact he even debated the possibility of completely doing away with badges of rank. To crown everything, he attended a Jewish veterans' reunion dinner at Konigsberg. Not in uniform, I'm happy to say. Somebody managed to dissuade him at the last moment."

"Minor flaws, perhaps," Hitler said with easy conde-
scension. "Better send for him all the same, Keitel—we'll
sound him out." His alert gaze zoomed in on Schmundt.
"You seem to have another idea up your sleeve, Major.
Let's hear it."

"This is what you might call a transitional situation, my
Führer," said Schmundt. "What we need under present
circumstances is someone with a capacity for compromise." And then he spoke the name Hitler had been
waiting for all along. "You might do worse than consider
General von Brauchitsch."

"Congratulations, Schmundt—another admirable suggestion. I'm sure you agree, Keitel? You do? Good, send
for him too. We'll see how things turn out."

3. Narrowing the field

General Keitel reappeared in Hitler's study the very
next morning, having spent the entire night gathering
information or getting others to do so. He now dumped
the proud result of his labours in the Führer's lap.

"Generals von Reichenau and von Brauchitsch are
already on their way to Berlin," he announced. "I've
booked one of them into the Esplanade and the other into
the Continental. They'll both be reporting to me on
arrival."

"My compliments, General. That's what I call staff
work." The Führer beamed approvingly. "But now tell me
how far you've got with your inquiries. Reichenau doesn't
interest me as much—I know enough about him already.
What about Brauchitsch?"

Keitel eagerly consulted his notes. "General of Infantry
Walther von Brauchitsch has had an exemplary military
career. He joined the Potsdam Cadet Corps as a boy and
subsequently became page to the Empress Augusta
Victoria. He was commissioned when underage and
decorated for his outstanding conduct at the Front. He

then served in the Republican Army, earning an unblemished record. His superiors have always described him as adaptable and dependable. Apart from that, he's noted for his smart appearance, chivalrous disposition, and compelling personality."

"He sounds promising," said Hitler, "but I see from your face there's a fly in the ointment."

"That's one way of putting it, my Führer. Early in October of 1935 Brauchitsch tendered his resignation to his immediate superior, General von Fritsch, for personal reasons."

"How personal?"

Keitel did his best to look troubled. "In Breslau about twelve years ago Brauchitsch became acquainted with a woman named Charlotte Ruffer, the wife of a brother officer. She divorced him but remarried soon afterwards without severing her ties with Brauchitsch, which can only be described as intimate. Her second husband was a banker named Schmidt, who drowned in his bath. Not long after that, Brauchitsch saw fit to go and live with this Frau Ruffer-Schmidt. He's quite prepared to marry her, but he can't, still being married himself."

"What's the Ruffer woman like?"

"Thoroughly presentable, my Führer—every inch a lady and a staunch National Socialist. She not only admires you but has frequently said so in public. Brauchitsch and she would make an ideal couple in the new German mould. Unfortunately, Frau von Brauchitsch seems averse to a divorce, even though she and her husband have been separated for years."

"Why won't she let him go?"

"Her motives are financial, I suspect. She appears to be demanding far more alimony than Brauchitsch can afford. He's nearly broke as it is."

…ed Hitler. "Of course,

…be to place him under a
…s instructed to deal with

…Brauchitsch, one of the
…lonel himself, visited his
…shrewd negotiator, had
…with him, pledged his
…red him the problem could
…l generous manner. This, he
…personal wish.

…sch junior with a battery of
…and his wife had become
…e of affairs but one which was
…However understandable it
…auchitsch declined to terminate
…an undertaking by her husband
to pay her a meagre monthly allowance, the Führer had
urgent need of the general's services. Patriotism and
personal advantage both prescribed that she should
release her husband immediately.

Frau von Brauchitsch greeted this request with the
same composure she had shown throughout twelve years
of marital humiliation. She evinced no bitterness towards
anyone, not even her honest broker of a son. Yes, she said,
she would welcome an equitable solution, but what form
would it take?

"A financial settlement, Mother. A lump sum of eighty
thousand marks payable on demand plus a monthly
income of one thousand marks for life—personally
guaranteed by the Führer."

It was too good an offer to turn down.

5. Clinching the deal

There was no more need for General von Brauchitsch to await his fate at the Hotel Continental. The Führer sent for him and greeted him with a brilliant display of warmth and charm. Keitel stood close by, wearing a winning smile.

"General," said Hitler, "I trust you and always have. I can't think of anyone better qualified to command the Army. Would you accept such an appointment?"

"Of course, my Führer, particularly if it accords with your personal wishes. However, I'm bound to point out that my own circumstances are ..."

"Your misgivings do you credit, General. I appreciate your honesty, but we've nothing more to fear from that quarter—isn't that so, Keitel?"

Keitel nodded. "If the Führer were assured of your consent, General, your wife would receive an extremely handsome settlement. She already knows this and has announced her willingness to divorce you. You would at last be free to marry Frau Ruffer-Schmidt. What do you say?"

General von Brauchitsch said nothing at first—he was speechless—but his initial relief and delight were succeeded by alarm. He could not help wondering what all this would cost. The fact remained that he was fast approaching an unexpected peak in his career just when he thought it had hit rock bottom.

"What other conditions would I have to fulfill, my Führer?"

Hitler did not go into this justified question. He parried it by saying he would need time to consider everything carefully and formulate his ideas in writing. "We should be able to manage that in two or three days, eh, Keitel?"

"Two days should be enough," Keitel said eagerly.

Two days were quite enough. Brauchitsch was meanwhile subjected to continuous pressure, mainly by Keitel but also by Hitler, whose manner was extremely friendly. He even prodded Göring into shamming delight at the general's advancement. As for the Führer's new Wehrmacht aide, Major Schmundt, he plied the prospective Commander-in-Chief Army with a mass of files and kept assuring him that nobody enjoyed more widespread trust or could do the job better.

Only then did Hitler unveil his principal demands, which he presented with considerable force. The Army must be steeped in the spirit of National Socialism, the influence of the conservative General Staff curbed, and the Army Personal Office purged. A new generation of officers must be deliberately promoted and the Army trained and equipped for war at far greater speed. The Führer concluded his ultimatum:

"And you and I, General, will maintain the closest possible working relationship."

Walther von Brauchitsch was quick to grasp the practical implications. The Army would be wholly geared to Adolf Hitler's wishes, and that would mean that all three services were finally under his thumb. Even Brauchitsch hesitated before signing the Führer's blank cheque.

"May I have time to consider?"

This request was promptly and flatly rejected. He would have to decide on the spot—yes or no. Which meant, in effect, that he could either become the German Army's most senior soldier and a man of means or a prematurely retired general with two women on his hands.

He said, "I accept, my Führer."

Now that the power game required it, Field Marshal von Blomberg was ostracized with disconcerting speed. All his contacts were severed. He received no more official callers and very few visits of a private nature.

His isolation was the product of a "confidential memorandum" distributed to every head of section and department, every senior staff officer and military administrator in the Wehrmacht High Command. Inspired by Hitler, though drafted and signed by Keitel, its contents were soon common knowledge.

This widely circulated document stated that Field Marshal von Blomberg had ceased to exercise his official functions. He was therefore no longer entitled to request or receive documents, reports, or information. From now on, he was to be excluded from all official briefings and conferences unless the Führer's express consent had first been obtained via General Keitel. Furthermore, it was strongly recommended that social contact with Herr von Blomberg, "Field Marshal, retired," should be restricted to a minimum—at least until all matters relating to his personal position had been finally resolved.

The reactions to this artful and insidious directive varied as widely as its distribution list. Curiously enough, most people were contemptuously hostile to its victim. Blomberg's pro-Nazi line had not endeared him to the traditionalists in the officer corps, the majority of whom thought it served him right.

Others, though not very many, sensed that the latest development might have fateful repercussions. If Hitler could subject his only field marshal to such treatment, what would he do next? There was a vague feeling that something should be done. Just what, no one could decide.

Thirteenth essay in dramatic reconstruction
... Subject: the final eclipse—

Eva von Blomberg noticed nothing of this, not even

when a uniformed naval officer called on her husband in Rome, where they were now staying after their sojourn in Capri.

The Blombergs had moved, still at Hitler's expense, into the Villa Medici, an elegant hotel near the Trinità dei Monti. With Eva at his side and Rome at his feet—or so it appeared from their luxurious vantage point—Werner von Blomberg continued to revel in his newfound happiness.

He greeted the naval commander warmly under the misapprehension that he was an envoy from Admiral Raeder. It delighted him to think he was to be "consulted" again at last.

"Welcome, my dear fellow," he cried jovially, only too eager for a discussion of official business. "What can I do for you?"

"For me, nothing!" The commander had halted near the door. "My only motive in seeking this interview is the hope that you may just possibly be prepared to uphold the honour of the German officer corps with a courage and determination proper to your rank."

Though visibly shaken by the commander's provocative tone, Blomberg lost none of his courtesy. "Would you mind explaining yourself?"

"Herr von Blomberg, I speak on behalf of many officers in all three services, not just the Navy."

"Well, what do they want?"

"They demand a convincing response on your part— the only one possible at this late stage. Your reputation is theirs. You must redeem it in the traditional way—the German way."

Blomberg was still smiling, even now, with a trace of indulgence. The smile proved to be gravely misjudged. "Really?" he said. "How?"

The commander advanced on him and drew his service automatic, a Mauser 7.65. He slammed it down in the middle of the table. "With that," he replied coldly.

"What can you mean, my dear fellow? What do you hope to achieve? You're obviously confused."

"Not about one essential point. The most senior member of our armed forces has disgraced himself by contracting an unworthy marriage which dishonours us all. That stain can only be removed by a final and conclusive display of personal courage."

"Young man," Blomberg said, struggling to retain his dignity, "I admire you as I would any conscientious officer, however, mistaken." A trifle nervously, he pushed the pistol away with the back of his hand. "However, you obviously have no conception of the forms public policy can take. I bow to the national interest. I readily make sacrifices for its sake—sacrifices whose magnitude is probably lost on you and your friends. But suicide, young man, is not among them."

"Herr Blomberg," the commander cried angrily, "I despise you!"

"And I can only pity you. Be good enough to leave and take your artillery with you."

Immediately after this incident, Blomberg rejoined his wife, who was waiting for him in the Café Goya at the foot of the Spanish Steps. She clasped his hands as he sat down beside her.

"You're looking tired," she said. "Has something happened?"

"Something rather terrible, Eva." He smiled at her tenderly. "Somehow, though, it's cheered me up. I suppose it's always heartening to feel you know something for sure."

Her face clouded. "Is it something to do with me again?"

"No, us," he replied, still smiling. "I've got something

absolutely straight in my mind, darling. Do you know what really matters in life? The unbreakable, indestructible bond between one human being and another. Everything else is either secondary or irrelevant, and that's all there is to it."

It was a realization which never faded for the rest of his life.

Blomberg did, for all that, feel justified in complaining about the incident, though not with any particular vehemence. One of his letters on the subject was shown to Hermann Göring.

Still unaware that Hitler had reserved the armed forces for himself, Göring was already picturing himself in Blomberg's shoes. As would-be Commander-in-Chief Wehrmacht, he staged one of his grandiose explosions of fury.

"Who do these imbeciles thing they *are*! My God, a dead field marshal is all we need! That would really put the cap on this damnable situation. What the hell did he hope to achieve, the interfering young busybody? He ought to be shot!"

He snatched up the phone and called Hitler, who seemed temporarily at a loss for words. His only comment was "What an unholy mess!" That was enough for Göring, who promptly got in touch with Heydrich.

"There's no time to lose. We must pull out all the stops if we don't want our scheme wrecked by some other idiot. You know who the enemy are. Get them!"

9

Fair Game

From the notes compiled by Counsellor Erich
Meller of the Prussian Ministry of the Interior—

"This is a real can of worms," Colonel Oster said,
trying hard to swallow his anger. "We've taken a thorough
beating." It sounded like a dig at me.

"I don't recall being asked to advise General Fritsch," I
said. "That was your job. If he hasn't bothered to fight
back, it's because he hasn't been adequately briefed on his
position. That's why we're in this spot."

"I see," said Oster, snappishly, "so it's all *my* fault.
What's the matter, don't you trust me any more?"

I could see where we were heading. It was always the

same with our crowd. We never felt entirely sure of each
other—that was our cardinal sin. I suppose it was the
constant strain and the growing threat to our survival that
fostered such self-destructive tendencies.

Oster seemed to grasp this too. He gave an apologetic
shrug. "Sorry, old friend, but this business is getting me
down. You ought to sympathize—I'm sure you feel the
same way. To tell the truth, I'm surprised you're still here
at all now Huber's been found out. After all, you were the
one who sold him to Heydrich."

I was able to reassure him on that score, or almost. I'd
been prepared for the worst when Heydrich summoned
me to Prinz-Albrecht-Strasse, but I found him in his usual
confidential mood. He simply wagged his head, with its
oversized ears, and grinned at me.

"Who the devil was that you sent me? I'd be downright
suspicious if the recommendation had come from anyone
else, but since it was you ..."

"I thought you could use a first-rate man, Reinhard, and
that's what Huber is."

"He's good all right—in fact too damned good for our
kind of work. He doesn't seem to get the hang of it, so I've
told him to take a break and think things over. Who knows,
Erich, you may be able to get his mind working along the
proper lines."

Oster's reaction to this news was spontaneously
delighted. "So the heat's off. Good for you and good for us
too, even if your policeman friend has been put out of
commission."

"Ah, but he hasn't. This'll leave Huber free to build
up an effective defence for Fritsch. Any exonerating
evidence he finds will be forwarded by me to you and by
you to whoever represents the Commander-in-Chief at his
trial. I suppose a court-martial's inevitable now, isn't it?"

Oster nodded gravely. "Did you know the Gestapo have requested another 'interview' with the general? They're being all very polite and official, which I find doubly ominous."

"Yes, and this time Huber's place will be taken by Meisinger."

"A tough customer, I gather."

"Tough but essentially stupid. Tell me, though, what are the generals doing?"

Oster gave another of his apologetic shrugs—he was getting good at them. "They're sitting on the fence and waiting to see what happens. Generals are only human, Erich. They've all got private lives and personal ambitions. Security means as much to them as anyone else. They don't see why they should stake their promotion prospects on a long shot."

"Is that what they all think?"

"Not all, fortunately, but the few who think otherwise are the exceptions—and the rule seems to be gaining ground. It's much the same lower down the scale, though there are a few junior officers rash enough to cling to their youthful notions of honour and integrity. They're eager to have their say, which means they'll bear watching."

Detective Chief Superintendent Meisinger had been compelled to forego the rest of his pleasure cruise. This had left him grumpy, irascible, and only too ready to jump on anyone he considered responsible for "lousing up" his leave, generals included.

On top of this, Heydrich had treated him to another harangue.

"All right, Meisinger, this may be your last chance. If you fall down on the job again you can kiss this place good-bye. I'll boot you out personally, understand?"

"Yes, Gruppenführer, but it'll go all right this time."

"It better. If there are any holes in our case, plug them—tight! I want that old man squeezed like a lemon. He's got to stop messing around. If you don't want a dose of the same medicine, settle him!"

"I'll soften him up, Gruppenführer, don't you worry. He'll be all ready for his trial by the time I've finished."

"God Almighty, man, are you crazy!" Heydrich looked thunderstruck. "You mean you still haven't grasped the object of the exercise, not even after that CID man nearly succeeded in wrecking all our plans? A trial could land us in deep water—we can't afford one."

"I understand, Gruppenführer." Meisinger backpedalled hurriedly. "My job is to work on Fritsch till he cracks."

"Yes, but that's not all. Just in case he does decide to risk making a public exhibition of himself, you've got to strengthen our case by feeling out his weak points. I'm relying on you, Meisinger. Don't let me down."

This interview with the Gruppenführer was sufficient to redouble Meisinger's efforts. It was his case alone now—the biggest in his career. He duly polished the performance of his two main prosecution witnesses, Schmidt and Weingartner, by consigning them to the mercies of his toughest, most expert interrogators. These "tidying-up sessions," in which he took a personal and active part, lasted several nights.

As expected, Otto Schmidt came through his ordeal in the Gestapo's chamber of horrors with flying colours. Being conversant with the methods of those in power, he clung to his testimony like a limpet. Meisinger almost hugged him afterwards.

"Bavarian Joe" Weingartner was another matter. He

simply couldn't withstand intense physical pressure and collapsed at once.

"Yes, yes, I confess!" he whimpered. "It wasn't the general—it wasn't him I did it with at Wannsee Station ..."

Meisinger glared down at Bavarian Joe's writhing form. Then he gave a contemptuous grunt and kicked him deliberately in the backside.

"You're useless, you degenerate bastard, utterly and completely useless!"

With that, Bavarian Joe Weingartner was deprived of his privileged status as a prosecution witness and banished to a concentration camp. Nothing more has ever been heard of him.

Before Fritsch voluntarily attended his next interview with the Gestapo, he received a visit from Oster. .

"You've no need to go, sir," the colonel told him. "They can't compel you to ..."

"My dear Oster," said the general, who still seemed pathetically complacent, "all I want is to settle this business as quickly as possible."

"Which is precisely why you shouldn't put yourself in their hands. If they want something, let them come to you. At least insist on a neutral rendezvous. We could protect you better there."

Fritsch indignantly shook his bullet head and lost his monocle in the process. "My life is based on faith in the people round me. I always hope they'll return it."

"Does your faith extend to me, General?"

This drew a prompt affirmative, whereupon several phone calls were exchanged between Army High Command and Gestapo Headquarters. The outcome was a compromise proposed by Heydrich and rejected by Oster but accepted by Fritsch, namely, that he should be interviewed in an empty villa beside the Wannsee.

Oster knew enough about the Gestapo's methods to feel apprehensive. The choice of this ostensibly neutral spot, which was well off the beaten track, offered them a wide range of options. They might, for example, claim that the general had threatened his interrogators with a gun and represent his murder as an act of self-defence. Alternatively, there was scope for a skillfully staged "suicide." Overwhelmed by the weight of the evidence against him, Fritsch had drawn his pistol and turned it on himself . . .

"Balderdash, Oster," was the general's response to these forebodings. "I never carry a gun."

"So? They could plant one on you!"

"My dear man, this isn't Chicago!"

"No, General, it's Berlin—the capital of a country controlled by Hitler, Göring, and Himmler, not to mention that jackal Heydrich. The sooner you get used to that idea, the better. It isn't just a question of your personal survival—the future of our nation is at stake."

"You're entitled to your opinion," Fritsch said simply. "My own concern is to squelch these ridiculous charges. Whatever else you consider important is your affair, but I sincerely hope you can justify any action you take as a result."

Encouraged by this tacit go-ahead, Oster surrounded the forthcoming encounter with every possible precaution. He had the landside villa thoroughly reconnoitred by agents from his own Military Intelligence department.

They reported that it was a secluded house enclosed by garden walls and additionally shielded by some tall chestnut trees which made it very hard to see inside. The house itself looked neglected. It was a fortresslike box of a building with small windows, some barred, but the approach road could be kept under observation. So could the drive from the gates to the main entrance.

Still taking the general's tacit consent for granted, Oster arranged for him to be driven there and back in an official Mercedes provided by Military Intelligence, a funereal black limousine with reinforced coachwork and bullet-proof windows.

The man appointed to chauffeur this monstrous hearse, a corporal named Benniken, was reputed to be equal to any road conditions because he had trained as a cross-country scout-car driver. The general was to sit beside him, this time in uniform, and the rear scat would be occupied by two carefully selected Army officers: a Lieutenant Kant, who had undergone commando training, and a legal officer named Siewert. Oster explained Siewert's function.

"You must insist on his presence at all times, General, and that means throughout this so-called interview. Siewert is absolutely trustworthy. He's also under strict orders not to intervene unless you ask him to. You can take it he's well versed in all the relevant rules of evidence and military regulations."

Although the general's gloomy silence was tantamount to a mute protest, Oster felt sufficiently encouraged to step up his security measures. He sent for Corporal Benniken and Lieutenant Kant.

"Each of you will be issued with a brace of eight millimetre automatics and two spare clips," he told them. "According to my records, you've both been thoroughly trained in the use of the weapon. If you need a refresher course, I can arrange one. No? All the better."

"Who do we use them on?" asked the lieutenant.

"If the Gestapo follow their usual routine, the house and grounds will be guarded by several men, probably in SS uniform. Keep your eyes peeled. If things go wrong—if they challenge you or actually open fire—gun down as many as you can."

Lieutenant Kant just nodded, but Corporal Benniken seemed to have a more practical turn of mind. "Very good, sir," he said. "But we don't have to get ourselves killed in the process, do we? Otherwise, I'd better make my will."

Oster ignored him. "The main thing is this," he went on. "Make sure you drive through the gates and right up to the front entrance—you've got to insist on that, Kant. The car will provide you with cover. It's virtually bulletproof."

The lieutenant looked dubious. "That's all very well, Colonel. Let's assume we have to shoot our way out. We take cover behind the car and blaze away, but then what happens?"

"As soon as the first shots are fired, you'll get some effective support—and I mean really effective. It's all arranged."

Oster had already persuaded a captain named Both to station his tank unit near the Wannsee villa at a time to be set by himself. Captain von Both was a staunchly patriotic young officer who had served under Fritsch and greatly admired him. His Military Intelligence rating was "utterly dependable and ready for anything."

"I want you to stage an exercise in the immediate vicinity of the house," Oster had told him. "Some of my men have already reconnoitred the grounds. I've instructed them to guide you and act as liaison officers. This is a red alert, Captain. Draw some live ammunition but don't forget that your role is precautionary. You're supposed to be a deterrent, so you can show yourselves at a reasonable distance from the house. The bastards we're up against must never be allowed to think they've got a free hand."

Both sides had made their preparations and the end game could begin precisely at the appointed hour. Even on this occasion, Fritsch was determined to be punctual.

His car purred up to the open gates, which were guarded by two SS men, and drove on unchallenged to the villa's main entrance. Here the general got out, looking impressive despite his medium height. Lieutenant Kant and Corporal Benniken took up their positions behind the car. Siewert, the lawyer in Army lieutenant's uniform, stuck close to the Commander-in-Chief's side.

Fritsch and his companion were greeted at the door by Dr. Werner Best, again with studious courtesy. Meisinger, who was introduced as "Detective Chief Superintendent Meisinger, my special adviser," lingered in the background trying to hide his excitement. He knew he was approaching the greatest watershed in his career—a crucial test which had to be passed, but how?

The proceedings opened in an atmosphere which suggested that only generous concessions on both sides had made them possible at all. Nobody objected to the general's companion, and Meisinger's presence was likewise accepted. The whole party disappeared into the empty house, Best on Fritsch's left, Meisinger and Siewert following at their heels. Passing through a hall guarded by two impassive SS men, they entered a small side room. All it contained was a heavy oak table and some ornate Prussian Baroque chairs which looked as if their designer had conceived them in a fit of extreme boredom. Two of these had been placed behind the table and two in front of it. Everyone sat down. Best politely inclined his head in Fritsch's direction.

"First, General, a word of explanation. I am only here today as an observer, so my function is purely peripheral. The interview itself will be conducted by Detective Chief Superintendent Meisinger, an acknowledged expert in his field. I would advise you to confide in him fully."

The Gestapo lawyer smiled, relieved he was temporarily off the hook. He had done his duty, demonstrated his zeal, and—to a large extent—covered himself. Meisinger could handle the dirty work—he looked the ideal person, Best thought, and he was right.

Meisinger began the interrogation, which was still dressed up as an "informative discussion," on a positively servile note, more than a little inhibited by the sight of one of the Third Reich's most distinguished figures in full regalia.

"You're already acquainted with the allegations made by Otto Schmidt. Do you still deny them?"

"Most certainly I do."

"So you're unaware of having committed any such offence?"

"I have nothing to hide, Herr Meisinger."

"Herr" Meisinger, thought the chief superintendent. In his book, courtesy implied a bad conscience. Metaphorically rubbing his hands, he persevered in his efforts to shake his exalted victim with direct but reasonably civil questions. The only result was a series of steadfast denials. He soon realized he was getting nowhere. If Fritsch was to be coaxed out of his shell, he would have to become even more direct. A little provocation could work wonders. He glanced at Best and caught an almost imperceptible nod. Then he let Fritsch have both barrels, acting on the long-established Gestapo principle that suspicion connotes guilt and every interrogation must lead to an indictment.

"Well, Herr von Fritsch, I suppose we'd better talk plain German—to borrow a phrase of the Führer's."

"Whatever that may mean, please proceed."

Meisinger embarked on an ostentatious and unnecessary perusal of his papers. This he accompanied by shaking his head, clicking his tongue, and hissing through his teeth with a mixture of derision, contempt, and menace.

"Right," he barked eventually, "so you deny the Wannsee Station incident ever took place, even though we have witnesses—or at least one witness—whose testimony is unshakable and would be quite sufficient to put you in the dock. But that's by no means all."

"You mean there's more?" said Fritsch. From one moment to the next, he looked tormented and dismayed. "Is this really necessary?"

"You decline to hear these further allegations?"

"Certainly not. I shall repudiate them whatever they are."

Lieutenant Siewert leant towards the Commander-in-Chief and stared at him. His face was a study in alarm. Why doesn't the general defy them, it said—why doesn't he stand up, deliver a blistering rebuke and march out? It was all Siewert could do to refrain from butting in before Meisinger turned to the attack.

"Very well," said the policeman, "since you insist on being confronted with further evidence, Herr von Fritsch, I can oblige you three times over. The first incident concerns the Hitler Youth members you so kindly entertain at your home. One of them, the boy named Heinz, has made a statement which gravely compromises you. It seems you tried to touch him, not only on the neck and shoulders but considerably lower down."

Fritsch looked hurt and appalled. "But—that's a rotten thing to say!" he exclaimed. He meant the alleged statement, not Meisinger's effrontery in quoting it to his face.

"Second," snapped Meisinger, "we have another equally incriminating statement from someone named Konstantin Krause. He used to be one of your grooms when you were a regimental commander, and he's prepared to testify that you subjected him to advances of an unmistakably homosexual nature."

"Absurd," Fritsch said in a strangled voice. His face turned grey, and he gripped the edge of the table. "Nothing like that ever happened."

"Third and last," Meisinger intoned with vulturous relish, "we have a statement from one ex-Lieutenant Kern. He used to be an aide of yours but was forced to quit the service at your insistence. He then transferred to the Party and has since become an SA brigadier in Pomerania. Can you explain why you kicked him out?"

"He wasn't kicked out, as you choose to put it. He was court-martialed, convicted and cashiered—for grave and persistent embezzlement of mess funds, as I recall."

"That's what *you* say! According to his sworn deposition, you made improper advances to him and he firmly rejected them. That's the only reason he had to go— because he wasn't cooperative enough for your liking. It's the truth, isn't it, *Fritsch*?"

The general stretched out both arms as though warding off an unseen blow. His faced looked numb and blank—even Dr. Best wore an expression of sympathetic concern. Meisinger felt victory within his grasp, but Lieutenant Siewert could contain himself no longer.

"I strongly object to these tactics. Every accused person is entitled to legal representation and all charges must be open to scrutiny, whatever their nature. Defence counsel must be guaranteed access to interrogation transcripts."

"Yes, yes," Best said soothingly. He sounded faintly perturbed. "I take your point, Herr Siewert, but you really must try to see things in perspective. We're clearing the air, that's all."

"But you seem to forget who you're dealing with. It's outrageous to insult the general by addressing him as 'Fritsch.'" Siewert turned on Meisinger. "I take the strongest exception to your manner, sir."

"You?" Meisinger retorted. "What gives you the right to interrupt these proceedings? Who the hell do you think you are?"

"That's enough!" said Best, firmly now. "It's time we settled this matter. General von Fritsch, may I respectfully request a word in private?"

Best's second "confidential chat" with Fritsch was also overheard, this time by Lieutenant Siewert. He refused to leave the general's side and was finally allowed to remain, provided he stayed well in the background.

"Ghastly business, this." Best spoke with honeyed regret. "Quite ghastly, General, but we'll have to face it. The Führer wants us to settle things as soon as possible."

Fritsch shook his head. "I simply can't fathom how anyone could do this to me—me, of all people..."

"This is merely a routine inquiry, General," Best assured him. "Policemen are like greyhounds—they have a built-in urge to chase hares. The finer distinctions are lost on them. They see no need to observe them, least of all when the national interest is at stake."

"And my good name."

"Of course, General. The good name of one of our most distinquished public servants. You and the German Army are one, and not in the public mind alone, so your reputation is identical with that of the service you command. Wouldn't it be irresponsible to jeopardize it? I ask you to consider that carefully."

Fritsch lapsed into dejected silence. His usual air of paternal authority had vanished, leaving his face wan. His head, with its lofty brow and sparse hair combed neatly outwards from a well-defined central parting, hung low. It was hard to escape the impression that he was placing his neck on the executioner's block.

The lawyer rammed his point home. "It mustn't come to a public hearing, General, not under any circumstances. Nobody wants that, the Führer least of all."

"But I insist." Fritsch's voice was low but distinct. "I insist on settling this matter once and for all."

"Think carefully, General!" There was nothing spurious about Best's imploring tone. "The consequences of a court hearing could be absolutely ruinous—for you, for the Army's reputation, for us all."

"Not if justice still exists in this country, as I hope and believe it does."

Lieutenant Siewert uttered a subdued "Bravo!" in the background. Best swung round.

"Kindly keep out of this, Lieutenant. You've no conception of the issues at stake." He turned back to Fritsch. "General, you've heard the evidence against you. Surely you must realize how destructive it would be to air it in front of a court of honour? The Führer doesn't want that—he respects you too much. You're a living symbol to all of us whose sole concern is to keep this country's reputation untarnished."

But Fritsch was possessed by an extreme, almost instinctive resolve. He did not raise his voice or speak with any detectable acrimony. All he said was, "I don't want this business swept under the rug. On the contrary—I want the truth officially established. My personal code of honour demands it."

"This is a Pandora's box, General. Nobody with your interests at heart could possibly advise you to open it. If you continue to press for a hearing, charges will have to be preferred. You'll also have to relinquish your official functions. Think it over."

"My mind's made up." Fritsch squared his shoulders. "I demand to be tried by a court of honour. I insist on a verdict."

From the Meller report—

I met Colonel Oster that evening. We didn't bother to cover our tracks but dined openly at Horcher's in the Kurfürstendamm.

"This time," said Oster, who was obviously in high spirits, "the sky's the limit. Only the best is good enough tonight."

"What are we supposed to be celebrating?" I asked.

"A belated revival of the old Prussian spirit," he said, and ordered champagne cocktails. "The general has finally shown he's what we always hoped he was—a cast-iron man of integrity."

"Has he really agreed to a court hearing?"

"Agreed? He *insisted* on one! He was great, apparently—firm as a rock."

"But what about the evidence against him? Didn't it make him think twice?"

Oster fanned this question aside with the menu. "The

old man was adamant. He doesn't seem to have grasped its implications."

"But he could find himself in very deep water."

"Not necessarily. I've already consulted General Beck and the Commander-in-Chief's aides. We're getting him the finest defence counsel bar none."

I could only marvel at his optimism. "What makes you think you can afford to indulge in these manouevres. You don't imagine they've escaped the notice of your boss, do you? Admiral Canaris is one of Hitler's leading advisers. He's always being called to the Chancellery for confidential briefings."

"Twenty-one times in the past nine months, actually, but you don't know Canaris. Plotting is part of his stock-in-trade. So is covering himself from every conceivable angle. Of course he knows what I'm up to, but not officially—not a breath of it. If all goes well, fine. If not, he'll come down on me like a ton of bricks."

"You're looking awfully confident in spite of it all. May I ask why?"

"Largely because I'm pinning a lot of my hopes on that weapon of yours—Huber, I mean. You told me he could be trusted all the way."

"So he can," I said, but not without a trace of misgiving. Why? Because I had seen Huber just before keeping my dinner date with Oster, and our meeting had left me feeling thoroughly apprehensive.

"Counsellor," the policeman had told me, "we're virtual strangers. You'd better get used to the idea, because that's what I'm going to say if anyone asks. You sent for some papers from the Berlin Police Department, and I delivered them to your office as instructed. We only met a couple of times. I didn't know who you were, not exactly, and the same goes for you. You certainly didn't know what I might or might not be capable of."

"What *is* all this?" I asked.

"Take every precaution you can think of. If you keep an appointments book with my name in it, burn it. Tear my phone number out of your diary. If there's anything on paper about me at your home or office, get rid of it fast. That should provide you with a little insurance against your old friend Heydrich. With luck, you'll survive."

"But good God, Huber, you can't expect me to write you off just like that."

"I expect you to be sensible, Counsellor. There's no point in two heads rolling when one will do. We'll take a leaf out of the opposition's book. For instance, I'll say I always mistrusted you—thought you were an ambitious careerist. You can say I always struck you as overzealous, but you'd never have thought me capable of surreptitious obstruction."

Huber produced this bombshell quite calmly, though he did look pale and weary—almost ill. His eyelids drooped, possibly with fatigue, possibly with some deep but nameless emotion.

"I won't be a party to what's going on here," he went on. "Not any longer. They're ganging up on a decent man—a pathetically decent man—and I'm going to try to see he gets the justice he deserves. If I succeed, my life will have been worth something even if I lose it."

I was overwhelmed by a depressing awareness that the Blomberg-Fritsch affair had claimed yet another victim—an anonymous figure burdened with a truly monumental sense of responsibility.

"Don't be too hasty," I advised him, pointlessly, of course. "The situation's still fluid, Huber. Pin your faith on

the other Germany. It still exists, you know, even now."
He gave me a pitying smile.

Adolf Hitler's hopes and expectations were soon confirmed: generals didn't go on strike, certainly not German
generals. They merely uttered rumblings of discontent,
which was a manageable reaction.

Even though this was probably the most dangerous
crisis in Hitler's sphere of influence since the so-called
Röhm Putsch of 1934, it seemed to be resolving itself in a
very satisfactory manner. The generals, at any rate, were
no great problem. They allowed themselves to be divided
and ruled with little difficulty.

It was true that General von Brauchitsch, the new
Commander-in-Chief Army, persisted in haggling over
minor prerogatives, but this was a predictable and easily
soluble problem. Besides, one good turn deserved
another. Brauchitsch yielded to Hitler's demand for the
dismissal of various military district commanders because
their political views were deemed suspect. Conversely,
Hitler sanctioned Brauchitsch's retention of General von
Rundstedt after Brauchitsch, in his turn, had agreed to
dispense with General von Leeb.

The Führer's horse-trading worked perfectly, much to
his gratification. He stated his requirements with less and
less ceremony.

"This major cleanup was absolutely essential, my dear
Brauchitsch. We mustn't forget Göring while we're at it.
He's been a tower of strength recently—to your advantage, among others. I think he deserves a reward of some
kind, don't you?"

"Of course, my Führer." Brauchitsch stared at his
master with a trace of alarm. "Are you planning to appoint

him Commander-in-Chief Wehrmacht?"

"You misunderstand me. All I had in mind was a small token of gratitude—an official pat on the back which will placate and flatter him without meaning much in practice. My original intention was to make him an air marshal. However, it was argued that several air marshals already exist on the other side of the English Channel. In view of that valid point, I propose to make him a field marshal instead. Any objections?"

"None at all, my Führer. From what you say, the appointment will be semihonorary in any case."

"Exactly. He'll hold the rank but continue to command the Luftwaffe only. And while we're tying up loose ends, Brauchitsch, what's your opinion of our present Foreign Minister?"

"Baron von Neurath? As far as I'm able to judge, my Führer, he's a very worthy man."

"Quite, quite—very worthy indeed, but the pace of events is quickening. I'm afraid he isn't young or dynamic enough to cope with them. We shall have to replace him with Herr von Ribbentrop. The Baron won't go unrewarded. I propose to appoint him head of my Cabinet Council."

Brauchitsch had no idea what that meant—nor, probably, had anyone else. However imposing the title "Cabinet Councillor," it didn't carry an ounce of political weight. The establishment of this body was just another attempt at obfuscation in a world already veiled in official smoke screens.

Hitler was determined to do a thorough job, using a technique which had proved its efficacy in the past; he always got others to endorse his views and so made them jointly responsible. He had decided to combine the replacement of his Foreign Minister with the dismissal of several ambassadors. One of them was the German envoy in Rome, Ulrich von Hassell, whose loyalty to the regime was not beyond doubt.

The Führer had also decided that his Minister of Finance, Hjalmar Schacht, was redundant. In place of this alleged financial wizard, who had become a thorn in his flesh, he proposed to appoint Walter Funk. Although Funk was a notorious homosexual, his ministerial appointment almost coincided with the drafting of the indictment against Fritsch.

On 4 February 1938, pursuant to instructions received, senior generals serving in every area command from East Prussia to Bavaria converged on Berlin. Obediently, some three dozen of them turned up for a 2 P.M. conference at the War Ministry.

Their mood was far from defiant. It might better have been described as subdued but not hopeless. Of the small groups that stood around chatting, a few looked moderately amused and continued to do so even when the three service chiefs marched in. Their entry followed an invariable sequence: first Brauchitsch for the Army, then Göring for the Luftwaffe, and finally Raeder, who had retained command of the Navy. The three Commanders-in-Chief stood rigidly at attention.

The Führer and Chancellor appeared immediately afterwards, accompanied by General Keitel and Major Schmundt. His head was slightly bowed, and his expression conveyed that he was labouring under a heavy burden of responsibility.

Face to face with his generals, he straightened up and fixed them with a piercing gaze—resolute and imperious, invincibly self-assured, and confident of his mission.

At first, he seemed to grope for words, painfully and laboriously. Then, as if a switch had been thrown, he picked up speed. His voice soared in accusation and entreaty, sank to a throaty murmur which seemed to plumb the depths of brooding meditation, then suddenly burst into renewed life, peppering his awed listeners with phrases as staccato as machine-gun fire.

It all sounded quite spontaneous and straight from the heart. Those who did not belong to his immediate circle were immensely impressed by this sort of performance. Very few realized that none of it, needless to say, was extempore. As usual on such occasions, Hitler had thoroughly rehearsed himself and may even have practised key lines in front of a mirror. He was Germany's finest character actor, and his performance on that day ranked among the most brilliant in his career.

He began by apologizing to his esteemed and distinguished audience for trespassing on their time. That he had done so was a token of his deep concern, but also of his implicit faith in them. He knew they were at one with him in their determination to preserve at all costs the honour and good name of the Wehrmacht. "The knowledge that you are behind me, that you have closed ranks around me, will surely enable me to surmount any conceivable difficulty."

Point number one: the position of Herr von Blomberg. He, Adolf Hitler, had always been predisposed to trust his judgement. Unhappily, the field marshal had not proved himself as bold an adviser or resolute a soldier as might have been expected. He had shown this early on, when the Rhineland was reoccupied by German troops in defiance of the Versailles Treaty. Sadly, Hitler recalled that

Blomberg had urged him against taking such a step because he grossly overrated the French and their motley bunch of allies.

"I risked everything, or so it seemed, and my decision proved absolutely correct. History has already borne me out, as I'm sure you gentlemen will admit."

This appeared to be a cue for applause, but none of the assembled generals followed it up. All three dozen continued to ruminate like a flock of meek but thoroughbred sheep.

He could have taken Blomberg's defects in his stride, Hitler went on, because the field marshal also had some fine soldierly qualities—like loyalty and obedience. For these he deserved gratitude, as the gentlemen present, who were made in the same mould, would undoubtedly agree.

Then, however, something deplorable had happened—something best described as a personal tragedy. "Several senior officers, including some from your own ranks, took the precaution of warning me in no uncertain terms that there might be a threat to national security."

Most of the generals grouped round Hitler looked thoroughly taken aback. There were a few variations, but only minor ones: here a touch of discreet surprise, there a hint of disbelief and bewilderment, but everywhere a look of stunned expectancy. Drawing encouragement from this, the Führer pressed home his advantage.

"After Blomberg's deplorable social gaffe, it became essential to find a replacement for him. The most logical candidate was General von Fritsch. In the meantime, however, certain facts have emerged—facts of which you may be aware and which I, difficult as I find it, must take into account. I'm sure you understand."

Very discreetly and politely, somebody standing near General Beck ventured a question, "May we take that as official, my Führer?"

"After examining the charges against him," Hitler replied, "Herr von Fritsch has asked to be tried by a court of honour. He has insisted on this, so we shall have to respect his decision."

Silence fell. The Führer always construed the absence of any discernible reaction as approval. There was no mistaking his listeners' air of disquiet, but that he ignored. It didn't count.

The generals tried hard to disguise their uneasiness. Professional integrity, love of power, considerations of national security—they wavered between all three, uncertain how to react. And then, seizing his moment with an instinctive sense of timing, Hitler made an announcement which left them speechless. He put a numerical value on their own importance.

"For you, gentlemen—and by you I mean the armed forces which enable us to attain our supreme national objectives—nothing can be too good and no sacrifice too great. I have made due provision for our Wehrmacht in the face of strong opposition from numerous sources. I have, in fact, managed to earmark a sum unique in the annals of military expenditure, anywhere, any time. It amounts to ninety billion marks."

This was a genuinely breathtaking piece of news. Hitler's audience, professionals all, realized that he had named a figure which defied comparison even with the enormous sums expended on the devastating artillery duels of 1914–18.

"Gentlemen," he concluded, "I ask you to trust me implicitly. I shall always do my duty. Do yours!"

They trooped off, still preserving a stunned silence. Hitler happily watched them go. The Wehrmacht was his at last.

The trial of General von Fritsch on charges under Article 175 of the Penal Code, ostensibly a straightforward legal hearing, opened on 10 March 1938. It was held in the so-called Preussenhaus, a palace which had once served as the Prussian House of Peers.

The supreme judicial authority was Adolf Hitler, though he never had to appear in person. This task he left to Göring, now a field marshal but still "only" Commander-in-Chief Luftwaffe, who had been deputed to attend the charade in his capacity as an actor of proven competence.

He was accompanied by the other two commanders-in-chief, Brauchitsch for the Army and Raeder for the Navy, plus two senior judge advocates who had been instructed to join the bench.

Göring's first contribution to the proceedings, which were clearly intended as a show trial, was to declare himself president of the court. This he did on the scarcely contestable grounds that his recent promotion to field marshal made him the ranking officer present. In assuming the presidency of this court of honour, he declared, he was acting against his personal inclinations but fulfilling his duty.

Led by Göring, the five-man tribunal filed into the makeshift courtroom. Everyone rose, as was customary on such occasions, with the sole exception of General von Fritsch.

In front of the accused, like a human shield between him and his persecutors, stood counsel for the defence.

Count Rüdiger von der Goltz was a distinguished advocate whose legal and military qualifications were as far above reproach as his personal character. He was also reputed to be a devout National Socialist, which might well prove an asset in present company. Nobody had ever disputed his loyalty to the regime, not even Heydrich. On the other hand, nobody apart from Oster and Meller knew that Huber had already furnished him with a substantial quantity of exonerating evidence.

Göring opened the proceedings on a note of massive self-assertion. As president of the court of honour, he sharply reminded all present that the hearing constituted an official secret. "Anyone broadcasting details of it outside this courtroom is committing an offence and will be prosecuted. I'll personally see to that."

The so-called witnesses paraded under Meisinger's direction, carefully marshalled, well rehearsed, and all primed with evidence of a more or less incriminating nature. The less incriminating testimony came from Fritsch's ex-groom and erstwhile ADC. Both of them made highly evasive statements prefaced by phrases such as "It seemed to me that..." and "I got the impression that..."

There was little to be wrung from these pathetic creatures, even when Göring bullied them, appealed to their sense of duty, and called their testimony "luke-warm." "How dare you produce this sort of stuff!" he thundered, glaring at the prosecution.

The picture changed when Meisinger's pet pupil took the stand. Everything seemed to stand out in sharp relief. Otto Schmidt stuck to his story with predictable tenacity and produced another fervent cry of "It was him!"

But then came Count von der Goltz for the defence. Conducting a dogged and skillful cross-examination, he succeeded in shaking Schmidt with the aid of Huber's evidence, which enabled him to brand the witness a habitual criminal and discredit his testimony.

At this, Göring stepped in. He fully sympathized with defence counsel's efforts to clear his client, but he must not do so by recklessly attempting to compromise a witness who had volunteered to testify in good faith. "It simply isn't fair, and this—I'm bound to point out—is a supremely fair trial."

Brauchitsch and Raeder swallowed this assertion in silence. So did the other two judges. They lay low and said nothing.

The prosecution immediately summoned Meisinger to the stand. "You are a detective chief superintendent and were assigned to investigate this case? I would ask you to comment on defence counsel's statements regarding the witness Otto Schmidt."

Meisinger swung into action, solemnly indicating his protégé. Yes, he said, Schmidt might have committed various youthful misdemeanours—who hadn't? Yes, he might even have had a few minor brushes with the law, but that was long ago. He had turned over a new leaf since then and become a valuable member of the German national community—a staunch supporter of the institutions charged with maintaining law and order.

"He's a human being, sir. Nobody can take that away from him."

At this precise juncture, when Fritsch's fortunes seemed to have reached a perilously low ebb, the trial was adjourned. On the second day, 11 March 1938, Göring consulted his fellow judges and turned to address the body of the court.

"For reasons affecting the national interest, this hearing is adjourned *sine die*."

The pretext was Germany's military swoop on Austria, alias "The Return of Hitler's Homeland to the Reich" or "The Campaign of Flowers." The Führer was radiant with success. The tide of world history seemed to have swamped all his domestic difficulties, including the Blomberg and Fritsch affairs.

But the break in the proceedings was urgently and successfully exploited for Fritsch's benefit by Huber, who managed to locate additional exonerating evidence with the aid of documentary research, former colleagues in the CID, and agents from Military Intelligence.

The trial resumed on 17 March 1938, only to reach a swift and unequivocal conclusion. For perhaps the last time in Nazi legal history, "justice," seemed to prevail.

Detective Superintendent Huber, granted temporary "leave of absence" by Heydrich's Gestapo, had succeeded in finding a needle in a haystack. Plumb in the middle of a stack of files at the Berlin Police Department, he unearthed an official memorandum complete with date, time, and full particulars. It read:

Wannsee Station, November 1933. Homosexual act observed. Paid participant: Weingartner, Josef, also known as "Bavarian Joe," listed as a male prostitute with several previous convictions. Source of payment identified as a Captain Frisch (ret.), Austrian origin. Not previously listed, so presumed to be a casual offender.

Also involved: Schmidt, Otto, nickname, "Otto-Otto." Known in the department as a habitual blackmailer and listed several times under the relevant heading. Has performed extremely valu-

able work as an informant. Appended is a list of the
sums extorted in this case: times, places, amounts,
method of payment, recipient, etc.

Action to be temporarily deferred while further
particulars are compiled.

But the most significant feature of this memo was its
pair of marginal notes. One of them read "Endorsed—
Brei" and had been added by the records officer,
Detective Inspector Breitner. The other was signed "Mei."
This, as comparison with numerous other documents
proved beyond doubt, was the abbreviated signature of
Detective Superintendent Joseph Meisinger, CID, now
Detective Chief Superintendent Meisinger of the Gestapo.

Counsellor Meller, who was the first to be shown this
prize piece of evidence by Huber, was ecstatic. He
planned to mobilize all the pro-Fritsch forces without
delay, not only Defence Counsel Goltz but Oster and his
trusted cronies in the High Command.

"This'll blow their case sky-high!" he exulted.

"No," said Huber.

"No? Did you say *no*?" Meller was taken aback. "What
more do you want?"

"I aim to do a really thorough job," the policeman said
stolidly. "That memo could be challenged in court and
rejected as a forgery. I want positive proof. That's why I'm
going to try and track down the mysterious Captain
Frisch. It ought to be possible as long as he's still alive and
living in Berlin, which seems likely."

"All right, Huber, say you find him. What happens
then? You seriously think he'll risk his neck by appearing in
Göring's state circus?"

"If I do manage to trace the man, he'll have to be taken
in hand by Goltz or people like him—you and Oster, for

instance. When I say taken in hand, I mean worked on until he agrees to give evidence. The prosecution case is only a house of cards, but they're sticky with dirt. You won't demolish it without Frisch."

Huber did manage to track down ex-Captain von Frisch, who turned out to be bedridden and suffering from a chronic complaint. His doctor pronounced him unfit to be moved and incapable of withstanding interrogation.

After a long and exhausting interview, Goltz succeeded in convincing the invalid that his testimony would be of the utmost importance. He also persuaded him that giving evidence would be advantageous rather than dangerous because the Gestapo would have no good reason to harass him once he had done so. Besides, a confession would not only clear the name of a decent man but ease his own conscience.

Achim von Frisch, captain of cavalry (retired), was escorted to the Preussenhaus by a male nurse and summoned before the court of honour. Once in the witness box, he drew himself up in a pathetic attempt to cut an honest and manly figure. His voice was so faint as to be almost inaudible, but his testimony was crucial.

"Yes," he admitted, "I was the one."

The one who had consorted with a certain Josef Weingartner at Wannsee Station—the one who had later been blackmailed by Otto Schmidt ...

"I'm prepared to repeat that on oath."

This brought a spontaneous interjection from the station barmaid whom the Gestapo had produced to confirm that General von Fritsch had paid Schmidt a second blackmail instalment of two thousand marks.

"That's right," she cried, "it was him! No doubt about it, that was the gentleman who slipped him the money!" She levelled a finger at the ex-captain, who was almost out on his feet, then pointed at the accused with an equally sweeping gesture. "It certainly wasn't him. I've never seen him outside this room—I'm absolutely certain now."

Göring emitted a theatrical bellow of rage. The court of honour's self-appointed president saw all his hopes melting away and looked around for a scapegoat. His plump fingers beat an angry tattoo on the judges' table.

"What *is* all this?" he thundered. "How dare the prosecution inflict such a witness on the bench! Remove that miserable swine Schmidt immediately. He ought to be shot!"

The only possible verdict came soon afterwards. Field Marshal Göring, who was obliged to read it out in person, announced the court's decision in a harsh and caustic voice.

"Not guilty. Charges dismissed for lack of evidence."

Ever eager to display himself in a magnanimous and comradely light, Göring wound up this abortive political drama with the following pronouncement:

"The Army's good name, and consequently that of its commander-in-chief, is now unblemished."

The Führer and Chancellor took a similar line in a letter to Fritsch dated 30 March 1938, which scaled the heights of mendacity. Its gist:

General!
    You are cognizant of the verdict which has established your total innocence. I have confirmed it with heartfelt gratitude, for, terrible though the burden of suspicion must have been for you personally, I too was deeply distressed by the ideas to which it gave rise ... I shall bring this to the nation's attention.

He never did so, nor was he expected to by the few real connoisseurs of the contemporary scene. The only certainty was that Hitler had gained another of his major objectives. The road ahead bristled with opportunities for further abuses of power. He proceeded to take the fullest and most unbridled advantage of them.

Sequel

Immediately after the foregoing events, Otto Schmidt was committed to a concentration camp. He languished there until July 1942, presumably hoping to survive, if nothing more, because he had the Gestapo's gilt-edged assurance that his life would be spared.

This guarantee held good until Himmler sought the Führer's permission to liquidate a number of individuals who had been medically certified as "creatures of a schizophrenic and antisocial disposition."

Hitler consented, and Otto was executed.

General von Brauchitsch, Fritsch's immediate successor as Commander-in-Chief of the Army, was divorced on 4 August 1938 after his first wife had received prompt and generous compensation. The general's marriage to his longtime companion Charlotte Ruffer-Schmidt took place on 23 September of the same year. Hitler and Göring, who both had experience of such functions, were present at the ceremony. It was as solemn and decorous an occasion as circumstances demanded.

The pecuniary side of this arrangement, which was only one of several designed to purchase generals and other human assets on Hitler's behalf, was skilfully and unobtrusively handled by the manager of his financial affairs, Philip Bouhler. Bouhler was a fixer *par excellence*, a wheeler-dealer who believed that nothing and no one without a price tag could possibly be worth having. It was a maxim which gave him plenty of scope.

Field Marshal Werner von Blomberg remained in virtual isolation, almost as if he were dead but refused to lie down. He was ignored even after the outbreak of the war which Hitler had wantonly planned and ruthlessly launched, aided by the deliberate removal of all who might have opposed it.

Blomberg had hoped, in the event of such an "emergency," to be entrusted with an active command appropriate to his rank. Hitler conveniently forgot his pledge when the time came. All he said was, "If I give that man Blomberg a command, I'll have to do the same for Fritsch, but why should I?"

So the first of Greater Germany's field marshals spent his declining years in idleness, a forlorn figure banished to the wings of the theatre where he had once played a leading role. He shared his ostracism with Eva, for whom he preserved an enduring affection—or infatuation, as interested parties described it. The slanders against her persisted.

When Blomberg was confined to a British prisoner-of-war camp in 1945, nearly all his fellow detainees cut him dead. They treated him like a leper, even when he lay dying in their midst.

His last recorded comments were made with an indulgent smile at himself and the world in general. "After all," he said, "I've been immensely happy for seven whole years—happy with Eva and because of her. What more could anyone want?"

General Baron Werner von Fritsch was appointed honorary colonel of the 12th Artillery Regiment a year before the outbreak of what soon became known as World War II. He received his commission on 12 August 1938 at an elaborate ceremony attended by his successor, General von Brauchitsch, and held at a training area in North Germany.

Hitler had sent him another letter. Couched in the most cordial language, it culminated in an assurance of "grateful appreciation for your meritorious efforts to rebuild the German Wehrmacht."

Some five hundred officers are reported to have attended a banquet to mark the occasion. Fritsch's speech to this gathering contained no word of reproach or recrimination, only the following profession of faith:

"A soldier is a soldier, nothing more, so he must always be ready to serve. He must do so unquestioningly and with an absolute disregard for self, come what may." There is no reason to doubt the general's sincerity. All sources agree that he wholeheartedly devoted himself to "his" regiment from then on. He wore its uniform, supervised its training and directed its field exercises. We are also told that he spent some happy and harmonious times—his last on earth—in the companionable surroundings of the regimental mess.

When war broke out, Fritsch accompanied his unit to Poland—"if only as a target!," to quote a remark made to one of his very few close friends. A bullet smashed his skull outside Warsaw on 22 September 1939.

It was openly surmised that the general had courted death, but this seems quite improbable—certainly as regards his presence in the combat zone. Fritsch was accompanied by an aide, and he would never have exposed another man to danger for his own sake. That would have been entirely inconsistent with his noble and unselfish character.

General Jodl, who was often accused of being brutally businesslike and devoid of finer feelings, opened his situation report on 22 September with the words: "Today there died one of the finest soldiers our country has ever known!" They were uttered in an unmistakably accusing tone and levelled straight at Hitler, who could not repress a start.

The Führer promptly ordained that Fritsch should be buried with full military honours but regretted his inability to attend in person. Arrangements for a state funeral were entrusted to Göring, who performed his duties with resounding insincerity.

Not for the first time in history, an age had dawned in which executioners were free to double as chief mourners.

Priests indulged in spiritual treachery, soldiers behaved like hucksters, and generals like whores.

It was all very "human."

Quite a few people, even including the more perceptive members of society, thought their only course was to accept these developments and hope for the tide to turn. Some behaved like hunted hares, and others engaged in deliberate and surreptitious conspiracy, inuring themselves to the idea that, from now on, their lives might degenerate into an endless series of intrigues.

Not so Huber. Recent events had sickened him—him, a man whose job had brought him face to face with every conceivable form of human depravity and the whole gamut of moral aberrations. Yet it was he who came to the most radical conclusion of all.

"Diseases are pernicious," he told his friend Meller. "Sick people are like diseased cattle. However much they deserve our sympathy, we have to quarantine them and attempt a cure. All right, but what if these diseased and infectious elements gain a political hold over their fellow men? Can we afford to look on idly? Shouldn't we do something positive?"

Meller tried to calm him down but didn't find it easy. The world was in a state of flux, he argued. Nothing could be regarded as absolutely final, so Hitler's proclamation of a "Thousand-Year Reich" was utter nonsense—just one more proof of his inability to see things in true historical perspective.

"What about you and your friends?" retorted Huber. "You gave the man a year when he came to power, then three years. Now almost six have gone by, and there's still no end in sight. Every day is a day too long."

Meller, who had grown attached to Huber, realized that

the policeman was in grave danger. He refused to heed the signs of the times and conspire in secret. He didn't want to be an underground fighter, he wanted justice, and he wanted to wring it out of the authorities openly—by main force.

The Counsellor tried to save Huber from the consequences of this suicidal behaviour by sending for Meisinger. He coupled his invitation with a hint that it might "pay."

Meisinger promptly appeared, looking as vicious as a caged tiger. "So you're trying to cover yourself, eh?" he snarled. "Getting jumpy, are you? I don't blame you. If all my suspicions about you are correct, which they are, and if I manage to prove them, which I almost have, your old friend Heydrich will finish you for good—and that goes for your inside man as well!"

"Don't be too sure," said Meller, handing him a sheet of paper. The policeman snatched it. To Meller's glee, his jaw slowly dropped.

"It's only a copy," Meller went on. "One of several, and the original's in a safe place. I don't have to tell you what a bearing this memo might have had on the Fritsch trial if you hadn't deliberately suppressed it. It demonstrates beyond doubt that you were fully aware of the true circumstances. In other words, it proves your willful complicity in the trumped-up charges against General von Fritsch."

Never a man to lose his grip on reality, Meisinger recognized the document's significance. "You aren't planning to show it to Heydrich, are you?"

"You'd be sunk if I did, sure as fate, but I won't—not necessarily. There's just one condition."

"Huber, you mean?" Meisinger caught on at once. "All right, it's a deal. As long as I'm fireproof, so is he."

So Huber was able to resume his duties with the Gestapo under Meisinger's wary eye. The chief superintendent, who watched him closely from then on, prevented him from tackling any of the Third Reich's bigger game.

Reinhard Heydrich rose to become acting "Protector" of Bohemia and Moravia, which he ruled with a rod of iron. Immediately after his assassination on the outskirts of Prague in 1942, Meisinger was promoted to senior SS rank and inflicted on the diplomatic corps. As police attaché at the German Embassy in Tokyo—a title which authorized him to spy on other members of the staff—he acquired another promising sphere of activity.

His transfer presented Huber with an entirely new range of opportunities. Now that Meisinger was no longer breathing down his neck, he succeeded in nailing a Gauleiter for rape. Soon after that, he shut down a Berlin brothel frequented by diplomats and senior Party officials. Last but not least, he made it his business to rescue a number of underage girls from the clutches of some Gestapo colleagues who had compelled them to engage in sexual orgies.

It was Heydrich's successor, Ernst Kaltenbrunner, who gratified many of his subordinates by giving the long-awaited order: in spring 1943, Huber was sent to Flossenbürg concentration camp, where he remained for nearly two years.

Only days before the end of World War II, an SS execution squad herded him naked into the yard with several other prisoners. One was a man whom Huber had never met but whose name and function were only too familiar. Indirectly, at the instigation of Oster and Meller, he had worked for him during crucial phases in the Blomberg-Fritsch affair. The man who stood beside him,

shivering in the dank dawn air, was a certain Admiral
Canaris, Hitler's erstwhile spymaster-in-chief.

They were hanged together.

Counsellor Erich Meller was detained, interrogated, and
tortured by the Gestapo after Hitler escaped assassination
on 20 July 1944. He admitted nothing and named no names
but one—Göring's. All he would say was, "Ask *him* what
he thinks."

They did so and earned themselves an indignant rebuke
from that worthy, who now held the unique rank of "Reich
Marshal." "How dare you fail to consult me!" he bellowed
in the presence of several witnesses. "How dare you lay
hands on one of my most valued associates—a friend of
poor old Heydrich's too! I flatly forbid it!"

Meller, commenting: "Göring's protest not only saved
my life but tickled my vanity more than a little. I've always
fancied myself a master of dissimulation—in my own
small way—and this proved me right. Even the Reich
Marshal, who was an actor of the first order, had found my
performance convincing."

Meller had yet to discover that his talent for acting
would cause him a lot of trouble after the war. At a time
when the Russians and their Western allies were still
conducting a joint investigation of the Nazi era, he
threatened to become *persona non grata* in both camps. "A
controversial figure" was the general verdict. "Hard to pin
down—not entirely above suspicion ..."

Meller greeted this with sovereign calm.

"To err is human, so they say, but it's possible to be too
human. I always feel uneasy when the would-be survivors
of this world oversimplify things in an effort to fit them for
everyday use.

"It's always black or white, left or right—nothing in between. Do we have to accept that?

"Certainly not!"

Just before his death, Adolf Hitler turned to the chauffeur who later helped douse his body in gasoline and burn it. "My epitaph," he said, "should be:

Here Lies
the Victim of His Generals."

Frau Eva von Blomberg, née Gruhn, has survived all these vicissitudes. She is living in Berlin as I write, in deliberate seclusion but not in total solitude. She may already have perceived that her historical "caricature" is, little by little, undergoing the modification it so sorely needs.

Hitler's description of her as a prostitute has been refuted by historical research. It was nothing more nor less than one of the most vicious smears and canards of the Nazi era, yet it continued to be broadcast, with many a nudge and wink, after 1945. The time has come to write finis. If Eva von Blomberg was guilty of anything, it was to have experienced the human yearning for love and happiness at a time when inhumanity had become an official creed. It was to have loved a human being who stood in the path of that inhumanity and, in company with his wife, became its victim.

This book is a belated attempt to make amends. It is dedicated to her in particular and, in general,

To Those
Who Die by the Word.

MASTER NOVELISTS